THE COTTAGE.

S.J.C. Ratcliffe.

1

S.J.C. RATCLIFFE

This Book is dedicated to:

My family, thank you for all your support .

Love you all.

Chapter 1. Eve.

The light is too bright; I want to open my eyes, but I can't.

'Eve, can you hear me open your eyes?' a strange voice says.

'Who is that and where am I?'

'Come on, Eve. Try again, open your eyes.'

'What's going on, where am I?'

Listening to the surrounding noises, I realise, I'm in a hospital. Everything that happened rushes into my memory. I have to get away.

'NOOOOOOOO.'

I try to sit up, but there's something pushing me.

'Calm down, Eve, you're in the hospital.'

Blinking my eyes, until I can finally open them. There's a nurse, a doctor, and someone dressed in a suit whose job I don't recognise.

'Eve, I'm Dr Walsh, and this is Dr Ryan our resident psychiatrist.'

'Hello Eve,' Dr Ryan said stepping forward.

'I want to go home.'

'I know, but first we have to make sure you are well enough. Do you remember what happened?' Dr Walsh asks.

I nod. I don't want to answer that question, and look away. I don't want to see Dr Walsh's face.

'I can't let you go home until I'm satisfied that you are safe. Firstly, I would like you to have something to eat and talk to Dr Ryan before I can consider discharging you. Ideally, I would like to keep you overnight for observations, but I will know better after you talk to Dr Ryan okay?'

I nod, and pain rushes to my temples. The more alert I become, the more aware I am of my head pounding and my stomach churning.

'Okay, I'll stay,' I say nodding.

Dr Walsh seems satisfied and tells me she will return this evening. Leaving me alone with Dr Ryan. Dr Ryan pulls up a chair and I realise that we are having the chat now.

'Eve, I would like you to tell me why you did what you did?'

I don't want to talk and ignore her question, turning to look out of the window. I watch cars drive in and out of the car park outside my window.

'Eve, we have to talk about this, or I will have no other choice than, to section you under the Mental Health Act. I need to know that you won't try to hurt yourself again. Tell me what happened.'

Glancing at the doctor, I don't want to talk to her, but know it's the only way I will get home.

'I don't really know. Everything was just too much. I just wanted the pain to go away.'

'What did you do?'

'I was drinking vodka, and I took some painkillers, then I took some more. Before I knew it, I had taken all the pills in the house. But the pain was still there, I didn't want any more pain. I just wanted to get a good night's sleep. That's the last thing I remember, feeling sleepy.'

'Did you know taking the pills could end your life?'

I nod.

'I hate my life, I'm so alone, I miss my mum,' I blurt out, pressure building, as the sobs escape.

My chest heaves as I gasp for breath. I try to stop it, but I can't, and the tears spill forth like water from a dam. My body shudders, I'm raw not just from the pills but from the past year trying to cope.

Dr Ryan doesn't say anything, just watches me, I feel like I need to explain.

'My mum died a year ago, it was sudden, she was in a car accident. My best friend, my housemate, she's drinking herself to oblivion, all day and night. I can't cope,' I exclaim, tears streaming freely down my cheeks.

'It's okay Eve, you've been through a traumatic event, anybody would struggle. But I think this is a cry for help, not an actual attempt to end your life.'

I watch Dr Ryan making notes in her notepad, I'm completely exhausted, like utterly wiped out. Who knew crying was so exhausting? Dr Ryan finishes whatever it was she was writing and tells me she will give her assessment to Dr Walsh. I don't know what she is going to say. Right now, lying in this bed feeling completely wretched, I don't care if she sections me. Lying back, I realise, for the first time since my mum passed away, I feel calmer.

Chapter 2. Recovery.

It's been a month since that awful day when everything got too much. Today is my last day with Dr Ryan. It took a while, but I trust her. She didn't section me, instead, she insisted, I come to the clinic every day and today is the last day. After today, I will only have to come once a month. Waiting to be called I watch the brightly coloured fish swimming in the tank next to me. My stomach flutters today is a big day.

'Eve Mullen,' Dr Ryan calls, poking her head around the door.

I'm always glad that I don't have to wait long at the clinic. I don't think my nerves could cope with waiting too long.

'Good morning, Eve. How are you today?' Dr Ryan asks, smiling when we're in her office.

'Good, a little nervous.'

'Why are you nervous?'

'I won't have the clinic to come to every day.'

'Why does that make you nervous?'

'In case I can't cope.'

'But you know I'm here. All you have to do is lift the phone, and I'll have you in the next day.'

She stares at me, waiting for me to respond, but I don't know what to say, and say nothing.

She waits a few minutes before asking,

'You were telling me yesterday that you're thinking about selling your mum's house. Have you thought any more about that?'

'Yes, I've had it valued and I'm going to sell it. Before mum died, I'd been saving to buy some land, I had wanted to build my own house, but after she died, it felt wrong to carry on.'

'But now?'

'It still hurts, but what can I do? She's gone, and she's not coming back. That's the hardest part, that I'll never talk to her again.'

'What about Emma, what does she think about your plan?'

'I haven't told her, we're still not talking, she's drunk all the time and very abusive. She's part of the reason why I'm selling the house, so I can move out.'

'How does it make you feel when she's abusive?'

'Sad, I miss my friend, I don't have any family left, she's all I've got. But coming here, has helped me understand, that she has to recognise her own problems and want to get help.'

Dr. Ryan smiles as she leans back in her chair.

'Well Eve, I'd say this past month, you've come on significantly and as long as you're happy, I'm happy to reduce our sessions to once a month. Or if you'd prefer, we can do fortnightly for a while?'

'I don't think I'm ready, just yet for monthly. Can we do fortnightly for the next month and see?'

'Of course, but you're stronger than you realise. Now go, get your land and build your new home.'

Chapter 3. The Land.

A week after my session with Dr Ryan, I found a piece of land for sale; The only problem is that it's in Northern Ireland. I love the look of it and my gut tells me that I should view it. The trip could double up as a mini break. I'm hoping Emma will come with me, it would be good to catch up. I miss her, Dr Ryan helped me understand that Emma's drinking is a reaction to mum's death. I know she needs help, but she has to make the decision herself.

A week later, Emma and I are setting off for a mini break to Northern Ireland. Emma's not happy. She thinks it's a ridiculous idea, telling me that I've lost my mind. Although that's not new, ever since I got home from hospital after my suicide attempt. She appears to take pleasure in telling me that I've lost my mind. I'm trying to make allowances for her, but my patience is wearing thin. We've been friends since primary school, but if she's going to continue to be such a bitch, I'm ready to move on. I'm hoping the trip will bring us closer again.

Who knew the roads in Northern Ireland would be so bendy? I'm navigating, using the Sat Nav. I'm wishing, with my heart and soul that I came alone. Emma has been a nightmare the whole way. I'm thankful when the Sat Nav shows that we have almost arrived. Finally. I don't want to admit it, but Emma is right; it really is a long way from home. The weather has been pleasant for the journey so far. Emma is snoring as I drive down a small back road.

'*You have reached your destination,*' states the Sat Nav.

'At long last,' Emma said jolting awake, letting out a long sigh.

Parking on a grass verge next to a flaking green wooden gate, hanging off its hinges. I'm grateful to have finally arrived; my body aches, it's been a long tiring journey. The sun is shining low in the sky; the land looks green and lush. My stomach does a flip, the reality of what I'm doing hitting home. Glancing at Emma holding her head in her hands, I wish I could tell her my fears. But I don't want to hear what she will have to say. Telling her my plans after she'd been drinking was a bad idea.

'That was stupid of me,' I thought, feeling slightly guilty at dragging her here, she's clearly hungover and pissed off.

I know, she sees me like a little lapdog and before, I didn't mind doing everything she said. But I know now that I need to do what's right for me even if it upsets Emma. She gave me a big lecture on the ferry over, telling me that this is a reaction to mum dying, that I'm just depressed. I'm sick of being told that I'm depressed. What does she expect? It's been a long journey and I can feel my anger rising ready to erupt.

'At least it's not raining. Are we ever going to get out of the car?' Emma asks sarcastically, smirking as she lifts her head to look at me.

She looks so unwell and pissed off; I really wish that I'd come by myself. 'Yes, let's do this,' I said, stepping out of the car, slamming the door.

I don't want Emma's disapproval here. My annoyance at Emma quickly subsides as the cool fresh pine tree and grass smell hits me. It's refreshing and instantly uplifting. The low winter sun feels warm on my face as a cool breeze blows my hair. I'm giddy, at all what this place could be? I feel home. Closing my eyes, I take deep breaths trying to inhale as much as I can. I know before I see the land that I want to experience that uplifting smell every day. Opening my eyes, I look up and see a slim, smartly dressed woman in her late twenties walking towards us.

'She must be the estate agent,' I said, turning to look at Emma, who's staring at me like I've got two heads.

'What is her problem?' I thought, irritated.

Emma is really pissing me off, but thankfully I'm distracted by the woman who is smiling broadly as she walks towards us.

13

'Hello ladies, you must be here for the viewing,' she said in a broad Northern Irish accent.

'My name is Mya Thompson; I own Thompson Auctioneers. This plot is a new listing; it only came to us last month,' she said.

Mya has a calm authority about her as she guides us around the outer of the land where there's a small dirt pathway.

'This is a well-appointed acre and a half site. It has just been granted full planning permission for a two story 3-bedroom family home,' Mya said.

'I can tell you that there has been a lot of interest already,' she continues.

'I didn't know it had planning permission' I state, apprehensive that the price may be bumped up.

'Yes, it was granted last week just before it was put up for auction,' Mya said, stopping in front of a small stream.

I'm enjoying the feel of the area as we walk around. The land is completely secluded; I can't see any other houses nearby. There's a thick wooded area to the north with what looks like a small stone outbuilding that has a broken tin roof. The overgrown meadow stretches from the woods to a shallow river that runs along the bottom southern boundary. Mya shows us the plans and where permission has been granted for the dwelling. I like it, it shows that the house will face south overlooking the meadow, river and the surrounding fields. I would probably keep the layout, just use sustainable building materials and natural sources for electricity.

'My aunt used to live here in that dilapidated cottage over by the wood there, before she died. Then my cousin inherited the land, but he doesn't live in Northern Ireland and just wants it sold. The cottage and land have been unoccupied for many years,' Mya tells us looking wistfully around the land.

'Would you mind if I explore by myself? I just want to get a better feel,' I ask.

'No problem. I'll wait in my car. Give me a shout when you're ready.'

I hand Emma my keys watching as she turns stropping off to sit in my car. Ignoring her, I turn back into the land to get a better feel. As I walk around breathing in the air, listening to the wind whistling through the trees. I realise that I want it, I want to buy this land and build my new home here. There's an excitement in my belly that I'm trying to subdue as I walk across to Mya's car.

'I live in England and this is my first time coming to Northern Ireland, everywhere is completely new to me. Could you tell me about the surrounding area?'

'Yes, of course, about two miles south down that road, there is a small town called Ramtree. Ramtree has a GP surgery, a convenience store, a pub, a church, a chemist and a police station,' she said before turning and pointing in the opposite direction.

'And to the North about four miles down that road you will arrive at the north Atlantic coast. This is a great location, you're rural and as secluded as you want to be. But you have the bonus of having amenities right on your doorstep,' she explains.

'There's a farm on up that road, they would be your nearest neighbours,' she said pointing in the direction of the farm.

'Sounds great' I said, feeling optimistic that I could make a life here.

'We're heading back home to England tomorrow afternoon; do you know if I can bid online at the auction?'

I'm glad Emma's in the car and doesn't hear the conversation, I can see in my peripheral vision her face is like thunder. I'm not sure she will ever talk to me again.

'This could be the end of our friendship' I realise trying to avoid looking at her.

I notice Mya looking from myself to Emma, trying to read the situation.

'Yes, yes, the auction has online bidding, here is the legal pack and good luck. Maybe I'll see you soon,' Mya said, smiling broadly as she shakes my hand before returning to her car.

It was an awkward journey home. Emma sat with her face in her phone and completely ignored me for the whole journey. I don't think she will forgive me if I decide to do this.

'Do I really want to risk losing a lifelong friendship, over a piece of land, in a place I don't know?' I wonder as I sit alone on the ferry home.

The trip to Northern Ireland has helped me realise how much Emma and I have drifted apart. Where once we did everything together, now I barely see her. Maybe it really is time to move on.

***

It's Thursday, and the auction is this evening. The past two days have been torture, firstly, because Emma's being a complete bitch, telling everyone and anyone who will listen, that I've lost my mind. She won't even speak to me when we are alone in the house. The atmosphere has been horrible in the house, but what's been even worse, has been the waiting. I can't stop thinking about the land, my gut is telling me, that it's where I'm supposed to be. The auction doesn't start until 7:30 this evening and I'm terrified that I will be outbid and lose the land. I keep remembering that first intoxicating smell when I first stepped out of the car.

'I want that to be my every day' I reflect knowing deep in my gut that this is what is right for me.

I would never have picked Northern Ireland as a place to live, but I loved it. I loved the greenery, the accent, and the friendliness of everyone we met. It was a wonderful experience and one I hope I will be able to experience every day in the near future.

It has been a long day, work dragged, and the evening has been even worse, but the auction site is finally open. I feel sick, I'm so nervous, I've got butterflies in my stomach.

'Am I really going to do this?'

I don't know how fast land auctions go? but the plot is Lot No. 75. I don't want to risk missing it, so I'm going to watch the whole auction. Preparing to spend most of my evening watching, to my surprise, however, the properties are going thick and fast. I'm amazed and excited at how fast the auction is going. Before I know it, Lot. 75 is up. The bidding has started, I've already put in my top offer, because I can't go over. I hope that it won't get that far. The bidding starts low, but the numbers are going up every couple of seconds before the bidding abruptly stops.

'What's happening?'

My hearts racing, I was leading, but the hammers down and SOLD in big red letters has appeared under the picture of the land. It looks like they're moving onto the next Lot. It was three thousand under my max budget, I check my account which has *Winning Bid* written in red stretching across a picture of the land.

'Does this mean I've won, that I own the land?'

I don't believe what I'm reading, my hands are shaking uncontrollably.

'It looks like I've won.'

As I sit staring at the screen, my email pings. I can't stop shaking and want to be sick, but I've got to check. Opening my email, I see *"Your winning bid of £37,000 for Lot No. 75 was successful"* written across the page. I can't believe how easy and fast it was. I keep reading the email over and over, I can't believe it. My bid was successful, I own the land, and it was under budget.

Chapter 4. New Beginnings.

I can't believe it, I don't actually believe it, but I keep looking and it's right there, in the email. That my bid was successful, that I won! After drinking a large glass of wine to calm my nerves. I spend the rest of the evening continuously re-reading the email. It takes a while but eventually I begin to realise that I've actually done it. I've bought the land. I can't believe it, I am delighted, my dream is on its way to becoming a reality. This is the first time since Mum passed away. I feel truly happy and optimistic and excited for the future. I decided to wait a few days before telling Emma, I just wanted to enjoy the moment without her disapproval. And I was right. She reacted exactly as I thought she would when I did eventually get around to telling her.

'You've lost your mind and need psychiatric help. You're gonna end up locked away,' she said, her words slurring as she takes a large gulp of wine that spills down her top.

Watching her as the wine spreads down her top. I find it strange that she seems to enjoy telling me that I've lost my mind. When she's the one who is drinking herself to oblivion every day.

***

It takes a full week for the reality of what I'd done to settle in. After which I begin to think about when I should move and how I'm going to begin building my new home? Initially I'd thought about renting, but I quickly decide it would be better to stay on the land. Mostly because I'm going to need all the money I can get, but also because I just want to be there, to enjoy the smell and feel of my new land. So, with the spare three thousand, I purchased an eighteen-year-old, four-birth towing caravan and I love it. I love everything about it. The decor is dated, but I love the flowery pink interior. It has a small bathroom with a shower and wardrobe. In the kitchen, there is a small fridge, along with a full-size oven and hob. At the front there are two long seats that turn into a double bed, with two small seats down the side that turn into bunk beds. I love my new caravan; My only issue is that towing is completely new to me. I'd never towed anything before towing the caravan home, and now I'm planning to use my ten-year-old Volkswagen Golf, to tow my caravan all the way to my new life in

Northern Ireland. I'm not only worried about towing in general but also about how I will get it on and off the ferry and hope I don't destroy my car and the caravan in the process.

***

It's February, and it's been a busy month since I purchased the land. This morning, I booked the ferry and I'm leaving for my new life in Northern Ireland next Wednesday. Everything has happened so fast that I've been almost too busy to worry about what I've done. I handed in my notice at work the day after I bought the land and today was my last day. I've spent the past four weeks selling most of my stuff. I'm only going to bring what is essential, and what I can fit into the caravan, and my car. The closer my moving day gets, the more excited I am about my new venture. I must admit I'm a little nervous about living in a caravan by myself in a strange country, a country where I don't know anyone but mostly, I'm excited. Everything is going to plan perfectly, apart from the fact that Emma is still ignoring me. She's barely spoken to me since we got back from Northern Ireland a month ago. I wish she could be happy for me, or angry or anything would be better than the silent treatment I'm getting. I miss my friend, but there's no talking to her; she's either drunk and abusive or hungover and abusive these days.

***

The week flew in and today is moving day. Today I leave the life I know to tackle the unknown. I've been up since the crack of dawn checking everything. The ferry is leaving at 11am and my plan is to get some breakfast and get going. I'd rather be too early than too late. I don't know what to do about Emma I'm contemplating waking her to say goodbye, but I am too excited and happy about my new venture. She came in late last night and I really don't want to have an argument right before I leave. I wait until I've finished breakfast before making the decision to leave her a note instead of waking her. I really don't want to deal with her drama this morning.

Hi Emma, you were sleeping when I left early this morning, and I didn't want to wake you. I just wanted to leave you a note to say that I hope someday you can forgive me. I love you; You are my best friend, and maybe when I'm settled, you will come to visit.

Take Care, Lots of Love Eve xxx.

Folding the note in half and placing it in the middle of the kitchen table, I take a deep breath in as I glance around the room one last time. That's it, I'm going, I've double, and triple checked that I've got everything, also, that the caravan is hooked up properly. I don't want to lose my new home halfway down the motorway. My hands are shaking and my stomach jittery as I set off on the first part of my journey. The journey is going smoothly, and I've been driving for just over two-and-a-half hours when I start seeing signs for the ferry port and realise that I've arrived. I'm delighted, the journey was uneventful, the car was fine, and the caravan is still attached. My next hurdle, however, is going to be getting the caravan onto the ferry.

'I really hope I can do it' I thought, walking back to my car after getting myself checked in.

My stomach is jumping and I'm beginning to wonder if this is a good idea? My nerves build as I wait and I feel sick, I've been waiting for about forty-five minutes when the ferry workers in their bright yellow jackets start calling for loading. My stomach lurches when I realise it's time to move, that this could be the end of my caravan! Of my dream! Looking at the incline of the ramp I'm wondering how on earth my VW Golf is going to pull the caravan up that ramp? The cars ahead of me are moving and I let off my handbrake and roll slowly forwards. My leg is shaking while I wait to watch the vehicles in front of me board the ferry. The line moves fast, and before I know it, suddenly it's my turn.

'What if I can't do it?'

Checking my wing mirrors, I can see rows and rows of cars behind me and realise that all these cars will be stuck, if my car isn't powerful enough to get the caravan up the ramp. I'm too hot, my heart is racing, and my palms are sweaty as I release my hand brake and begin to roll forward. My front tyres have landed on the bumpy ramp, I check my extended wing mirrors again and wait for all the cars in front to drive on, until the ramp is completely clear. Increasing the pressure on the accelerator, the engine rev's and the car begins to move up the ramp. My car strains loudly as it struggles with the weight of the caravan. There's no going back now, I keep my foot on the accelerator, pushing on. I keep checking my mirror, delighted that every time I look the caravan is still there and before I know it. I'm up and over the ramp, quickly catching up with the car in front of me. The car has quietened down, and the caravan is still behind me. I can't believe I've done it; I want to do a happy dance, following the car in front, I notice a ferry worker, in a yellow jacket directing me into a parking space. I can't believe that I've done it, I probably look ridiculous, grinning from ear to ear, but I don't care, I don't even care about the strong smell of fuel wafting through my open window. My first major hurdle is over now I only have to worry about getting the caravan off when we dock, but, for the next three hours all is good and I can relax.

Chapter 5. Northern Ireland.

Exhausted after my early start, I slept for most of the ferry journey. Only waking when it is announced over the tannoys that the ferry is ready to dock at Belfast harbour. All drivers have been called to the parking decks ready for unloading. Be calm, you can do this, I tell myself over and over as I look for my car and caravan my palms sweating, and my heart racing. The strong smell of petrol fumes turns my stomach along with my ever-increasing nerves. Waiting patiently, I notice the back of the ferry opening, and the light seeping in. The line is moving quickly and before I know it, it's my turn.

'Oh crap, I hope I can do this.'

It's a bit bumpy, but the caravan is still behind me and the car sounds okay. I'm nearly there, I just have to keep moving. Before I know it, I'm rolling down on to land and feel delighted to have landed in Belfast as I follow the traffic towards my new life. Well, I would be, if the traffic hadn't abruptly stopped just around the first corner. After more than an hour of being stuck in traffic. The cars are finally moving, and the road has cleared. Finally, I'm heading north towards the coast noticing bits of a mangled car at the side of the road realising that it had been a car accident that was causing the holdup. My new home is only four miles from the North Coast, and I'm looking forward to exploring all the famous sights when I get a chance.

***

I've been driving for almost an hour and a half, but I'm beginning to worry I don't remember any of these roads and feel completely lost. I'm trying to find anything that I recognise, but I can't and convince myself that the Sat Nav must be wrong when it suddenly announces that I should be arriving soon.

'You will arrive at your destination in 200 yards' states the Sat Nav.

I don't trust it but follow the instructions anyway and turn onto a road that I finally recognise. My body aches, but I'm delighted to have made it and feel myself welling up. Sitting in my car looking around, the land is exactly how I remembered it. I'd been worried that it would be different and wouldn't live up to expectations. I open the green rickety gate and manoeuvre the car and caravan down the small dirt trail before parking up.

'It will do for now, I'm too tired' I thought stretching my stiff shoulders as I get out of the car.

I take a big breath in, whilst taking in the views surrounding my rugged new home.

'I love the smell of this place, it's intoxicating,' I thought welling up at actually being here.

It's been a long day travelling and it won't be long until the sun sets. Lifting the last bottle of water out of the car I take a swig and realise I'm gonna need to get some. The auctioneer mentioned something about the land having a water and electric supply. But I have no idea where the water is? I decide to explore before it gets too dark, but I don't know where to start. I'm panicking wondering if moving here was a good idea? Standing beside the caravan, scanning the area my eyes, stop on the crumbling building over by the woods, it seems the most likely place to have water. The temperature has dropped, and I pull my heavy coat on before setting out across the meadow. The cold damp grass is as high as my waist, I'm trying to be brave, but I'm freaking out about what I can't see in the long grass as the light quickly fades around me. I'm startled when I hear movement behind me. Spinning around, looking for what made the noise? I spot the tall grass moving and follow the trail which is heading in my direction. I'm trying desperately to calm my racing heart, but instinctively I want to run.

'Oh, thank goodness' I said looking down, feeling instantly relieved, when a friendly looking sheep dog bursts through the grass in front of me.

Scanning the meadow as I pet the dog; I spot a smartly dressed elderly gentleman who I assume must be the owner. He stops by the gate and waves; I wave back before wading through the tall grass towards him bringing the dog with me.

'Well, how's it going?' he said in a thick Northern Irish accent, smiling.

'Hello, I'm Eve, I've just moved in, well sort off, I'm staying in the caravan for now,' I said, indicating my caravan.

'Well, that'll make us neighbours then,' he said, smiling.

'I'm John and I own the farm next door. It's just me and my partner Morag.'

'If you need anything just call up.'

'Thank you. I don't want to be a pain, but there is something I could do with some help with. Would you happen to know if there is a tap or water supply on this land?'

'Well, this used to be Mrs Thompsons place. She died a number of years ago now, but you see the stone building near the trees over there, that's where she lived and where the tap would be,' he said, pointing towards the woods, as the dog sits obediently at his leg.

Following the direction, he's pointing; I realise the light is fading fast and don't want to go near the building in the dark. Maybe I'll be okay until the morning, there's a small amount of water left.

'It doesn't look very safe,' I said.

'Listen, I don't want to intrude, but it's getting far too dark to be messing about looking for water. If you want? I'll bring

31

you a barrel of water that will keep you going until the morning,' he said, smiling.

'Thanks, John. I don't fancy exploring that building in the dark. In fact, I wasn't going to bother.'

'Give me ten minutes,' he said, heading off in the direction of the farm.

The light is almost gone as I walk back to the caravan, I'm struggling to find all my torches and warm clothes when I spot car lights coming down the road through the caravan window.

'That must be John' I thought pulling my coat on as I quickly head back outside to meet him, as he parks up and gets out of his land rover smiling broadly.

'Well, young lady, here's your water. I've also brought you some of Morag's homemade vegetable soup and soda bread. Thought you probably would need something warm,' he said, kindly handing me a large pot of soup along with some bread.

'Thank you so much. It smells delicious. I wasn't looking forward to battling with the caravans gas cooker,' I said, grateful to my new neighbour.

I'm exhausted and suddenly feel overwhelmed with emotion; The soup is exactly what I need. John stays to help me hook up the caravans' water and gas bottle before leaving as the daylight disappears completely. It's so dark here, I don't think I've ever been anywhere that is so dark, there are no lights anywhere. I turn all the lights off in the caravan and sit on the doorstep looking up at the stars. It's amazing and I'm completely awestruck; I've never seen, so many stars; it's magical. While the stars are magical, it also feels very eerie being on my own, in the pitch-black in a strange place. As I look out into the darkness, my imagination begins to run wild.

'There could be anything out there and I wouldn't be able to see it' I thought, certain that I'll not be getting any sleep at all tonight.

Turning the lights back on, I lock the door, close all the blinds, and listen to the noises outside the caravan. The wind has picked up and the trees are blowing wildly outside, making the caravan rock. It's still early, just after 9pm and despite feeling completely exhausted. I can't settle and get my television set up; the background noise is a welcome distraction from my imagination, the wind and the outside noises. Lying down on one of the long seats at the front of the caravan, I close my heavy eyelids listening to the TV. As I listen, I can feel myself beginning to relax, finally. My body is heavy as I listen to the trees blowing in the wind outside.

***

Blinking several times as I open my eyes, I'm confused about where I am? My vision clears and I suddenly sit up, remembering I'm in the caravan. Glancing around as my eyes adjust, I can see that it's daylight outside. I notice the TV has turned itself off and reach over to turn it back on. BBC breakfast fills the screen. The clock in the corner of the TV shows that it is almost 6:30am. I can't believe I fell asleep so early and slept right through. I've slept well, really, really well and feel great, my body doesn't ache anymore. I'm rejuvenated and excited about exploring my new land today. My first goal for today is to find some fresh water and I'm going to start with the stone building. But before I do anything, I need a shower and then some food. I'm hoping and praying that the hot water will work, pessimistically assuming that it won't. It's freezing in the caravan and I lean over to turn the gas heater on. It's my only source of heat, I don't like the smell and it makes me feel nervous but at least it's warm. I wait to let the caravan heat before attempting to get up, but there's still a chill when I step away from the heater. The shower was grand, it was, dare I say it, nice. I feel clean and refreshed, ready to start my day as I make myself a cup of coffee and some toast. The sun is shining low in the winter sky as I sit in the doorway of the caravan, watching the trees blowing in the wind. As I finish the last dregs of my coffee, I set about looking for my purple sparkly wellies, warm coat and torch. Even with the sun shining there's still a chill in the air, as I set off determinedly towards the stone building. I'm not as nervous now that I can somewhat see where I am going? As I trample through the overgrown grass, listening to the cows in the nearby fields. I remember that I must thank John and Morag for the water and soup. As I get closer to the building, I can feel that the ground is more stable here, almost like there is a pathway somewhere beneath the vegetation. As I reach the building, I'm not sure where to start? It's completely covered in ivy, but I notice a gap and pull a large chunk of it away. Removing the ivy has revealed a really charming stable door. The green paint is flaking off, but it looks sturdy, nothing a lick of paint wouldn't fix. I could sand it down, paint it and try to use it on the new build. It would be nice to incorporate some reclaimed pieces. I try turning the door handle and pushing, but when it doesn't budge, I realise that it's locked and wonder how on earth I'm going to get in? I don't want to ruin the door; it only needs a lick of paint, and I really do like it. Perhaps the key has been hidden somewhere? I begin lifting nearby rocks and get lucky when I lift a stone placed next to the step. It's light and I immediately realise that it's a fake stone and there's a key inside.

'Awesome' I said, laughing unable to believe my luck.

The key turns inside the lock without a problem, but when I try to push it open, it's stuck. The thick ivy is stopping it from moving, I begin pulling as much as I can off, and use all my strength and body weight to shove the door with my shoulder until it opens a small way. I continue to push until it opens enough that I can squeeze myself in.

THE COTTAGE

Chapter 6. The Stone Building.

Cobwebs and dust hit me in the face as the door swung open. I panic, spluttering and choking as I stumble back out of the building.

'Aghaaa, waaaaa get off me' I shout, frantically swiping at the cobwebs.

I run as fast as my legs will take me away from the building screaming, waving my arms all around. I don't stop until I'm in the middle of the long grass coughing from the dust while jumping up and down, swiping at the cobwebs and spiders that are crawling all over me. It takes a while, but when I've calmed down a little, I look back at the building, grateful that I'm alone, and no one saw my meltdown. Shivering, I continue to swipe at imaginary spiders and realise how ridiculous I'm being. I take a minute to calm down before gathering myself up and marching across to the caravan to find my umbrella. Hoking the umbrella out from the under-seat storage in the caravan I'm satisfied that it will protect me if more dust, cobwebs and spiders are going to fall. Trying to calm my racing heart and stop myself from jumping at every little thing, I inhale several deep breaths before heading back through the long grass. Slowly easing the stable door open, more dust and cobwebs fall as I try to see in. Reluctant to enter, I stand in the doorway, still swiping at imaginary spiders as I lean as far as I can in through the door without actually entering. It's very dusty and hard to see, but there is a beam of light coming through a large hole in the roof. Stepping backwards, I tread carefully around the side of the building to inspect the roof from the outside. I can see that it's an old corrugated tin roof with the whole corner missing. It's not just the roof that's missing but also some large wall stones. There's ivy growing out of the roof, and it looks like there might even be a tree growing from the inside out. Heading back around to the front door, I begin clearing as much dirt from the outside step as I can and use all of my strength to push the door completely open. When the door is fully opened, it's a lot brighter and I can somewhat see inside the building, but I'm too afraid to actually enter and lean in through the doorway. Peering in, I spot an old ceramic sink on the opposite wall, in front of a large window that is covered in ivy. Taking a small tentative step through the door, I push my umbrella up, hoping that it will stop whatever is falling from landing on me. My heart is racing, and I can't stop shaking, imagining that spiders are crawling all over my back and hair. Glancing around, I'm terrified that the building is going to collapse, and I will be crushed. The dust is dense, and I pull my jumper up to cover my mouth and nose, but I still can't stop coughing and can barely see what's in front of me. The building smells of damp concrete and my heart does a flip when I notice movement out of the corner of my eye. I quickly turn to see a mouse running along a shelf. Too afraid to move, I freeze and sweat trickles down my back as I watch the mouse stop to preen itself on the shelf. This whole building feels like it is alive. There're spiders everywhere, mice running around and plants growing all over the windows. I'm trembling but trying desperately to stay calm by taking deep breaths through my jumper. Too afraid to do anything else, I watch the mouse as the dust begins to settle and my heartrate begins to slow. Scanning my surroundings, I notice that it is a large room that has been divided into a sitting area at the far side and a kitchen on the other side. I can see that it was, at some point, someone's home. There's a small wooden dining table and two wooden chairs against the wall beside the sink. There are also two single armchairs facing away from me. I can't see to the back of the room from where

I'm standing. It's too dark, but I can see that there's the outline of a large window. I look up at the shelf and can see that the mouse hasn't moved. Holding my jumper over my mouth and nose to filter the dust, I take some deep breaths to compose myself before stepping back outside. Walking through the long grass to where I assume the kitchen window is located. I can't find any sign of any windows anywhere. In fact, standing here looking at the building, you can barely see any sign of a building at all. It's completely covered in ivy with only a few stones showing. I use all my might to pull the ivy away, but it's really thick and difficult to shift. It takes a long time but finally, after breaking a big chunk off, I can finally see the rotten wooden window frame. Feeling determined, I pull more and more ivy and plants away until the window is completely exposed. Using my sleeve, I wipe the window until I can see through to the open door on the opposite side. Heading back to the front door I look in and can see that it's a lot brighter inside, the light is streaming in through the newly exposed window and the hole in the roof. Still feeling very jumpy and nervous, I stand in the doorway trying to calm my racing heart as I step through the door. Walking further into the building, I spot two more doors I hadn't noticed before. The doors are next to each other on the left-hand side of the living room area. Now that it is brighter, I realise that the building is a lot bigger than I originally thought. Taking care, I walk through the rubble and open the nearest door. The door is very stiff, and I use my shoulder to shove it, unsettling a pile of dust that makes me start coughing uncontrollably. It takes a while before I am able to look into the room. I'm pleasantly surprised when I poke my head in through the door and find a bathroom. It smells damp, and it's difficult to see, but there's a small window on the far side, that like the rest of the building is completely covered with ivy. As my eyes adjust to the darkness, I'm surprised to find a large cast iron bath, a toilet and sink. Stepping in through the door, I flush the toilet that is right in front of me and I'm delighted to find that it works and immediately try the taps. I can't believe it when rusty looking water comes pouring out of them. Standing in the dusty room, I realise that the building has a fully functioning bathroom.

'This is awesome' I thought, cautiously stepping back into the main living area.

I try the next door which also needs a lot of force to get it open. Leaning in through the door, I find a small bedroom that is dusty, cobwebby and probably bigger than it first appears. It has been completely filled with a large double bed and an imposing dark wooden wardrobe. Looking around, I spot a small single radiator below a large window which like the others is covered with plants. The room is covered with cobwebs and as I step through the door, I walk face first into one. The cobweb has covered my face and in a complete panic I jump up and down screaming and swiping in front of me, as I frantically wipe it from my face. Backing out of the room as quickly as I can, terrified that large spiders are crawling all over me. I'm jittery as I stand in the living room area, waiting for my heartrate to regulate and notice a large window on the far side wall that is filthy and covered with plants like the others. Walking deeper into the room, the texture has changed under my feet. I assume that there must be a rug on the floor, but there's too much rubble and dust to tell. The dust is dense and choking me, hanging heavy in the air. Turning toward the door, I begin to panic, I need to get out of here, I'm struggling to breathe and need some fresh air as I make my way carefully out of the building. It's sunny outside and I sit down on a large rock, taking deep breaths desperate for some fresh air. Looking at the walls covered with ivy, I decide that my next job is to find and clear all the windows.

'At least then I will be able to see inside better and hopefully I'll be able to open them.'

Sitting with the sun warming my face, I'm beginning to think that if I fix the roof and clean the place up, I could stay here instead of the caravan for the rest of the winter. The caravan was freezing this morning, and it would be nice to have water on tap. Looking at the building, I realise that it is going to be a lot of work and to be any benefit it will need to get done quickly.

'It doesn't have to be perfect, just watertight to see me through the rest of winter.'

'I'm going to need to get myself some cleaning supplies, a ladder, and some corrugated iron to fix the roof' I thought, looking forward to my new project.

'I'll ask John where to go? he's bound to know somewhere.'

Closing my eyes and looking up at the sun, enjoying its warmth on my face, I'm feeling energised at the prospect of my new project. It's nice sitting in the winter sun but I'm filthy. Standing up, I stretch and dust myself off before walking back through the long grass to the caravan. I want to get cleaned up and get some lunch before heading over to see John. The sun is shining, but the air is cold as I walk up the road towards John's farm. As I approach, I spot a short stout woman with wild grey hair sweeping the yard and assume that it is John's wife Morag. The woman stops what she is doing and shouts what do you want? she has an odd sounding Northern Irish accent. I'm taken aback I didn't expect her to be so abrupt.

'I'm Eve, I've moved in next door, I wanted to thank you for the soup and soda bread' I said, trying not to offend her, but she doesn't look pleased.

'What do you want?' she repeats scowling as she turns away, continuing to sweep the floor.

'I was looking for John. Is he around?'

I'm standing at the gate unsure what to do when she doesn't respond. I'm about to leave when I see John coming from the house towards us.

'Thank goodness' I thought, wondering what Morag's problem is?

'Well, Eve, nice of you to call' he said warmly, walking with a stiff gait to let me in.

'I'm glad to see that you survived the night in the caravan. Not sure I'd want to be camping out in this weather' he said chuckling.

'I was just thanking Morag for the food, and yes, I survived, it was noisy with the wind though' I tell them both.

'I wanted to ask, if you would know somewhere local, where I could buy corrugated iron and outdoor cleaning supplies?'

'Well, you're in luck, I have some corrugated iron that might suit you. I don't need it and I'm sure there's everything you need for cleaning here. Come on, follow me' he said.

He turns and begins walking towards a large wooden shed. I thank Morag for the soup again and follow John.

'We can load up the truck with everything you need. Then you can show me what mischief you're up too?'

I'm delighted, John has everything I need, and he's happy to let me have it, refusing to take any payment for anything. John insists on helping me unload when we get back to the land, even though he looks like he is in a lot of pain when he moves.

'I wonder if I should ask if he is okay? or would that be rude? I hardly know him after all' I thought.

I don't say anything choosing to help him unload the truck instead. After everything is unloaded, I bring John over to the small building and show him inside.

'It was a long, long time ago, that I was in this cottage' he said, looking around.

'Old Mrs Thompson was a very private person, she kept herself to herself, but she was a good person.'

I get the impression that he was fond of her.

'I'm thinking, that if I can tidy the place up, maybe, I could stay here for the rest of the winter, instead of the caravan.'

'You might find that you want to stay here for good, it used to be a nice place' he said, nodding his head in approval.

'I know it needs a lot of work, but I do like it. It does have a nice feel about it.'

'It does indeed, my dear' he said patting me on the back.

'While I would love to stay and help, I have to love you and leave you. But please, make sure that you be careful' he said pointing at the broken roof.

'I'll try, and thanks again for all of this.'

'No problem' he said heading back towards the truck. I wave as John drives away, standing in the long grass looking at the crumbling building. It occurs to me that I want to build an eco-friendly house.

'Well, I can't get much eco-friendlier than recycling a whole building, can I?' I thought.

The more I think about it, the more the idea grows on me. Standing in the long grass outside I'm thinking about all it will take to make it liveable. It will be cheaper than building from scratch. Doing this place up, could save me a fortune. The building has a water supply, it also has an open fire for heat, and I can see some dodgy looking electrical wires. It will definitely need a proper roof eventually, but for now, patching the roof will keep it dry for the rest of the winter.

Chapter 7. The Big Clean Up.

My first job will be the roof. I need to make this place watertight. There's no point cleaning inside if rain can get in. Although as I look around what I assume to be the kitchen, I'm a little overwhelmed and apprehensive. It's going to be a mammoth job. Stepping outside, I lift John's ladder and place it against the side of the building. It's a bit wobbly but I don't think it'll move. I've never done anything like this before and grip the ladder tightly as I slowly climb high enough to assess the damage. The ladder is unsteady as I climb, but when I reach the top and assess the roof, I realise it's not as bad as I first thought. By the look of things, I should only need one, possibly two sheets of the corrugated iron John gave me. From my elevated position, I notice that the top of the stone wall that supports the roof is also damaged and will need to be secured. Looking at the damage, I'm wondering whether I will need to get someone in? But it's only a small area of the wall that needs built-up, just a couple of the big stones. I can see them on the ground below me. Glancing across at the stuff John left yesterday, I realise that I could just have a go myself and if I can't do it, then I can get someone in.

'Get down, before you fall and break your neck' I hear a male voice with a broad Northern Irish accent shout from behind me.

Turning in the direction the voice came from, I spot a scruffily dressed man with wild brown hair escaping from under a flat cap striding towards me.

'Who are you?' I call, amused at the rudeness of the slightly dishevelled but wiry figure striding towards me through the long grass.

He ignores my question and continues to stride in my direction until he gets to the bottom of the ladder. He holds the ladder steady as he looks up at me. I'm instantly distracted by his vivid blue eyes, which stir something in me.

'I'm Tom, I work for John. I'm his farm hand' the rude stranger tells me. 'Now get down, before you fall down', he said, gesturing with his muscular arm for me to get down.

Amused at his abruptness, I feel a flush of excitement crawl beneath my skin when I tell him that I'm going to fix the roof. I stay where I am up the ladder, refusing to do as I'm told.

'John gave me cement mix and some gravel, so I can build the wall up. It's only a few large stones,' I said, pointing towards the materials on the ground.

'I know, he told me to come over here and help you before you do something stupid like kill yourself. Don't make me climb up there and carry you down,' he said, a lopsided grin filling his face.

I burst out laughing, noticing the muscles in his arms flexing as he gathers the bags of gravel and water. I watch as he begins to mix the cement.

'You want to get down? and help me?' he said.

Felling a little guilty at my thoughts, I slowly ease myself down the unsteady ladder, I don't actually know what I'm doing and just do whatever Tom says and eventually we begin mixing the cement. Making and mixing cement is back breaking manual work and I'm very glad for the help this rude, surprisingly handsome stranger has given me.

'John was right to send you. There was no way I could've done this by myself,' I said, grateful that Tom is here.

I'm exhausted but proud when the cement is finally ready to use. Tom fills a bucket with the cement mixture and looks very unsteady as he clambers up the ladder. I want to help but he orders me to stay on the ground and pass him up whatever he needs. It doesn't take long before he's got the wall stable and he carefully adds the new piece of corrugated iron before securing it. It's been a long day, the sun is starting to set, and it's getting chilly by the time Tom gets the last of the roof fixed securely. When he's safely down on the ground, I thank him for fixing the roof and wall. He has done a great job.

'I couldn't have done it by myself that's for sure. How much do I owe you?' I ask.

'No need, we look after each other here' he said smiling, refusing to take any payment for the work. I thank him again for what he has done, but I feel a little awkward that he won't accept any payment.

'No problem, but I really need to go and help John bring the cows in for milking,' he said dusting himself off. 'Are you okay to clear this up?' he asks, gesturing at the mess on the ground.

'Yes, yes, of course, thank you again', I said, watching as he strides back across the long grass.

Looking up at the newly built-up wall, I'm proud of what has been accomplished today, but I'm also exhausted and starving. As I set about clearing the mess, I tell myself that I really must remember to eat in the future. The long grass tickles my arms as I walk back to the caravan my stomach grumbling. As I impatiently wait for my cheese and ham toasty to cook, it dawns on me that this will be my second night in the caravan. So much has happened in such a short space of time. I've done so many things that I'd never done before. Sitting on the caravan doorstep, I'm enjoying listening to the birds as I eat when I suddenly remember that I haven't checked my phone since I was on the ferry. I can't recall the last time I saw it? and wonder where on earth it could be? After a frantic search, I eventually find it in my coat pocket. Immediately, I can see that there are three missed calls and four text messages from Emma. The first message I open is a load of abuse for not waking her before I left. I'm sure she must've been drunk when she wrote the second one because I can barely read it. I delete the other two without reading them There's a voice mail and I momentarily consider listening to it but choose to delete it along with the text messages instead.

'What's the point? It will only be a load of abuse,' I thought, feeling tired and irritable. 'It's not like she made it easy for me before I left. I've had such a good day today, trust Emma to bring me down.'

Looking at my phone, it dawns on me that the wedge between Emma and me is continuing to grow wider and wider and I'm not sure we will ever get back what we had. Opening the caravan door and sitting back down on the doorstep, I resent Emma for ruining my day and feel glad that I'm away from her, and all her drama. She needs to cut back on her drinking until she does that this is how she's going to be. Thinking back, I realise, she started drinking heavily after my mum died but it's getting worse, I can't remember the last time she was sober.

'I'll phone her tomorrow sometime in the afternoon hopefully she'll be sober' I thought, wishing ironically that I had some wine or any kind of alcohol to calm me

55

down. I decide to go into Ramtree in the morning to stock up on supplies including alcohol.

***

My second night was a lot quieter than the first. I could barely hear the trees and slept like a baby. It's almost 8am when I wake, it's the first time in a long time that I've slept all night, without having nightmares.

'It must be the country air' I thought happily, my body aching after the manual work yesterday.

I'm stiff and my muscles ache, but I'm satisfied and happy as I put the kettle on and pull out a Pot Noodle for breakfast.

'Now, that was delicious,' I thought, happily enjoying my new routine of doing whatever I like, whenever I like. I take my time getting washed and dressed and when I'm ready to go, I try to do a Google search on my phone, hoping to get directions to Ramtree. But quickly realise that I have no signal. I hadn't noticed before, but I've barely any signal at all, for calls or internet. I'd noticed yesterday that the cottage has electric cables running to it, but it's not connected. If I get the cottage connected to the grid, I could get the Internet installed. I have to walk out into the middle of the meadow before I can get enough signal to phone the local power company. I'm pleased when they tell me that someone will be out today to look at the wires. When I'm ready to go, I program Ramtree into the Sat Nav and drive slowly and carefully, manoeuvring my car down the narrow and bendy road. I'm only driving for about five minutes, when I see houses and a large church.

'This must be Ramtree' I thought feeling a bit silly using the Sat Nav and turn it off.

Driving through the town, I'm delighted to find a large grocery shop with an off-licence and manoeuvre my car into a narrow parking space outside. After I have stocked up on groceries and most importantly wine, I take a drive around Ramtree just to get my bearings. There's a large church at the top of the town, many small shops along the main street, including a chemist and a library.

'It's pretty' I thought, feeling happy to have so much right on my doorstep.

As I'm driving back down the narrow windy road towards the cottage, I spot a Power NI van parked up blocking my way in. I pull in and park up behind the van.

'Is this your place?' a male voice yells from somewhere up above.

Looking up, I see a man at the top of an electrical pole.

'Yes, I called earlier.'

'These wires are old, I'm going to replace them, then get you hooked up,' he said.

'Okay thanks, I'll be in the caravan, if you need me.'

Grabbing my box filled with groceries I head to the caravan, happy with my productive morning. The winter sun is shining low in the sky, which makes it feel warmer than it is. Most of the meadow is covered with cobwebbed dew, it was a frosty night and there is still frost on the grass where the sun hasn't reached yet. The birds are singing, and I can hear machinery in the distance. After unpacking my groceries, I sit on the doorstep enjoying my surroundings and sniff the air; it smells just as good as the first time. I'm truly loving my life and my new home when I spot movement in the trees. I'm delighted when I see a red squirrel jumping across the branches right beside the caravan.

'Wow, that is awesome.'

It's the first red squirrel I've ever seen, and it makes me realise that the world really is astonishing when you get a glimpse of it in its purest form. It's fresh this morning and a chill pricks at my skin as I look across the tall wild grass. I love just about everything about my new home. Listening to the machinery coming from John's farm, I remind myself to visit him later to thank him for sending me Tom. Although I'm hoping his wife won't be around. My thoughts are disrupted when I hear someone calling.

'That's you connected' a male voice calls from behind the caravan.

'That was quick, thank you' I said, walking him back to his truck. I wait until he pulls away before bringing my car in.

'I will probably need to get an electrician; all the switches look dodgy in the building,' I thought.

Walking across to the building, I want to see if the electricity will work? Although, when I look at the switches, I quickly change my mind; none of them look safe. I don't want to cause a fire and decide to ask John if he knows any electrician. Now that the roof has been patched, and the ivy cleared from the windows, it's a lot easier to see that the crumbling building is in fact a small cottage. My plan for today is to clean the windows, to let as much natural light into the building, then get started with properly clearing the inside. Looking out of the grubby kitchen window I realise that I should also clear a proper path from the caravan to the cottage, it will make it easier than tramping through the long grass every time. Tom helped me clear all the ivy from around the house yesterday, and it's making it a lot easier to walk around the building. This time I easily find all the windows, and when I'm done cleaning, it makes such a positive difference. All the natural light coming through the now clean windows floods the inside. Looking around, I can now see what a lovely bright space it will be when I'm done. Standing in the living room with a mask over my face, I'm grateful the dust has finally started to settle, it's making it a little easier to breathe. Even with the sun shining in through the windows, it's still freezing inside, and I wonder if I should try to light the fire?

But on closer inspection, I can see that there are lumps of dirt and what look like bits of bird nest falling down the chimney.

'No, I will need to call a chimney sweep,' I thought.

Chapter 8. Finishing up.

It's early November, and it's been nine months since I first arrived here in Northern Ireland. I find it hard to believe how quickly the time is passing; Today it has been 23 months since my mum passed away. I think about her and miss her every day, but my life has completely changed since I made the decision to move to Northern Ireland. I don't know exactly when it happened? but I no longer feel angry. There's still a massive hole in my life where she belongs, but I'm surviving. Slowly but surely over the last nine months I've been living here, things have got easier. At times I'm furious with myself for not being miserable, but as the months have passed, the darkness has gradually brightened. I can't pinpoint exactly when it happened, but I now feel like I have something to live for. I haven't started a job yet, or even bothered to look for one. In choosing to renovate the cottage rather than building a new house. I was able to save a lot of the money that I'd put aside for building work. I've worked out that I can live off my savings for at least another year before I'll have to think about getting a job. I know eventually I will have to get some sort of paid employment, but for the time being, not having to go to work every day has given me the opportunity to get back to my old passion of writing. I always enjoyed being creative and have recently started working my way through the manuscript I'd started whilst at university. I try to write most evenings after I've finished my day working on the cottage. My life in Northern Ireland is good, and along with writing, I also enjoy watching all the lovely wildlife I regularly see here at the cottage. Red squirrels are a regular visitor looking for nuts in the trees, and I often hear the cry of buzzards or red kites soaring high in the sky. I've spent every day for the past nine months, repairing, cleaning and making the cottage habitable. I'd hoped to spend the last few months of last winter in the cottage, but it needed too much work. Thankfully, I was lucky the weather was mild, and spring came early, which meant I stayed comfortable living in the caravan. I managed to save some money by keeping most of the furniture that was left behind. The original floor of the cottage turned out to be beautiful white quarry stones, that just needed a good clean and a polish. The quarry stone floor is beautiful but freezing to walk on, so I've placed a large fluffy cream rug in front of the fire to keep it cosy. It's taken a lot of work, but the cottage now looks and feels like a home. I've kept costs down by doing most of the work myself but one of the more expensive jobs was getting the cottage completely rewired, but it needed done and it's safe now. I kept most of the original wooden kitchen, just updated the worktops, sink, and added a few extra cupboards. I also kept the green cast iron AGA stove. I love it. It stays warm for ages and heats the whole house.

***

I've been living in the caravan since I arrived and it's been very comfortable, but with November came the strong icy winds. The winds have been so strong that several trees came crashing down in the wood behind the cottage. It's been a couple of weeks since the weather took a turn for the worse and I've been terrified most nights that a tree will come crashing down through the caravan. Along with strong winds, there has also been relentless heavy rain. The dramatic change in the weather has pushed me to make the decision to move into the cottage before I'm properly finished. I'd hoped to get a proper roof on, before moving in, but it can wait until the weather improves. I'm not worried about keeping the corrugated roof a little longer, it may be noisy, but it's watertight, and the cottage is still lovely and warm, and more importantly, safe. Shortly after I started working on the cottage, I got the chimney swept and it turned out that my open fire had a back boiler, and it heats two radiators along with the water. I've been lighting the fire every day for the past couple of weeks since the weather changed. I'm really pleased with how the cottage has transformed over the past nine months. Last week, the cottage got dragged into the 21st century when I had a house phone installed along with a broadband connection. The cottage is now connected to the Internet and the rest of the world. Although, the first thing I saw when I logged in to Facebook, after nine months was that Emma has been bad-mouthing me every minute she gets. I don't know what her problem is, or why she's still so pissed with me? But it annoys me that she is being so childish. I'm beginning to wonder if there is actually something wrong with her. Some stuff she has written is like she is possessed or mentally disturbed. It's more likely that she was drunk, but even if she was, it doesn't make what she has said hurt any less. Putting all thoughts of Emma aside, I glance around the cottage's transformation and it fills me with awe how much it has changed. It was a dilapidated old building that was ready for demolition when I first arrived. There's been many changes at the cottage, but I kept the front stable door, I love it and painted it a pillar box red, replacing all the old rusty hardware with reclaimed black cast iron hardware, including a new letterbox. It looks amazing. In the spring, I want to add a small porch to finish the front entrance and add a little more protection from the weather. Renovating the cottage has been a lot of hard work, but over the past nine months it's become unrecognisable as the crumbling building that was here when I first arrived. It now looks bright and smells lovely and clean. As I stand admiring all my hard work, I realise that along with the cottage, I've also transformed. When I made the decision to move to Northern Ireland, I was in a sad, dark place and had no desire to live. I didn't expect my life to change as much as it has. I never thought that I would find a reason to live or that I would make new friends, but John and Tom have become people who I enjoy spending time with. We have developed into an unlikely trio of friends and I know that I wouldn't have settled as well without them. They've helped me with almost every part of the renovation. I always enjoy their company and look forward to their daily visits, especially Tom. I've been having feelings for him; I don't know how he feels? but I'm too shy to say anything for now.

The weather has become very unpredictable recently and I don't think I'll be able to get much more done outside until the spring. Even so, I'm pleased with all that I've achieved in the last nine months. The cottage is now a warm and cosy home and I'm looking forward to starting my new life here.

Chapter 9. Moving In.

It's official, I now live in the cottage. I moved in last weekend and to celebrate, I've invited Tom, John, and his wife Morag over for a small house-warming party this evening. The rain has been relentless for days and it's pelting heavily on my windscreen as I travel home from Ramtree. My car is full of groceries, snacks, red and white wine along with some beer for the party. The weather is shocking; I need to have the wipers and blowers going full blast in an attempt to keep the windscreen clear as I drive along the small narrow road back to the cottage. After I have unpacked my groceries, I decide to take some photos of the cottage now it's finished and post them on Facebook. There's a secret part of me that wants to annoy Emma. It works, a few minutes after I post my photos, I get a notification that someone has commented.

'Proof that she's lost her mind and is living as a hillbilly hick!!' Emma comments under one of my photos.

'Living the dream and I love it, lol' I comment below, knowing it will annoy her, but I don't care.

There was a time when I would just put up with whatever bullshit Emma was dishing out. But putting some distance between us has helped me realise that I'm far better off away from her negativity. Even so, it still irritates me that she's being so bitchy. Shutting the laptop down a little too forcefully I go to the kitchen and pull all the vegetables I'd bought earlier out of the fridge. I'm making homemade vegetable soup along with some soda bread for my guests this evening. The soup has only started cooking, and the cottage smells divine. Last week, when the rain let up for a short while. I used a piece of the left-over corrugated iron to make a shelter big enough to stand under beside the front door. I've placed a garden table under the shelter and I'm using it to store the extra bottles of white wine and beer. I'm hoping they will stay nice and chilled out here.

It's almost 7pm I've been so busy getting everything ready that I hadn't noticed that it's almost time for my guests to arrive. Looking down at my clothes, I wonder if I should wear something nice tonight, realising that I've been in outdoor work clothes since I arrived in Northern Ireland. I'd almost forgotten that I had anything other than work clothes. It's my first party in the cottage and I'm going to get dressed up. Opening the wardrobe, I realise I haven't even unpacked most of my clothes. I open a box and pull out a lovely blue sparkly top and team it with some black skinny jeans and high heels that I find at the bottom. I hadn't thought about it before, but I haven't been to the hairdresser since I arrived. My thick wavy hair has grown almost to my shoulders. I've always had a short pixie cut but looking in the mirror I realise how wild my hair has become with its natural wave. I must fix this. Opening another box, I dig around until I find my hair straighteners. It takes a good ten minutes of working the straighteners through my unruly hair until it is all smooth and sleek. To my surprise, I'm pleased with the result; my hair now looks long and glossy. I've always had a short pixie crop and liked it that way but examining my new glossy hair in the mirror. I like my new longer look; it's a new start, a new home, a new life and new hair as I run my fingers through my silky hair. Heading back into the kitchen, I realise that there's still half an hour until my guests arrive. The smell from the soup is filling the whole cottage, and it's making me very hungry. I'm wondering if it would be rude to have a bowl before my guest get here, stirring the pot as my belly grumbles.

'No, I must wait' I tell myself, stepping outside into the darkness to my temporary shelter and pour myself a glass of wine instead.

I can barely see what I'm doing; it's so dark with no light pollution nearby. On a clear night, the stars look so much brighter than I ever remember seeing them before. But not tonight, tonight it's even darker than normal with the heavy rain clouds. Enjoying the sound of the rain thundering on the roof, I stand in the dark sipping on my wine.

'Don't drink it all.' I hear someone shout from the darkness.

'Tom,' I call, delighted to have some company laughing as he emerges from the darkness with his enormous colourful umbrella and torch.

'What do you think?' I ask, showing off my make-shift wine and beer shelter.

'I'm impressed. All homes should have an outdoor alcohol chiller,' he said, placing a box of beer into the shelter.

I probably should've had a bowl of soup before drinking, as a warm glow from the wine makes me feel a little reckless. I watch

as Tom grabs himself a beer before heading
into the cottage that smells delicious.

'I hope John and Morag aren't late. I
don't want to wait too long before tucking
in' he said, stirring the soup. Turning to look
me up and down. 'Well, don't you spruce up
rightly, I feel underdressed' he said a
lopsided grin filling his face.

My cheeks are burning, and I'm flustered
when I say, 'Not at all, there wasn't a dress
code. I just wanted to wear something nice.'

I don't know if it's the wine, but I feel as if
he's looking at me differently as his vivid
blue eyes lock with mine. Suddenly, there're
voices outside, and we turn towards the
noise as a gust of wind rushes in, along with
John, followed quickly by Morag. After
shaking off his enormous umbrella, John
offers me two bottles of red wine, and
Morag hands me a basket filled with eggs.

'Good to see you guys, now let's get
some food, I'm starving' I said, beginning to
dish out large bowls of soup, as my guests
settle around my small table.

I've had to bring in a couple of tree stumps
as extra seats, but no one's complaining.

Before we tuck in, Tom nips out and returns with a couple of bottles of white wine and several bottles of beer.

'So, we don't have to keep running outside to refill' he said smiling.

I'd been a little worried about Morag coming, but thankfully, she's been friendly, even complimenting me on my soup. The food has gone down well, and the drink is flowing. I'm enjoying spending my first evening since I moved to Northern Ireland with my new friends.

'Here's to your new home, Eve' John said raising his glass.

'Cheers' everyone said raising their glasses.

Everything was going smoothly until John mentioned that he was thinking about selling the farm.

'I'm getting too old and want to enjoy more evenings like this, without worrying about the early mornings' he said his cheeks flushed.

He can't see Morag's face, but she's right in front of me and it's difficult to avoid the

73

fact that she's furious. The atmosphere instantly changed, no one wants to look at Morag her whole demeanour has transformed. I don't know if it's the amount of wine that she's drank, but she can barely control her anger. I don't know what she's saying, but she's turned her back to us and is muttering under her breath. I catch her glancing at John and I'm certain, if looks could kill, John would be a dead man. The atmosphere is toxic, I don't know what to do? Almost as if she remembered where she is, Morag turns to face us again and tries to make light of John's comment. But it's clear she's not happy, and John will pay when they were alone. There's an awkward silence for a while, and nobody knows what to say to lighten the mood? As host, I know I must do something and grab my phone to get some photos to remember the first party in my new home.

'Come on everyone, squeeze in, I need to get some photo's' I said trying to ignore the look on Morag's face.

My distraction appears to work, with the mood instantly lifting and everyone except Morag happy to pose.

'Does anyone mind if I post these on Facebook?'

'Not me, I don't want any pictures of me put on Facebook' Morag snaps, turning away from us again.

'I don't think you're in any of them' I said flicking through the photos on my phone, trying to avoid looking at her grumpy face.

'Let me see your profile, so I can add you as a friend, then you can tag me' Tom said, tapping away on his phone. It doesn't take long for his friend request to come through and I accept and tag him in the pictures.

'Who's Emma?' Tom asks sounding disgruntled.

'We used to live together before I moved here, we've been best friends since primary school.'

'Best friends, my arse' he said dramatically,

'She's a nasty bitch, that's what she is' he said, continuing to swipe his phone.

75

'Have you seen all the bullshit she's posted on your page?' he said looking annoyed.

'Yeah, I've seen it, but she's just jealous, I don't care about whatever Emma has wrote.'

'She's calling you everything under the sun, what's her problem? She's not your friend, let alone best friend. You should block her, no one needs that kind of negativity' he said.

Glancing at what he is talking about, I don't know if it is the wine that's making me not care, but I burst out laughing, I genuinely don't care what Emma has posted on my page.

'I know, you're right, I should block her, but then I wouldn't be able to annoy her with all my awesome pictures, also she's only showing herself up' I said, laughing.

'Ah, yes, and I can comment with loads of awesome things about you, and your lovely new cottage as well. That'll piss her off' he said, raising his glass.

'I think, we should head soon' John said looking at his watch.

I watch as he pats Morag on the back, but she shrugs him away her face like thunder. I don't want to look at her, she looks like she might kill John on the way home.

'Us oldies will leave you kids to enjoy your Facebooking' he said, a big grin on his face as he stands wobbling slightly.

'Thank you so much for the soup and bread, the food was delicious' Morag said, struggling to stand, but refusing to accept any help from John.

'Thanks for coming, we should do it again soon' I said walking them to the door.

'See you in the morning boss' Tom calls.

The rain is pelting outside, and I'm grateful I don't have to go out. After seeing John and Morag off, I notice Tom has moved from the table to the rug in front of the fire. The atmosphere has changed, it feels strange just the two of us, but he looks nice and comfy and I plonk myself on the floor next to him. We sit in silence listening to the noise from the rain pelting onto the cottage roof.

'I hope John survives the night' I said eventually before bursting out laughing.

'I know, she wasn't happy, was she? I felt sorry for him; I don't think he was expecting that reaction' he said smiling before we both burst out laughing.

'If John sells the farm, will that mean you will lose your job?

'Yeah, I suppose, unless whoever buys it, hires me? I'll worry about it, when it happens,' he said looking at his phone.

'So, tell me, what are you going to comment?' I ask pointing to his phone, laughing.

'Already did' he said, handing me his phone.

I glance at his phone and notice that he's commented on the picture of the two of us grinning like Cheshire cats.

'My new friend Eve, the most funny and beautiful woman I know.'

'Why thank you' I said laughing.

'I mean it' he said looking serious, and I realise that I like that he means it.

Chapter 10. First Christmas in the Cottage.

It's the morning after the party, and I wake with the pounding of my head. I'm tired but happy. Not wanting to move, I'm grateful Tom and I stopped drinking wine and moved onto coffee after Morag and John left. Otherwise I'm certain that I would have felt a lot worse this morning. I had such a great time last night, but I'm worried that Tom will regret what he'd said this morning. I don't want things to be awkward between us. He's been such a good friend, since I first arrived.

'But, could we be more?' I wonder, my head pounding with every movement as I get out of bed.

Going straight to the kitchen, I get some aspirin and a strong cup of coffee. My brain is fuzzy and I'm tired after last night. I can't be bothered getting dressed and spend my morning scrubbing the cottage in my pyjamas. It didn't really need it, but I needed to do something to distract me from worrying about Tom. I've been worrying all morning about last night, but my worry soon diminishes when he texts me at lunch time asking how my head is?

'*Surprisingly good, what about you?*' I reply glad to hear from him.

'*Not too bad, just tired.*'

'*I'm at work. John is alive lol. I'll call in later if that's okay?*' he texts.

'*Glad John is alive, lol, yeah, call in, I'll be here,*' I text back delighted that he is coming.

I spend the rest of the afternoon snuggled up on the sofa, too tired to do anything but watch the TV. It's early evening and I still have a head that feels like there's an axe planted in it when I hear Tom calling from outside.

'Eve, Eve, are you there?' he calls.

'Yes, come on in.'

I have butterflies in my stomach, but I'm delighted to see him and pull him into a hug as he enters.

'Listen, I'm not one to beat about the bush. I was thinking, after last night, that I would like to take you out on a proper date,' he said, smiling.

'What do you think?' he asks looking uncertain.

'Oh', I exclaim, blood rushing to my face, delight and shock coursing through me.

'That would be lovely. Where are you thinking?' I said my cheeks burning.

'Nothing too formal, there's this new bar in Ramtree which has started serving food. I thought we could try it tonight,' he said.

'Wait. I need to check my imaginary diary here,' I replied, smiling as I flick through imaginary pages.

'It would seem that I have a very busy schedule this week, that includes watching TV, then watching some more TV,' I said smiling.

'I would love to go out tonight. What time were you thinking?'

'I could book us a table for about seven. Would that be okay?'

'Seven's perfect, I'll meet you there,' I said, leading him to the door.

'Well, I didn't expect that' I thought, wondering what I should wear? excitement bubbling as I look through the boxes at the bottom of my wardrobe.

After much deliberation, I chose my new dark blue skinny jeans and a silver slinky top. Teaming my clothes with bright blue high heels, enjoying getting dressed up. The rest of the day flies by and before I know it, it is time to go and meet Tom. It feels a bit weird to be going on a formal date. Normally, we're working on something together and are very relaxed in each other's company, but this will be our first time out on a date together. I'm apprehensive as I arrive at the pub and I've butterflies in stomach when I spot Tom sitting at a corner table waiting for me. As I walk towards him, I notice he's had his hair cut.

'I like it, it emphasises his masculine angular features' I thought, walking a little unsteadily on my heels towards the table.

'Well, hello you' he said smiling broadly, standing up as I arrive at the table.

'You look nice' he said looking me up and down.

'As do you, I like your new hair,' I said, giving it a ruffle as I sit down opposite him in the booth.

'I hope you don't mind, but I've already ordered us a bottle of wine.'

'Not at all' I said, wishing it was already here. I could do with a glass to calm the ever-increasing butterflies in my stomach.

I'd never felt apprehensive around Tom before. I just hope this doesn't ruin our friendship. Thankfully I didn't need to worry it doesn't take long before my nerves calm, and we settle into a comfortable companionship. Our first date was great, and the evening flew by. I find Tom so easy to be around. He makes me laugh all the time.

***

After that first date, Tom and I begin seeing each other regularly. He usually calls to see me after work most evenings. I've been living in the cottage for a month now, and I love it. But, as we move into December, I realise that it's coming up to the second anniversary since Mum passed away. There isn't a day that goes by that I don't think about her and I'm finding it difficult to believe that it has been a whole two years since that awful morning when the police arrived on my doorstep. I don't know how I've survived when I remember how bad things were in the days just after her death, those were dark, dark days. I still have days when the darkness descends but renovating the cottage has been good at keeping the darkness at bay. I've been so busy, writing and spending time with Tom these past few weeks that I'd barely noticed that Christmas was in two weeks. I should definitely decorate the cottage. Glancing around my undecorated living room, I'm wondering if I should get an artificial tree or a real one? Christmas is going to be weird this year, last year being alone and doing nothing for Christmas suited me just fine, but this year, well things are different this year. I'm not miserable in the same way I was last year, but I will still be alone over the Christmas period. I don't know what I'm going to do this year. I should try to make some sort of effort, perhaps attempt to make myself a small Christmas dinner. I'm not looking forward to being alone. Tom hasn't said what he's doing for Christmas? but it's likely that he'll be spending Christmas with his family. The thought of being alone at Christmas makes me feel very lonely. It's all very well, moving to another country and living the dream. But when you don't know anyone and you're sitting alone on Christmas day, eating a dinner for one.

'It's just sad' I thought, my mood darkening.

My mood has shifted these past couple of days and it's ready to tip over into the darkness and it terrifies me that I don't have Dr Ryan here. Not wanting the dark mood to linger and overwhelm me, I decide to distract myself and head to Ramtree to get a real Christmas tree. I'll just pretend it's the same as any other day. I'm determined not to dwell on the dark mood that is ready to engulf me. Choosing my Christmas tree was fun, the guy selling the trees delivered it to the cottage, bringing my new tree right into the living room, helping me place it in the corner. Before leaving, he reminds me to keep it watered.

'If you keep it watered, it will hold its needles for longer' he said, before waving me goodbye.

The tree is a bit too big for the room, but I love it, and the wonderful pine smell it's giving off fills the room. I'm so glad I chose to get a real tree. It takes a while to find where I put the Christmas decorations and sorting through the box. I find a small set of lights that I'd brought with me. After draping them around the tree, I love how it looks. I don't want to use artificial decorations and spend the next half an hour scouring the woods behind the cottage for pinecones and holly and use what I find to make homemade ornaments for the tree. After placing the last of the homemade decorations on the tree, I'm finally feeling a little more Christmassy.

***

Despite doing my best to be positive, over the past fortnight the dark thoughts continue to blacken my mood, I've absolutely no interest in anything. It's Christmas Eve and Tom has just left to go to his parent's house until the New Year. He was worried about me before he left and wanted me to go with him, but I felt that it would be too weird. We've only been seeing each other for about a month after all. I feel a bit guilty because I didn't buy any Christmas presents and notice after he left, that Tom has left a present for me under the tree and John left me one yesterday. I really should have brought some presents, disliking myself for being selfish and not thinking about my friends.

It's early evening, and it's already dark outside and I'm all alone. This will be the second Christmas in a row that I'm all alone. I really can't believe that it has been more than two years since Mum passed away. Glancing around the cottage, the room looks beautiful there's a lovely glow from the lights on the tree. I wonder what my mum would think of all of this. Tears run down my face. I wish she could come back, even if it is just for a day or two. I need to distract myself, but I can't be bothered. The more I think about Christmas, the more unhappy I become. I realise I'm more miserable today than I was, this time last year. As the tears flow freely, I'm worried about how quickly my mood has changed and wonder how I can stop this darkness from overwhelming me again? I'm in no mood to do anything but stay in bed until all the festivities are over. Maybe I can find some box sets to binge watch, hoping they will distract me from this blackness that's threatening to overwhelm me.

Since arriving in Northern Ireland, I've kept myself busy. In fact, I've barely stopped since I got here. The busier I am, the less time I have to think, but that's a problem when everywhere is closed for the holidays. I hate being idle and realise that keeping busy has been instrumental in my mental wellbeing. Being alone with nothing to do, the darkness descends and my heart hurts. I miss Mum and Emma. I was going to attempt some sort of Christmas dinner, but I can't be bothered. It's just disheartening cooking a Christmas dinner for one. What's the point? It just emphasises how depressing my life is. I remember that I've got plenty of wine. I can drink wine and watch TV for the next two days. That's what I'll do, positive this is a good idea as I pour myself a large glass of Sauvignon Blanc. I know I'm drinking too fast and before I know it, I'm starting my third glass as tears trip down my face, when I think of Emma, I feel like I lost her, as well as my mum two years ago. I just wish she would stop being such a bitch and get over herself. Tears run freely down my cheeks, but I can't be bothered wiping them away. Lifting my laptop, I check Emma's Facebook profile, but seeing her posts and photos emphasises how much I miss her. Setting the laptop down, I lie down next to it, my swollen eyelids heavy.

***

I blink my eyes open and can hear an annoying noise; it takes a second before I realise that my phone is ringing. The room spins and my stomach lurches, as I sit up to quickly. Where is it?' I follow the noise and eventually find it buried under a blanket buzzing loudly next to me; I answer without looking at who is calling.

'Hello' I mumble, trying to focus my vision.

'Hey there, what ya up to?' I recognise Tom's voice and can tell that he's slightly rightly.

'Sorry, I was sleeping, how's you? Are you having a good time?' I ask slowly waking up, wondering what time it is?

Checking the clock on the mantel, I notice it's almost midnight.

'Yeah, I'm having a good time, just wanted to talk to you and make sure you're okay' he said, his words slurring.

I can hear someone calling him in the background.

'I'm fine, go and enjoy yourself. We'll talk tomorrow,' I said, yawning.

'Happy Christmas,' he said laughing.

'Happy Christmas to you' I reply, realising that it is after twelve and is Christmas day. It took me ages to fully wake up for the phone call, but now I'm wide awake, and no matter how much I try, I cannot get back to sleep. I took myself off to bed after the phone call, but three and a half hours later I'm still wide awake and at half three I drag myself out of bed to get a cup of tea. It's cold in the living room and I quickly set about making a small fire, listening to the rain thundering loudly on the roof. I find the noise therapeutic as I sit in front of the fire sipping my tea, willing the hours to pass. I'm tired and feeling very sorry for myself, as I begin nosing on Facebook. I consider sending Emma a message, but when I scroll through my newsfeed, and see all the abuse she has posted since I moved, I change my mind, however as I look through the posts, I'm pleased to see that it's been a while since she posted anything. She appears to have stopped harassing me. Thank goodness, maybe she's fed up with this, as well. My vision blurs with the tears that have filled my eyes again. My chest jerks up and down as I fight to control the sobs. I never wanted to fall out with Emma. We've been through so much together. I don't know what I did wrong other than move on with my life? I don't think she understood that after Mum died, I changed. She dealt with my mum's death by getting drunk every night which upset me. It was horrible dealing with her bad mood and hangovers the morning after. But the move wasn't anything about her. It was about me. I was unhappy and needed to change my life. I'm desperately missing my friend, realising I probably irritated her as well, I was miserable for a long time after Mum died, I couldn't snap out of it, remembering the darkness, I couldn't shake.

***

It's the day after Boxing day, and I've survived the Christmas holidays. It wasn't easy I spent the whole time feeling lonely and unhappy. I tried to block out my loneliness by getting blind drunk, which only made me feel even worse. Being alone these past couple of days has made me realise how much I need people in my life. I don't like being alone, or if I'm going to be alone, I need to make sure that I'm busy. My mood has lifted slightly, knowing that Tom is coming over later. He got back from his parent's house this morning and I'm looking forward to seeing him. Determined to get back to normal, I'm going to cook us a nice steak dinner later this afternoon and have picked a nice bottle of Merlot to go with the steak. My stomach grumbles loudly when I begin thinking about food and I realise, I've barely eaten anything for the past two days, suddenly feeling starving hungry. In fact, when I think about the past couple of days, I realise that all I've done is wallow in my own self-pity and watch TV in my bed. I haven't even showered since Tom left on Christmas Eve.

'I will make sure that things are different next year,' I thought, glad to be feeling more like myself.

'Hellooo' I hear Tom calling from outside the front door and rush to answer it, pulling him into a big hug.

'Glad to see someone missed me' he murmurs, placing light feathery kisses on my neck.

'I really did' I said, heat swirling through my body that has nothing to do with the nearby fire.

Tom bends his head and kisses me with a fierce passion as we stumble down onto the rug in front of the fire. As Tom continues to kiss my neck, I never realised how sensitive my skin could be. Immediately distracted by the whisper of his breath, the warm brush of his lips, the raw sensation of his body pressing me deep into the rug. It all combines to stir my desire to a fever pitch. I stuck in a breath as he tugs my jeans and underwear down my legs, tossing them on the floor. Then, with one smooth motion, he tugs my t-shirt over my head, tossing it on the chair behind us. Taking a moment to appreciate my lacy black bra before undoing it with one hand and tossing it to join the t-shirt. His breath hisses as he lifts his hands to cup the soft swell of my breasts. Holding my gaze as he slowly presses himself deep inside and starts to move, slowly at first then gaining speed as I wrap my legs around his waist and my fingers tangle in his hair. His tongue gently strokes my nipple, the pleasure that streaks makes me gasp, it's that intense, it almost boarded on pain. Inspired by my reaction, he did it again.

'Tom,' I groan my breath coming in small pants as he leans over kissing me with a maddening sense of urgency. The light from the fire flickers on our hot bodies as we groan in unison like a rising crescendo in our own magnificent symphony.   Lying spent in front of the fire, my body is still pulsating as I enjoy being held in his arms.

'I should go away more often' he jokes running a finger down my waist towards my bellybutton.

'It was horrible being on my own over Christmas, I should've gone with you to your parents' house,' I said, as the smell of the steak wafts around the room.

'I thought you might be lonely,' he said, squeezing my shoulder. 'Which is why I chose to come back early, and why I'm going to stay until after the new year. We can see the New Year in together.'

Leaning over, he gently kisses me while running a finger over my nipple. My body shudders, I am utterly delicate, fragile and utterly feminine under his touch.

'That sounds lovely,' I gasp, reaching up to kiss him delighted that he is staying.

'Every New Year's Eve, there's always a big firework display in Ramtree. We should be able to watch them from the meadow unless you want to go into town?' he said, running his hands down my stomach.

'No, I'm happy to watch them from here,' I tell him, my body throbbing as I squirm under his touch, desperate for him to enter me again.

We make love again before Tom adds more wood to the fire, pulling a blanket down for me to wrap around myself.

Now, what's that you're cooking? It smells delicious,' he said, walking naked to the kitchen to look in the oven.

***

My mood has improved but, in the future, I must make sure not spend too much time alone, especially around holiday times. It's just too easy for all the joy to disappear and I know how dark it can get. I watch Tom pottering around the cottage and realise how much I've enjoyed having him stay with me for the last couple of days. New Year's Eve was magical. After such a long run of wet weather, it was a clear frosty night. The stars were magical and despite the chill, Tom and I were snug and warm wrapped up in thick blankets, drinking hot chocolate. At midnight, we saw the New Year in, watching the fireworks with a bottle of sparkling wine.

'I don't think I've ever had such a nice New Year's Eve,' I said the following day.

'I'm a lucky man. I got to see the New Year in with my favourite person,' he said, wrapping his arms around me.

Sinking into the warmth of his side I realise that I don't want him to leave. I like having someone else in the cottage. On New Year's Day, I ask if he would consider moving in with me?

'I know we haven't been seeing each other for very long, but I like having you around, you make me happy' I said, hoping he doesn't think I've lost my mind.

His vivid blue eyes meet mine, but he doesn't say anything. Just sits quietly, I can't read his face and after several minutes of silence. I'm worried I've annoyed him when he suddenly says,

'Okay, let's do this, let's live together,' he eventually said, smiling pulling me toward him. 'I don't particularly want to leave either, also you make me happy' he said leaning over placing a gentle kiss on my lips. Squealing with delight I do a little happy dance as he continues to place gentle kisses down my neck causing my body to tremble with a passion, I didn't know I had.

'Thank you,' I said, lifting his shirt and running my hands down his chest, a knot of desire in my stomach ready to erupt, delighted he has agreed to move in. 'We can get your stuff later if you want?' I said kissing his neck.

'I can't move just yet, my rents paid up to the end of January and I'll have to give a months,' notice' he said pulling me close, pushing my hair back and kissing me with an urgency I can't resist. 'But I can start bringing my stuff over, and I should be good to move in by the end of February,' he said lowering his hand to find the hem of my T-shirt before pulling it over my head and tossing it on the floor.

Chapter 11. The Storm.

It's early March and Tom, and I have been living together for a week now. I love having him living with me; I didn't realise how much I missed having someone around, especially at night. Everything would be perfect apart from some strange things that have been happening recently. Such as not receiving any post for a week, then finding a pile of it dumped in the hedge. I asked the postman what had happened? And he told me that a woman who said she was my friend was waiting for him every day?

'What friend? I don't have any friends here' I said, confused about who would take my post and dump it in the hedge?

'Sorry I won't do that again,' he said looking confused.

I don't know if it's my imagination, but I also keep getting a spine-chilling feeling that I'm being watched. It happens again as I'm walking back to the cottage after speaking to the postman. My eyes scan all around, but I can't see anyone.

'Who would be watching me?' I thought, realising it's very unlikely I'm actually being watched, and it's probably just my imagination.

This spin-chilling feeling that I'm being watched is new; it only started shortly before Tom moved in. At first, I thought it was because I was on my own again, after Tom went back to his flat, but the weirdness with my post, well, that has unsettled me again.

'Who is this woman that has been taking my post?' I thought.

Ever since I began renovating the cottage, I've kept a spare key under the fake stone, I don't normally worry, because this place is so quiet, my only neighbours for miles are John and Morag. But this morning I removed it, choosing to keep it on a hook in the cottage. I don't know what's going on? but I'm on edge.

There was a weather warning from the Met Office this morning predicting a storm, but it's not due to hit Northern Ireland until tomorrow evening. I've wanted to get the grass cut since I arrived over a year ago and while the sun is still shining, I'm going to get it done before the storm comes. John lent me his ride-on mower, and it takes me all morning to get the grass cut. I love the cut grass smell, which is filling the air. Scanning the newly cut grass, I'm delighted at how big it looks and spot Tom walking towards me.

'What do you think?' I ask as he approaches.

'It looks great. We could have a nice garden here; you've done a good job,' he said.

'I was thinking that I'd like to get some hens. Come on let me show you where we could keep them,' I said, showing him a flat patch of land in the woods behind the cottage.

'We could put a coop here and the hens could be free range.'

'Absolutely, I'll talk to John. I'm sure he has a spare coop somewhere and I know he'll give us some of his hens. I'll ask after lunch. I didn't say anything before, but John is definitely selling the farm. He's getting it valued this afternoon. His health is getting worse. It'll mean I'll lose my job; I don't think I'll ever find another boss like John,' he said as we walked hand in hand back to the cottage.

'I'm sorry to hear that' I reply, shocked at what I'd just been told.

I'd noticed John looking pained when he's walking; He also lost a lot of weight recently.

'Do you think you could afford to buy the farm yourself?' I ask.

'No, it would be too expensive, it might not look like much but there's the house, loads of out-buildings and all the machinery. It all bumps the price up,' he said looking at his watch. 'I have to get going, I'm trying to batten down the hatches before this storm arrives tomorrow,' he said, kissing me on the cheek before leaving.

I'm wondering how long he's known that he might lose his job. As I watch the dark clouds move in through the kitchen window. The wind has picked up and I watch a leaf as it blows swirling through the air toward the caravan. I'm completely lost in my thoughts when I'm startled and let out a small gasp as I jump backwards, spilling the rest of my coffee. I can't be sure, but it looked like there was a movement in the caravan. Wiping the spilt coffee, my hand shaking as my heart thumps rapidly in my chest.

'It was probably just a shadow' I tell myself taking slow deep breaths to calm my racing heart and an overactive imagination.

I don't know what to do. I want to call Tom, but he's only just left, and it does sound a bit insane. Too afraid to look in the caravan by myself, I stand at the kitchen window watching. I don't want to leave in case I miss something. It takes a while, but my breathing and heartrate finally begin to calm, and I feel a bit daft, convincing myself that it was just a shadow or my imagination. The wind is whistling through the trees and the thick black rain clouds are hanging heavy in the sky, but the rain is yet to come. Desperate to distract myself, I head outside to mark out an area for the chicken coop, before the storm arrives. I lock the cottage, something I don't normally do when I'm on the grounds, but I'm still spooked after what I thought I saw. For a brief moment, I consider getting the caravan keys and having a look but decide to wait until Tom is home. As I walk around the cottage to where I want to put the coop, I can't help but keep a half eye on the caravan. I'm trying to remember the last time I was in it and realise I haven't been near the caravan since I moved into the cottage four months ago. It's just been sitting there, unoccupied.

There can't be anyone in the caravan; it was just a shadow. I keep telling myself feeling foolish at how afraid and jumpy I am. The wind is getting strong, and it's difficult to work in, but after a couple of hours, I get a large area for the coop fenced off. I've just about finished when I hear a large vehicle pulling into the meadow. Stepping out to where the noise is coming from, I spot John in his tractor, immediately noticing he has a chicken coop in the trailer on the back.

'Hi John, I see you've been talking to Tom,' I said, grinning.

'Certainly have, now where do you want this?'

'Just behind the cottage, you'll see there's an area that I've penned off,' I said, pointing.

I watch as he backs the trailer up towards the woods, surprised at how easy he makes it look, and it's not long before the coop is in place.

'You've done this before' I joke.

'Once or twice' he said, laughing. 'Anyway, that should keep you going, I'll bring you a few hens in the morning, maybe three or four to get you started' he said, before climbing stiffly into his tractor, giving me a wave as he goes.

I watch John navigate the tractor out through the green gate, feeling concerned about his health, he's lost so much weight and so quickly. I'm admiring the new coop when the first heavy drops of rain start to fall, just as a forceful gust of wind, whips my hair around my face. I gather my tools as fast as I can, as the water droplets grow larger and more frequent, before returning to the cottage. Later that evening, I tell Tom what I thought I'd seen in the caravan, and he reassures me that he checked the door after I moved out and it was definitely locked.

'It was probably just a shadow, it's too dark and wet now, but I'll check it in the morning before I head to the farm' he said.

***

The storm hit hard overnight, and both Tom and I had a restless night's sleep. The bedroom window rattled in its frame all night, and the rain thundered on the roof. I heard several branches breaking in the wind right outside. It wasn't just the storm keeping me awake, I kept playing what I thought I'd saw over and over in my head. I don't know when I fell asleep? but, I'm woken early by the noise of rain pelting forcefully off the roof. Without looking I can feel that Tom has already left. A noisy gust of wind blows fiercely around the cottage and I'm worried the roof is going to lift. As I walk into the kitchen, I don't know if it's the wind, but suddenly, I get a tingle down my spine as if I'm being watched. My heart begins to race as I set my coffee down and look through the kitchen window. I scan the meadow for any kind of movement, but I'm instinctively drawn toward the caravan.

'There's no way anyone can get in there, not without a key' I tell myself, remembering locking it when I left with the last of my stuff in November.

But I can't settle and continue to look out, my heart speeds when I realise that someone could potentially see me in the cottage from the caravan. My hands begin shaking uncontrollably as my heart throbs loud and irregular in my ears. I know I'm being irrational, but I just can't shake the feeling I'm being watched. Gathering all the bravery I can muster; I decide to call Tom to come with me to inspect the caravan. My stomach lurches but I'm determined to find out what is going on? Lifting my phone, I dial Tom's number, but it just rings and rings; he's not answering. Suddenly there's a deafening cracking sound, spinning toward the noise I watch as a large branch falls as if in slow motion from an old tree, blocking the road. Looking out toward the road, I notice several of John's cows wandering in the rain.

'What are they doing there? They must have escaped,' I thought, grabbing my waterproof coat and trying Tom again.

Pulling my coat on, I don't know what I'm planning to do? but I intend on directing the cows back towards the farm. I make sure to lock the cottage door behind me before striding against the wind and rain toward the cows. The wind is worse than I thought; it's forcefully slamming the rain into my face. It takes me longer than it should to reach the road, but I notice the gnarly branch hasn't damaged anything, in fact it's stopping the cows from going any further. The wind near blows me over as I lift a small section of the fallen branch and use it to move the cows back to the farm. Pulling out my phone, I call Tom again, but it just rings and rings.

'Answer your phone' I said frustrated wondering where he is and why he isn't answering?

I've only been out for about five minutes, but I'm soaked through to my skin and thankful the cows are moving easily. It doesn't take long before I have them all back to the farmyard. I can't see anyone and pull the gate closed, locking the cows in the front yard. The wind and rain slam into my face as I run back towards the cottage. There's no way I'm standing around in this weather, waiting for John or Tom to appear. As I approach the turn off for the cottage, I spot the branch blocking the way and decide while I'm already soaked, I might as well try to clear as much of the road as possible. Leaning over the branch I wrap my arms around it grabbing the thickest part, but it snaps, and I stumble backwards. I realise it's rotten and shouldn't be too heavy to move. I can't see with the rain is pelting hard and fast into my face and use all my strength to stand up against the force of the wind. Grabbing as much of the branch as I can, I dig my heels into the ground and pull using my body weight to pull the branch off the road. I'm gasping for breath as I stand up and look up and down the newly cleared road. I realise my efforts could be in vain because it's likely that more branches will break off and block the road again. Turning into the wind, I fight to get a breath as I push myself forward toward the cottage. I stand in the makeshift shelter, surprised it's still standing shaking myself down and try calling Tom again, before unlocking the front door. But when I enter, something feels wrong. The cottage feels weird and there's a nasty smell.

'Someone's been in here' I thought scanning the room, noticing a tea towel draped across the back of one of the chairs in the living room.

'I didn't do that; I know I didn't. But maybe Tom left it there this morning.' I reflect feeling very uneasy, wondering how I could have missed it?

I don't know what it is? but there's a nasty smell lingering in the cottage. I break out into a cold sweat convinced my imagination has gone crazy. How would someone get in here? I locked the door. I know I did, I just unlocked it. My heart's racing as I make my way to the bedroom, thankful that everything looks the same in here as I quickly change out of my soaking clothes into warm dry ones. Pouring myself a hot cup of coffee I use the cup to warm my hands, wondering why Tom's not answering his phone? I'm trying to stay calm, but I need to do something and decide to get the caravan keys and have a look, but, when I check the key hooks, I realise that they're gone.

'Where are they?' I thought, staring at the space on the key hooks where the caravan keys are normally kept.

Something's not right. The rain is distracting me pelting off the roof as I frantically try to remember if I put them somewhere else. But, where other than the hook would I put them? My heart is racing, and panic overwhelms me as I stare at the key hooks trying to make sense of what is going on? I suddenly notice it's not just the caravan keys that are gone, but also the spare cottage key.

'but I put the spare cottage key there yesterday' I thought, fear and confusion coursing through me.

My hands begin shaking and I phone Tom again, hoping and praying he will answer and tell me he has both sets of keys.

'Hey Babe' he answers, almost immediately.

'Why don't you answer your phone?' I yell.

'Sorry, I left it in the tractor. What's wrong?'

'Did you find the cows? They'd escaped, I brought them back.'

'We wondered how they got there. Thanks for doing that, are you okay? you sound stressed.'

'No, I'm not okay. Do you have the caravan and spare cottage key?' I ask, trying not to sound hysterical.

'No, they're hanging on the hooks, where they always are. You sound strange, what's the matter?

'The keys are gone, and I think someone has been in the cottage,' I said, my hands shaking as fear courses through my body.

'I'm on my way, stay there.'

I hang up my hand shaking and glance around, realising that all the walls in the main area of the cottage have windows on them. My heart thumps loud and irregular in my head and my breathing labours as I try to see through each of the windows. But I can only see my own reflection. I'm terrified and convince myself, someone is out there, watching me. I don't know what to do and feel thankful when I hear a vehicle pull up outside. The wind rushes in as the door opens, and Tom and John men step in.

'What's going on?' Tom asks shaking the rainwater from his coat.

I show him the key hooks, relaying what has been happening.

'Thanks for bringing the cows back' John said.

I'm shocked at his appearance; I can't believe how unwell he looks. His skin is ashen white his eyes sunken with dark circles and he's lost so much weight.

'Are you okay John? Sorry if I've worried you, it's probably nothing.'

Seeing how unwell he looks, I try to hide how upset I feel, not wanting to worry him more than I need too.

'No dear, it's just that there's been some strange things happening to me as well' he said, looking up at me.

I gasp, looking to see if Tom knew? but he won't look at me, he's staring at the floor.

'Why is he being so weird?' I thought, staring at him, willing him to look up.

Turning my attention back to John, I take a deep breath in, trying to regain my composure. 'Tell me what happened?' I say gently not wanting to upset him further.

'There's been a few odd things happening, but the incident just before the New Year is the worst. I thought I saw someone going into the milking parlour, a few days before New Year's Eve' he said quietly.

His heads down, looking at the floor, and after a few minutes of quiet, he looks up, his eyes full of tears.

'What happened John?' I ask trying to sound calm. A feeling of dread coursing down my spine, as it dawns on me, that what I've been feeling recently, has not just been my imagination.

'At first, I didn't see anything, but I noticed blood pooling on the ground, and when I looked into the pen, my dog Max was lying covered in blood. His throat had been slit.' he said, his body slumped, and his eyes filled with tears.

'I couldn't believe what I was seeing, I love all my animals, but Max was special' he tells me.

'Poor Max, he was a good dog' I reply softly guiding him to the kitchen table.

'I asked Tom not to say anything to you. I didn't want to upset or frighten you. But with these strange things that are happening to you' he said, looking up tearfully, his face full of concern.

The rain thunders on the roof and the wind howls as we sit in silence, none of us sure what to do?

'We should call the police' I said, looking at John then Tom and back to John again, unsure why neither of them are reacting?

'I don't think it will do any good. Tell her John' Tom said finally meeting my gaze.

'I phoned the police after I found Max, and they came to the farm, looked around and said they would look into it, and that was the last I heard from them. They didn't want to know, you could phone, if it makes you feel better, maybe you should. But nothing has actually happened, apart from some keys going missing and a feeling that you're being watched' he said sounding disappointed.

'How often do you lose keys then find them again?' he continues.

I know he's right, but I'm very uneasy that there is someone watching us right now and check my phone signal. My blood runs cold when I realise, I've no signal.

'Me neither' Tom said, looking at his phone.

Sitting at my small kitchen table, I'm very worried and pessimistic about this situation.

'My spare keys are missing, there's a storm coming and we've no phone signal' I said wanting Tom and John to realise how bad things are.

The rain suddenly pelts even more heavily on the roof, the noise is deafening, it's difficult to hear anything above the noise.

'It sounds like the storm is here sooner than expected. What about Morag, where is she?' I ask worried.

'She's still at the farm, I'm going to head back now' John tells us, pushing himself stiffly into a standing position.

'I'll drive you, better safe than sorry in this weather' Tom said looking pessimistic.

'Lock the door behind me' he said.

I don't need told twice and lock it as soon as they leave. My heart is racing as I stand with my back pushed against the door, realising that I can't be seen from any of the windows if I stand here. I really wish I'd put curtains up. If there's someone out there? they can see in, but I can't see out. The wind is blowing under the door, and I'm cold, but I don't want to move from my hiding place. My feet are like two blocks of ice, and slowly and cautiously I step out and run to the kitchen table. I can only be seen from one window here.

'Hurry up, Tom' I thought looking at the door.

I'm too distracted to do anything but sit listening to the weather outside. I'm startled by a loud rapping at the door. I don't know who it is out there? but I'm almost certain it's not Tom. I didn't hear the car return.

'Tom, is that you?' I call.

Standing behind the door listening, but there's no answer. I can only hear the wind and rain.

'TOM, is that you?' I call again, but there's nothing.

A loud rapping at the kitchen window startles me. Spinning around to face where the noise came from, but all I can see is my own reflection in the window. My heart thuds loudly in my head and I'm certain it's not Tom. He wouldn't do that to me. But who is this and what do they want? Fear courses through my every pore, I feel trapped I don't know what to do? Crouching down I crawl behind the chair in the living room, hiding where I can't be seen from the kitchen window. In my crouching position, I realise that I'm now in direct view of the large living room window, and swiftly pull the other chair around to hide behind. Sitting between the two chairs, I'm a little calmer knowing I can't be seen from any of the windows. The rain is thundering on the roof and I'm certain no one would still be out in that weather.

'You would have to be completely crazy to be out in that' I thought, feeling a little calmer and a bit ridiculous sitting behind the chairs.

I'm about to stand up, when the handle on the front door is shaken as if someone was trying to open it. In my crouching position, I don't take my eyes off the door, my heart racing as I clamp my hand over my mouth to stop myself from screaming. It's not Tom; he would just unlock the door and come in. I suddenly remember that the spare cottage key is missing. I don't know what to do. The wind is howling, and the rain has suddenly got heavier again pelting even louder on the roof, the noise is deafening and disorientating. Whoever is out there must be soaked to the skin. What sort of person this is? Apart from the noise from the storm it's gone quiet outside, my knees are aching in this crouched position, I check the time. It has been fifteen minutes since the door was last rattled. Whoever this is can't have a key, or they would have come in, especially in this weather. I check my phone signal again.

'Still no signal.'

Above the noise, I hear a vehicle pull up and a door open and close. A few seconds later a key is inserted into the lock and I stay perfectly still as I watch from under the chair as the door opens a rush of wind gusting in.

'Eve, where are you?' Tom calls.

'Someone was here' I shakily tell him, poking my head above the chair, noticing the water running off him onto the floor.

'You're soaked,' I said.

'Yeah, it's wild out there', he said, shaking the water out of his hair before removing his coat.

'Lock the door and sit down here, so they can't see you,' I said, relieved to see him back.

'Is Morag okay?' I ask, remembering why he left.

'There was a bit of a panic. We couldn't find her anywhere in the house when we first arrived. But she's okay, she'd heard a noise and was terrified, so hid under a tree round the side of the farmhouse. She didn't know that we were there and stayed out in the rain, too afraid to come in. The tree didn't do much to protect her; she was completely soaked when she finally did come in' he said looking concerned.

'Who is this nut job? and what do they want?' he said looking around the chair at the window.

'We can't just sit on the floor worrying. We should open a bottle of wine. It'll calm us down. There's no way someone is gonna stay outside in that' he said.

'Do you have any signal?' I ask, too worried to think about wine.

'No, my phones the same as yours, no bars' he said standing up pulling a bottle of red wine out of the wine rack along with two glasses.

'When I was driving John home, it looked like some more trees had come down' he said.

'It's possible we won't have any connection if cables have been taken down.'

'I'm going to try the house phone; I think we should phone the police' I said crawling on the floor and lifting the handset.

'It's dead. Tom, the phones dead, and neither of our mobiles have any signal' I said, the reality of our situation setting in.

I'm hysterical, my heart is racing, and my palms are sweaty as tears stream down my face, not knowing what we can do?

'Calm down, we just need to sit it out until the storm passes, we'll be fine, come on, have some wine, you need to calm down' he said, pouring me a glass of Merlot.

'Why are you so calm?' I ask, lifting my bleary eyes to look at him.

'Well there's not a lot we can do, right now, is there? Do you know if your generator is working?' he asks.

'Because if the electric goes, I don't know about you? but I don't want to sit here in the dark' he said, taking a sip from his wine.

'Yes, it's working, the electrician checked it and filled it with fuel, before I moved in. It's a pain though, you have to manually start it. It's behind the cottage, in a small shed' I said, hoping we won't have to worry about using it.

'Why? tonight of all nights does there have to be a storm?' I thought annoyed.

I know Tom makes sense in what he said, but my nerves are shot, and I don't want to move from my hiding position behind the chairs. My knees ache from crouching, as I watch Tom, sitting comfortably in front of the fire drinking his wine. After a while, I realise the wine may help to calm my nerves. I know I can't stay like this all night and crawl out from behind the chairs and sit down next to Tom in front of the fire. Lifting the wine, he's poured I take a large gulp. The noise is deafening, but we're startled by a sudden loud cracking noise, which is followed by another cracking noise. The lights flicker briefly, before darkness envelops us, with only the light of the fire dimly lighting the room.

'A tree must have fallen. I'll nip out and try to get the generator working' Tom said, standing up to peer through the window before grabbing a torch and his coat.

'Just to be on the safe side, you should lock the door until I get back. There's no point taking unnecessary risks' he said.

The storm is raging as he leaves and locks me in the cottage. It doesn't take long before I hear the motor of the generator and the lights flicker back on. Tom returns dripping water all over the floor. The wind howls, and the lights flicker with the generator, but I'm grateful to have electric. I try the TV hoping to get an update on the weather, but there's no signal. I don't know if it's the wine or logic kicking in, but I stop fretting about our intruder.

'There's not much chance that someone is going to stay out in that weather, is there?' I said, hoping for reassurance.

'Na, I wouldn't think so' he said, drying his face with a tea towel.

'I'm so happy you've got a generator, it would be a long night, sitting in the dark' he said, sitting down next to me in front of the fire, raising his glass.

'Here's to the generator' he said, smiling.

'To the generator' I agree raising my glass, watching the fire flickering, feeling my eyelids heavy as I start to relax and drift off to sleep.

***

I wake with a start and it takes me a second to realise I'd fallen asleep on the mat in front of the fire. The wind is still howling and the rain thundering on the roof. It's pitch-black, the only light is coming from the low fire embers.

'Where's Tom?' I thought trying to see in the dark.

I panic when I can't find him and begin to stand, I spot movement and notice him crouching in the kitchen, waving his hand at me to get down.

'What is it?' I whisper.

'I saw someone' he whispers.

'Where?' I ask my adrenalin surging.

'At the window, someone was looking in, so I turned all the lights off' he whispers, pointing in the direction of the kitchen window.

I peek at the window, but I can't see anything, it's too dark.

'We should call the police,' I whisper.

'How?' he whispers back, the reality of our situation dawning on me.

'What are we going to do?' I ask realising this time he's as worried as me.

'We should just sit tight for now, but I think we should arm ourselves' he said, looking around for something to grab.

'Whoever is out there is up to no good.'

It doesn't take long before we're startled by a loud bang and the sound of glass breaking.

'That came from the bedroom' I state.

My heart is racing as I crawl across the living room and push the bedroom door open slightly. The wind rushes at me and I spot a rock on the floor surrounded by broken glass. I panic when I realise the bedroom window has been smashed intentionally, turning as quick as I can, crawling back to Tom to tell him what I saw.

'Who is this fucking nut job and why are they targeting us?' he said as I sit down next to him on the kitchen floor.

I watch the bedroom door worried that whoever is out there will come in through the window. A loud blast of wind makes us both jump. Everything is closing in on me, I feel isolated and trapped, I can't hear over the noise of the storm.

'We need to get out of here. I think we should get into the car and drive,' I said, looking at Tom.

He nods in agreement, 'yeah, we should do that' he agrees

'We'll go to John and Morag's. I'm sure they're worried as well. Come on, let's go now' he said glancing at the kitchen window before moving into a crawling position.

'Yes, let's get out of here' I said, following closely behind as we crawl to the front door.

Tom has the keys and we listen for any noises outside, but all I can hear is the wind and rain.

'Can you hear anything?' I whisper.

'No, I think we should just go. What do you think?

'Just do it already, open the door. Let's get out of here,' I said.

The wind blasts in, and the door swings open, slamming against the wall. I don't bother to take the time to lock the door, just pull it behind me, and we run to the car getting in as quick as we can. As I'm running, I notice what looks like a light in the caravan and show Tom.

'Look, there's a light on in the caravan?' I said, as I pull the car door closed.

'Yeah, we'll deal with that another time, let's just get out of here.'

I watch intently for any movement in the darkness as Tom starts the car manoeuvring us towards John's place.

Chapter 12. Devastation.

It's difficult to see where we're going even with the wipers going full blast. But it doesn't take long before we're pulling into the yard at the front of the farmhouse. Immediately, I notice something isn't right when I see a large tree has crashed through the upstairs window.

'I hope they're okay,' I said, looking across at Tom.

My heart races as we sit in the car looking at the farmhouse, wondering what we're going to do? Glancing across at Tom, he's in shock staring up at the tree.

'We can't just sit here', I said, opening my door, hoping Tom will follow.

The wind almost knocks me from my feet as I step out of the car, I don't hang about waiting for Tom, instead run as fast as I can to the farmhouse door. I'm glad when I reach the front door and feel Tom behind me as he leans over and starts banging loudly.

'John, Morag open the door' he calls, trying the handle, finding it unlocked.

'That's strange,' I said, noticing Tom's worried face as we step through the door, immediately noticing a nasty smell.

'What is that? I said, screwing up my nose, wiping rainwater from my coat and pulling wet hair from my face.

'Shush' Tom whispers.

I notice how on edge he is.

'Keep quiet, there could be someone here' he whispers.

Tiptoeing cautiously around the downstairs of the farmhouse, I'm alert for any movement, but there's nothing, the house is silent except for the noise from the wind. Something doesn't feel right, it's pitch-black and too still. I keep hoping any minute John, Morag or both of them will appear.

'Where are they?'

'Shush' come on follow me!

It's dark and my heart pulsates loudly in my ears as we finish our search of the downstairs.

'They must be upstairs' Tom whispers.

The stench is disgusting as we pause at the bottom of the stairs before cautiously beginning to climb. I stay close to Tom not wanting to be left behind.

'They can't be asleep, not after a tree has crashed through the side of your house' I whisper, a feeling of dread creeping down my spine.

It's too still, there's no sign of life and the smell. The smell is getting stronger the higher we get, it's so overwhelming as we reach the top of the stairs, my stomach lurches and I start to gag.

'Shush' Tom whispers, pulling me close.

'What's that disgusting smell?' I whisper trying desperately to stop my stomach lurching as we stand on the landing.

I notice the door to the room where the tree has gone through is wide open. There's a strange crackling noise and I can see something sparking, but it's too dark to make out exactly what it is? The wind and rain are gusting through the broken window.

'Be careful. It looks like an electric cable has been brought in with the tree and it's sparking,' Tom said cautiously, stepping forward to get a better view.

Tom moves forward towards the door, I'm too afraid to go any closer. My eyes are still adjusting to the darkness when I spot something.

'Tom,' I gasp, leaning forward to grab his arm.

'What's wrong?'

'Over there, look. I think there's a hand hanging out of the bed,' I said pointing.

He follows where I'm pointing, 'looks like it' he said leaning over to get a better look.

'What are we going to do?' I ask, barely able to believe everything that has happened this evening. 'We could get electrocuted; that wire is still sparking.'

Instinctively stepping backwards away from the room, I desperately try to think of a solution.

'What can we do?' I repeat shivering with the cold, realising that at least one of them and most likely both have been electrocuted when the tree came crashing through the window.

'We've no phone signal. What are we going to do?' I said my heart racing as panic begins to overwhelm me.

I can't move, I'm rooted to my spot, watching as Tom moves cautiously towards the room, leaning in through the doorway.

'Who it is?' I ask.

I don't want to know, but I can't take my eyes off Tom as he turns to look at me. I'm only able to make out his silhouette in the dark.

'It's John' he said his voice cracking. 'He's been electrocuted while sleeping by the look of things' he said.

'What about Morag?

'She's not here. It's just John.'

'Come on, we need to get out of here, there's nothing we can do, I don't want to get electrocuted, we have to get help, we have to go to the police station in Ramtree' I said, unable to believe what has happened.

Tom agrees, and we slowly but cautiously make our way back down the stairs. The front door is slamming into the wall in the wind. I pull it closed behind me before running to the car. Tom begins driving, but we've only got as far as the farm gate when he stops the car and looks at me.

'What are you doing?' I ask fear coursing through me.

'Something's wrong' he said.

'Everything's wrong. John is dead. Why aren't you driving?' I said sick with fear, desperate to get away from the house and to the safety of the police station.

He's scaring me, I can't see his face and I'm confused about why he has stopped the car?

'What do you mean? Why aren't you driving?' I ask, trying to calm my racing heart.

'Stay there,' Tom said, getting out of the car, slamming the door.

I watch as he's knocked sideways with the wind and rain lashing into him as he circles around the car.

'What's going on?' I ask when he gets back.

'The tyres have been slashed' he said, pushing his wet hair out of his eyes.

'I didn't notice initially because I was focused on getting away but as I started to drive, I could feel something was wrong' he said.

'What, but how?' I ask, unable to comprehend what is happening as we both get out of the car.

'Look,' he said, pointing at the tyres as we circle the car.

Every tyre is completely flat.

'What's going on? Someone has done this while we were in the house?' I said panicking as the rain pelts into my face. 'Who is doing this to us?'

'We have to get to the police station. This isn't someone messing around. We're in danger and I don't want to hang around' Tom said, a grim look on his face.

'But how?'

'We have to walk. There's no other way, come on. Let's get going. I don't want to hang about here whoever slashed the tyres is still out there' he said.

I don't want to leave the car; it feels safer being here than out in the storm with a maniac on the loose. But I can't think of any other way.

'Okay let's do this' I said using all my strength I push the car door open and follow Tom in the direction of Ramtree.

I'm soaked to the skin within minutes, and the icy rain is stinging as the wind repeatedly slams into my face. I'm afraid of who has been targeting us and don't like being so exposed. I try with all my might to stay as close to Tom as I can. Our progress is slow, and every step is difficult as we continuously fight against the wind and rain. There are fallen branches scattered all over the road, and it's difficult to know where to step without falling. Despite my discomfort, I'm determined to keep going until we get to the safety of the Ramtree police station. It's only two miles is what I keep telling myself as my strength fades and I struggle to breathe when another gust of wind slams into my face. I'm exhausted even though we've only been walking for about fifteen minutes and want to stop. Taking a second to gather myself, I look up and notice something glinting in the hedge up ahead. As we get closer, I realise it's an abandoned car that's ploughed into the hedge. I have to move out into the middle of the road to avoid a large branch that is lying next to it, however, as we pass the car something bothers me, I'm sure I recognise it. Gasping for a breath as the rain smashes into my face, I'm struggling to carry on, my legs don't want to keep going.

'Can we stop for a break?' I shout, as another gust of wind knocks me sideways causing me to gasp for breath. 'I need to catch my breath' I call, as I catch up with Tom who has stopped to wait for me.

'Get into the hedge' he said pulling me close as we push ourselves into the hedge to get some shelter for a few minutes.

'Did you see that car in the hedge?'

'Yeah, it looks like someone has crashed in the storm' he replies panting.

'Do you know who it belongs too?'

'Na, I don't recognise it, why? he shouts looking back down the road we've just come.

'I don't know? there's something about it that's bothering me. I'm sure I recognise it, but I can't think who it belongs too?'

'I don't recognise it, and we have more to worry about right now. Are you good to get going again?'

'Yeah, let's do this' I said, and we step out into the wind and rain again.

It has been the most difficult journey, and it takes about forty minutes before we finally arrive at the police station. I'm so happy we've made it, I could cry, but as I step through the door, I'm blinded by the overly bright lights. Tom begins explaining to an officer what has happened to John. I can't stop my teeth from chattering and my body from trembling. I'm grateful when a police officer ushers us into a waiting room bringing towels and hot tea.

'I think this might be the best cup of tea I've ever had,' I stammer, unable to stop my teeth from chattering and my body from trembling.

'Could I get that in writing? We're not known for our tea making skills' he said chuckling.

Tom is telling the officer about the intruder and all the strange things that have been happening, also about what happened to John's dog. He also explains that Morag wasn't home when we found John.

'She was terrified earlier in the day when the intruder was lurking,' Tom said.

'Morag has most likely taken shelter somewhere; Do you know if she has any family nearby?' the officer asks.

'I'm sorry I don't know anything about her, only that she's John's wife' I said, unable to stop my teeth from chattering in the cold.

I watch as the officer writes everything down. He tells us they have already deployed officers to deal with John's body and look for Morag. They're also going to do their best to check the cottage and car.

'But with the storm we may have to wait until tomorrow. Could you both stay at the station until the storm has passed, and we've finished our checks. I will have someone from my team bring you home when the cottage has been checked,' he said.

We've been sitting at the police station for hours and my patience is wearing thin.

'I wonder how long we will have to stay here?' I said hoping it won't be too much longer.

Suddenly there's a blast of wind and rain causing the temperature of the waiting area to drop significantly as the door opens. I watch as two officers, a male and a female push their way through the door wiping rain from their coats. The female strides across the room until she is standing in front of us. Water runs down her coat and forms a puddle at her feet as she explains that her team have checked the area around the cottage.

'As far as we can see in this weather, there doesn't appear to be anyone there now. However, the caravan door was unlocked and there are signs that someone was in there. I'm also very sorry to tell you that your chickens have been killed, it was difficult to see with the storm, but it looks like they have had their necks wrung' she said.

'We don't have any chickens yet' I said glancing at Tom.

'There were eight dead chickens in the coop in the woods' the officer tells us.

I don't know what to think, I'm confused and look at Tom who shrugs and scratches his head.

'I don't understand, where did they come from?' Tom asks.

'Are you sure you went to the right place?' I said, immediately realising how patronising I sound and quickly apologise.

'Don't worry, I wasn't offended' the officer said, showing me on her iPad map the area where they searched.

'Yes, that's the right place' I said, unable to comprehend what is happening?

'Where did the chickens come from?' I thought, yawning, realising how tired I am.

The officer walks away from us to talk to her colleague and after a few minutes they turn and walk towards us.

'We need to recheck the cottage, but there's that much going on with the storm and for the safety of our officers we want to wait until the morning' she said. 'Oh, before I forget, the press are at the farm. They're already reporting that a person has been killed by a fallen tree. We don't know who contacted them? but they are there and will probably be there for the rest of the night' the officer said her face giving nothing away.

'It would be best if you stay in a bed-and-breakfast tonight. Just until we have finished our checks in the morning' the male officer said.

Sitting in the police station in my wet clothing, I'm trembling and feel cold to my bones, but I have no desire whatsoever to go anywhere near the cottage, I'm not sure I'll ever want to return. The thought of staying in the safety of a bed-and-breakfast, has me suddenly feeling completely exhausted, my body feels heavy as relief washes over me.

'I don't know about you Tom, but I'm happy to stay in a bed-and-breakfast, at least I'll feel safe' I said, blinking back the tears that have instantly sprung to my eyes.

141

The wind is noisy and whips the rain into our faces as we leave the station to get into the police car. The storm is showing no signs of stopping, in fact, if anything it looks like it's getting worse. As the officer drives us towards the bed-and-breakfast, I notice the storm has hit Ramtree hard, there are trees down all over the place. It's difficult to see where we are going, but I don't care, I'm just relieved that we are going to a bed-and-breakfast and not back to the cottage.

The bed-and-breakfast is clean, tidy and functional. When we get settled down for the night, I realise how exhausted I am. I glance at Tom who looks ashen, he has barely said a word on the journey from the police station.

'He's in shock' I thought my heart heavy and my body weary.

'I can't believe he's dead' Tom said, his voice shaking.

Ignoring my weariness, I cross the room and wrap my arms around him.

'Me neither' I said unable to believe that any of this situation is real.

My head spins when I think about everything that has happened in the past couple of days.

'He was my boss, but he was also my friend, like a second father to me.'

'I know he meant a lot to you; I didn't know him that well, but he was the first person I met when I moved here. He was always very kind to me I counted him as a friend' I said laying my head on Tom's shoulder comforted by his rhythmic breathing. I don't remember falling asleep and wake to the sound of Tom talking on his mobile. Immediately I notice it's quiet outside. Sitting up suddenly I get out of bed and open the curtains to look out. The destruction left behind by the storm is obvious and it's still raining, but I'm glad the fierce wind has settled.

'Who was that?' I ask, when Tom hangs up.

'The police, more bad news I'm afraid.'

'Morag?' I ask, panic instantly rising.

'Not Morag, she's still missing, but the police checked the cottage early this morning and it's been trashed overnight.

The officer said someone has smashed everything up. He asked if we've any enemies? Also, that John's body was removed and taken to the morgue for autopsy' he said his eyes tight with worry as he runs his hands through his hair.

My body trembles with each gut-wrenching sob unable to believe what is happening as tears freely roll down my cheeks.

'Why is this happening to us?' my voice quivers as I sniff into Tom's chest. 'What are we going to do? why would someone trash the cottage? we don't have any enemies; I don't even know anyone here' I said sniffing.

'When can we go home?' I ask, even though I'm not sure that I want to go back to the cottage yet.

'I'm not sure, give me a sec and I'll find out' he replies, before turning away to call the police back. 'The officer said we are to stay away until they've finished their investigations, hopefully it won't be more than a couple of days' Toms said rubbing my shoulders.

'I told them, I need to go to the farm to milk the cows, and if you're okay to stay here by yourself? I'll head over in a while. Maybe Morag will be back?' he said.

'Yeah, I'll be okay, I don't want to go out.'

After Tom has left to check on the farm, I turn the TV on instantly wishing I hadn't, every channel is showing John's farm, along with other places devastated in the storm. It's peculiar seeing the farm on the T.V, according to the news reporter at least three people have been killed.

Chapter 13. Strange Happenings.

It's been a long week living in the bed-and-breakfast, but two police officers have just arrived to let us know we can go back to the cottage.

'Do you know who trashed the cottage?' I ask.

'We don't have any leads, but we've been keeping an eye on the cottage and farm and no one has returned during our investigation.'

'What about the dead chickens and John's pet dog being killed?' I ask, worried that they are not taking this seriously.

'I'm sorry but I can't discuss details of the investigation, but I can reassure you that we are still investigating' the officer said, her face giving nothing away.

'But John is dead, and our home has been trashed' I state annoyed at her attitude.

'Yes, I'm sorry for your loss. Unfortunately, John wasn't the only casualty that night. Three other people in the local area also died' the officer replies.

'What about Morag?' Tom asks.

'Morag has not come forward, but when we searched the farmhouse, our officers found emptied drawers, it looks like she packed a bag and left. We have no reason to believe she is in any danger.'

'I know this is difficult, but the storm has been hard on the whole community, the whole town has suffered some sort of loss' she continues dismissing my concerns as she closes her notebook walking with her colleague to the door.

***

When the police finally leave, Tom and I begin packing our stuff ready to go home, but I'm uneasy, I don't believe they're taking this seriously. Someone was watching us from before the storm. Whoever that was? is likely to be the same person who killed the chickens and John's dog Max. I'm irritated and brooding at not being taken seriously.

'What if the person who was outside the night of the storm comes back? and where has Morag gone? people don't just decide to leave during a storm. Do they?' I exclaim, hoping Tom has some answers, because I'm not even a little satisfied with what the police have just told us.

'The last time I saw Morag, she was completely freaked out, so much so that she had been hiding outside in the rain, too terrified to come in, but I can't think where she would go? I don't know anything about her only that she's from Scotland' he said.

'She's from Scotland. Oh, that's why her accent sounds strange. I just thought it was a strange Northern Irish accent,' I said, feeling foolish.

'I don't actually know where she's from, but she definitely has a Scottish accent. Come on let's get this over with, the quicker we get home the less time we have to stress' he said roughly shoving the spare clothes he'd bought in Ramtree into a bag.

I'm agitated on the taxi ride home, worried about what sort of mess to expect. The police didn't go into detail only telling us the cottage had been trashed. My heart is thumping as we park up outside the cottage. It looks fine on the outside, but I'm worried about what we're going to find inside. As soon as the door is opened, the smell hits us.

It's disgusting, both Tom and I back away from the open door and cover our faces.

'This is gonna be rough,' Tom said, taking deep breaths before we both cautiously stepped through the front door.

I can't believe the mess, everything is everywhere, all the drawers have been upended and emptied; every piece of crockery has been smashed all over the floor. The smell is horrendous, my chest feels like it could cave in, the only thing stopping it are the gasps of air I'm taking with each heart-wrenching shuddering sob. I take a minute to scan my puffy eyes over everything when I spot something brown that has been spread all over the walls. From the smell permeating the room, I can only assume that it's faeces. Our clothes have been thrown all over the floor. Sucking in my breath, I sniff and wipe my nose before cautiously stepping further inside. The smell of urine and faeces is overwhelming as I step cautiously through the filth. The rug in front of the fire is squelching as I walk across it to enter the bedroom. The smell of urine is strong in here. I immediately notice the bed is soaking wet in what I can only assume is urine. Treading cautiously back into the living room, I watch as Tom rubs his neck before shoving a pile of our clothes into a black bin bag.

   'Everything is covered with urine and there's shit spread on the walls; what sort of sicko does this?' he said, his shoulders slumped as he stands holding the black bin liner in the living room.

   I glance around the room taking in all the destruction and genuinely don't know where to begin.

   'A psycho, someone sick in the fucking head. That's who does this?' he said his eyes flashing as he threw the bag of clothes down and marches out of the cottage.

   He strides out the front door and I watch through the window as he heads in the direction of the chicken coop. Staring at my hands, I don't know what to do? or where to start? But I need fresh air, I have to get out of here, the smell is overwhelming. Stepping out into the fresh air, I remember that the police had thought someone was in the caravan. In need of some comfort I cross my arms and hold my shoulders squeezing myself as I walk across the grass to inspect it. Cautiously opening the caravan door and stepping inside. I'm surprised it hasn't been trashed; it's messy and smells bad, but it's okay, it's obvious that someone has been in here. The thought of someone being in my caravan sends a shiver down my spine, glancing around I realise the caravan will need a good clean, but Tom and I will be able to stay here until the cottage is liveable again. Using my spare key, I make sure to lock the caravan door when I leave. Walking across the newly cut grass I join Tom at the coop.

'How is it?' I ask as I approach.

'Not too bad, but I don't understand why someone would do this?' he said, indicating the blood on the ground.

'I know, everything about this situation is strange isn't it?' I said trying to avoid looking at the blood spattered all around the coop.

Seeing the amount of blood makes me very thankful the police removed the bodies before we came home.

'How's the caravan?' Tom asks.

'It's okay, it's messy and there's a nasty smell lingering, but it's nothing a good clean won't get rid of. Someone has definitely been living in it' I said watching his reaction. 'But it should be okay for us to stay in until the cottage is ready to move back into. Come on let me show you' I said turning to walk back to the caravan.

Tom's shoulders are slumped, and his eyes focussed on the ground as we walk silently to the caravan. He takes his time walking up and down the inside of the van without touching anything.

'You're right, someone has definitely been here, it's fucking stinking' he said his eyes flashing.

His chest is thrust out and his eyes are cold and hard as he joins me outside, but as he's closing the door, I notice something out of the corner of my eye, it's a photo sitting partially hidden on the side.

'Tom wait.'

'What's wrong.'

'The photo on the side there' I said as he steps back in lifting it and holding it up for me to see.

'This is what's worrying you?'

The photo is of Emma and me, we've our arms wrapped around each other and look very happy, grinning like Cheshire cats. It's a nice photo, of happier times, taken before my mum had passed away.

'Yes, it's just…, I don't know?' I said running my fingers through my hair.

'Maybe it's bringing back memories?' Tom interrupts, placing the photo back down before we begin walking back to the cottage.

'Maybe, but I don't think so.'

It suddenly dawns on me that I don't remember bringing the photo with me.

'Tom, I want to look at the photo again, I don't think I brought it with me, you go on, I'll be there in a minute.'

'Okay, are you okay though? You must've brought it; otherwise how did it get here?'

'I don't know? but I want to look at it again, give me a shout if you need me.' I said, as the wind blows my hair across my face on the walk back to the caravan. As I step back in, it takes me a minute to

153

compose myself when I glance at the photo, I don't want to touch it, I've a feeling of dread creeping down my spine. As I stare at the photo the more certain I am that I didn't put it there.

'It's like it was placed in a way it wouldn't be seen right away.'

It's odd, the photo is random, the only people who had it are me and Emma, and she's not here. How is it here? I must've brought it with me. I'm very confused as I continue to stare at the photo. There's a noise behind me and I turn and spot Tom.

'What is it? what's wrong?' he asks

'I'm okay, it's just the photo is freaking me out.'

I know this sounds weird, but I don't remember bringing it here. The last time I remember seeing it was back at the house I used to share with Emma.'

'You must have brought it with you, how else would it have got here?' With everything that's happened, we're stressed and on edge' he said glancing at the photo.

'I know, I know I must have brought it, but something isn't right' I said.

'We should start clearing the mess' he said, locking the caravan door.

'You're right let's go and get started' I agree.

But as we're walking across the grass, I've a horrible spine-chilling feeling that I'm being watched again. I'm not sure I'll ever feel safe here again. As we head back to the cottage, I'm secretly wishing I'd never come to Northern Ireland. Back at the cottage, I watch as Tom pulls on gloves and begins lifting all the urine-soaked things, throwing them onto a pile he's made in the grass.

'I want to burn everything, if that's okay with you. We can buy new things; I don't want someone's stinking urine on our stuff' he said.

'No, you're right, we'll burn everything.'

Pulling on a pair of marigolds I begin helping him throw everything onto the pile. It takes us a good couple of hours before everything is piled high. Tom covers it all with fire-lighter fluid before flicking the match in his hand. There's a split second before a whoosh and everything is engulfed in flames. It's sad watching our stuff as it burns.

'What sort of sicko does this?' I said, as Tom places the last of our stuff onto the fire.

'Someone who is fucked up in the head, that's who. Tom said, angrily kicking the ground.

***

It was devastating burning all of our things. The smell of smoke is lingering but at least it smells better than urine which was permeating the cottage. We've taken the past two days to do nothing but scrub the cottage, the worst part was scrubbing the faeces that had dried rock hard and clung to the walls. This morning we're up early to begin painting, determined to finish as quick as possible we plough on barely speaking to each other as we focus on our task. I'm surprised but pleased when at lunch time, we've finished the first coat. I step outside to get some air, and while I'm standing looking across the fields, I begin thinking about John, remembering that he will need some sort of funeral.

'What do you think will happen with John? with Morag missing, do you think we should organise a funeral?' I call into the cottage.

When he doesn't reply I'm unsure if he's heard me or not, and poke my head through the door, spotting him knelt on the floor, his head in his hands. He glances up as I enter his eyes brimmed with tears.

'You're right, someone needs to do something for John' he said looking crushed. 'I've been so preoccupied with all of this, that I forgot, I mean how can you forget that someone will need a funeral?' he said, sitting on the floor with his head in his hands.

'Are we allowed to organise something, without Morag?' I ask, not knowing how things work, when a spouse is missing?

'I'll phone the police and ask what we can do' he said, his eyes scanning the room, looking around for his phone. 'The officer that I spoke to, said that we can have our own private service, but John's body cannot be released. The autopsy has shown some discrepancies that need investigated' he said.

'Discrepancies, what sort of discrepancies?' I said shocked at what I'd heard.

'They wouldn't say, just that there were discrepancies that are being investigated' Tom said his brows furrowed.

'And Morag still hasn't come home? Where could she have gone?'

'If she'd been harmed in the storm, you'd think she would've been found at a hospital or somewhere, don't you think? I said, unable to get my thoughts straight.

I've been very uneasy since the storm, there're many things unsettling me, from the photo of Emma and I. Morag going missing and now discrepancies over John's death. I've a bad feeling and wish things would go back to normal.

'What about we plant a tree?' I said, trying to offer something more positive to focus on.

'Yes, I like that idea, we'll go to the garden centre later today and pick a tree' he said, looking the most enthusiastic I've seen him since this all started.

'I remember Morag mentioning that she loved cherry blossom trees, before she lost her temper at my housewarming. Do you remember?'

'Yeah,' Tom titters.

'If John had died that night, we would be thinking that Morag did it' he said, laughing.

'I know, she was in a foul mood, wasn't she?' I agree laughing.

Sick of the smell of paint, we down tools and head to the garden centre. We pick a lovely cherry blossom tree and plant it at the bottom of the meadow where we can see it from the kitchen window.

'It's beautiful, this is a lovely way to remember him. And when Morag gets back at least we'll know she will like the tree' I said hopeful, that things would soon get back to normal.

'It is, isn't it' Tom agrees, smiling?

Walking hand in hand back to the cottage Tom asks what I think he should do about the farm? 'I mean, I can't just leave the cows, but they're not mine. I sold some heifers at the market last week and some eggs to the local farm store. I made enough that I could pay my own wages, but what am I going to do long-term?' he said looking at me for an answer.

I'm shocked I hadn't thought about the farm or what would happen to the animals.

'I don't know what you should do in the long-term? but for now I think you should just carry on as normal. I'm sure Morag will come back soon' I said not knowing what else to say?

'I suppose I'll just continue to do my job until she gets back' he said looking uncertain.

'I suppose' I agree not knowing what else he can do?

Chapter 14. Someone's Watching.

It's been a month since Tom, and I moved back into the cottage after the storm and while I was devastated that all our stuff had to be burned. I've enjoyed picking and buying nice new furniture together. Apart from the fact that Morag still hasn't come home, everything has gone back to normal. The caravan, however, is still giving me the creeps. It's probably just my imagination, but I thought I saw a shadow in it again the other day.

'I think I should sell the caravan; It's freaking me out, I keep imagining there's someone in it' I tell Tom later that evening.

'I know what you mean, it creeps me out at times as well, but everything has settled down and it's handy having that extra room.'

During breakfast the following morning, I tell Tom that I'm going to clear all our stuff from the caravan. I'm hoping it will help ease my anxious mind.

'Do you want me to help?'

'No, it's okay, I'll take my time and if it gets too much, I'll leave it' I said.

'Be careful, text me if you need a hand, I'll be around, I'm not going anywhere today' he said, kissing me on the cheek as he leaves for work.

I don't know why the caravan is scaring me so much, but it's probably because no one was ever caught for trashing the cottage. The grass has grown and is reaching almost to my knees, as I walk through it towards the caravan. I'm trying to stay level-headed, but I'm on edge and feel like I'm being watched again. Glancing around I can't see anyone and try to ignore it.

'It's just my imagination' I tell myself walking purposefully through the grass.

I'm dreading going inside, my gut is telling me that something isn't right.

'I must do this. If I don't, I'll never know.'

Unlocking the door and leaning in, I instantly know there has been someone in the caravan again. I'm sure of it; there's that smell again, and something is different; it looks tidy but smells unclean. I can't see what it is, but something is definitely different. I scan what I can see from the door. My heart begins to race, and I am too afraid to enter. I know Tom hasn't been here, he would have told me. I'm on the verge of phoning the police, but I don't know what to tell them? That I think someone has been in my caravan, there's nothing missing, it's just a feeling I have.

'I can't phone the police' I thought feeling stupid and unnerved.

My spine tingles and I look for movement in the fields surrounding the cottage. I'm trying to convince myself that I'm being ridiculous, that no one has been in here again, but I can't shake the feeling that something is wrong. I haven't yet plucked up enough courage to enter the caravan and realise that standing outside isn't going to get me any answers. Gathering all the bravery I can muster, I cautiously take a step inside looking all around, and as far as I can initially see, everything looks okay. Stepping deeper inside, I recognise that bad smell again. My heart is racing, and I turn desperate to get out heading for the door. I'm about to leave when I notice the photo again, only now, it's not the only one. Now there's another photo next to it, it's another picture of Emma and me. The second photo shows the pair of us at Glastonbury festival with glow paint on our faces smiling. I gasp loudly stepping backwards almost falling out through the caravan door. That was not here the last time. I know it wasn't.

'What's going on? How on earth did that photo get there? Am I going crazy?' I thought struggling to breathe as fear takes over, I have to get away and turn and run in a complete panic away from the caravan not stopping until I'm back inside the cottage.

I'm gasping, and my heart's thumping loudly in my head as I burst into the cottage. The door ricochets as it slams into the wall and I take a minute to catch my breath before glancing out the window in the direction I've just came. I'm horrified when I realise in my panic to get away. I've left the caravan door wide-open, but right now I don't care. There's no way I'm going anywhere near it alone. I take deep breaths trying to calm my racing heart. I'm struggling to make any sense of what's happening and sit down at the kitchen table, frantically trying to remember if I brought those photos with me. They used to sit on a bookcase in the house I shared with Emma. No matter how hard I try, I just can't remember packing them. Also, Emma wasn't talking to me at the time and was unlikely to let me just take them. I'm unnerved and jittery realising that the only person who had access to those photos is Emma.

'I need to talk to her, something weird is going on' I thought shakily dialling her number, but...

'*The number you have dialled has not been recognised*' plays over and over in my ear.

'She's changed her number.'

Determined to have it out with her, I check Facebook, but I can't find her profile. She's gone! I can't find her anywhere and realise she must have blocked me. Sitting at the kitchen table unable to control my trembling hands, I can't make sense of what is going on? Why is Emma being so weird? and why have those photos suddenly appeared? I'm certain I didn't bring them. But, if I didn't bring them, does that mean Emma is here in Northern Ireland?

'Surely I would know if she was here? wouldn't I?' I thought, feeling worried and confused, trying to think of a more reasonable explanation.

I don't actually believe Emma is here, but I'm certain someone has been in the caravan and someone put those pictures out. But who? And why? I phone Tom, I have an overwhelming need to know that he's okay?

'Hey, you, you'll never guess what's just happened' he said mysteriously.

'Just tell me' I said abruptly my hands shaking waiting to hear what he has to say.

'A solicitor phoned about ten minutes ago and I have an appointment to meet with him tomorrow. It's about John's estate. What do you think it's all about?'

Relief floods me, I thought he was going to tell me something awful had happened.

'I don't know. It could be anything, but when a solicitor phoned me shortly after my mum died, it was because she had left me her house.'

'It's very strange, I suppose I'll find out tomorrow' he said.

'Yeah, no point worrying about it until then, I'm heading up to the farm now see you in a bit' I said, not wanting to be on my own any longer.

'Great see you in a bit' he said.

As I leave, I double check that I've locked the cottage door.

'I'm not taking any chances' I thought my senses on high alert as I scan the meadow.

My heart races as I walk towards the farm, I don't know if it's my imagination, but I feel like I'm being watched again. My blood begins pounding in my ears and my heart thuds in my chest. I quicken my pace and keep checking behind to see if I can see anyone. Only this time when I check behind me, I realise I'm actually looking for Emma.

'She can't be here in Northern Ireland, can she?' I thought wishing I could just shake this feeling that I'm being watched.

I'm uneasy and jumpy when I reach the farm and spot Tom waving with a huge grin on his face, as he walks towards me. I instantly forget my concerns when he pulls me into a big bear hug and swings me around.

'I can see why John wasn't worried about giving us a few chickens' I said, pulling away as several gathers at my feet waiting to be fed.

'Can we bring some to the coop' I ask, enjoying throwing the hens some food.

'Yeah, I don't see why not, John was going to give us some anyway' he said showing me how to catch and lift a chicken.

Tom lifts two hens easily, holding one under each arm. I, however, spend the next ten minutes chasing hens around and only manage to catch one.

'This will do me' I said, breathless and laughing, pleased that I'd managed to get it.

'We should go through the wood it'll be quicker than using the road.'

He guides me in the direction of the wood and as we enter, I realise that I've never been this way before.

'Do you normally go this way to get to the cottage? I ask, noticing a pathway that has formed where the grass has been flattened from someone regularly walking this way.

'Never, I normally use the road, it's too mucky to use the wood every day, why do you ask? he said from behind me.

'There's a pathway here?' I said, stepping aside to let him see what I'm talking about?

'This pathway is definitely new' he said, the furrow on his brow deepening.

'That's strange, if you're not using it, then who is? I ask, my heart beginning to race again.

'There's something I forgot to tell you. I found another photo of me and Emma in the caravan this afternoon. I tried to contact her, but she has changed her number, and she's blocked me on Facebook' I said, blurting everything out.

'What? why didn't you say something before now?' he said, raising his eyebrow in confusion.

'I don't know. I thought I was overreacting, I keep getting a horrible feeling that someone is watching me, but I thought it was my imagination' I said, turning away blinking back the tears that have sprung to my eyes.

'Now that you mention it, I've had that feeling as well' he said, scanning all around.

I'm glad when we've managed to get all the hens in the new coop and agree to help Tom finish the last of the jobs on the farm, before walking back to the cottage. However, as we reach the cottage gate, I notice Tom has stopped and is staring at the caravan. I suddenly remember about leaving the door open and realise I've forgotten to tell him.

'Did you leave the caravan door open?' he asks a tightness in his eyes as he glances at me

'I did, I'm sorry, I forgot to tell you, but I ran out in a hurry and accidently left the door open. I was panicking at the time and too afraid to go back and close it' I exclaim, annoyed with myself for causing more worry.

Tom's face is hard with irritation as we start walking along the path toward the cottage. I don't know how I didn't see it before, and it takes me a second to realise that the cottage door is also wide-open swinging in the wind. Tom and I turn to look at each other.

'I definitely locked the cottage door. I double checked' I said, my heart thudding in my chest.

'I'm positive I locked the door, I made sure of it' I continue, desperately wanting him to believe me.

But he just stands silently scanning the surrounding area.

'I locked the cottage door' I repeat, knowing he doesn't believe me.

Chapter 15. Who's Watching Us?

As we cautiously step through the door, I notice it hasn't been damaged and on first impression everything looks fine. As far as I can see, nothing is missing or damaged like the last time.

'I definitely locked the door' I keep telling him feeling foolish and on the verge of tears.

'Well, it was definitely not locked, or even closed. You did leave the caravan unlocked' he said crossing his arms tightly, a hardness in his eyes.

'Yes, that's true, but only because I panicked after I found the second photo. I didn't think, just ran as fast as I could away from the caravan.'

I'm feeling very foolish and afraid, because even if Tom doesn't believe me. I know that I locked the cottage door.

'I definitely locked the cottage door,' I say again desperately wanting him to believe me.

I'm frustrated with myself for leaving the caravan door open and that he doesn't believe me, but I can't figure out how it's open without any damage? it must have been opened with a key or left unlocked. I know I left the caravan door open; I remember doing that. Pacing back-and-forth, I'm trying to remember what actually happened and beginning to doubt myself. Did I leave the door unlocked? I must have, otherwise, how is it open without any damage? Deep down, I know I locked the cottage door. I remember that I checked it twice.

'Come on, let's go and check the caravan' he said, making a big show of locking the cottage door behind us.

The caravan looks the same as it was when I left in a panic earlier. The photos, including the new one, are still in the same place as they were.

'Why would someone put these photos out? What are they hoping to accomplish?' he said, checking that everything is still where it should be.

When he's satisfied that nothing is missing, he makes another big show of locking the door before setting off across the grass. He's walking that fast I have to run to catch up with him.

'I didn't mean to leave it open,' I said breathlessly.

'I don't know what is going on? but someone is playing mind games with us' I said.

I almost run into Toms back when he abruptly stops his face hard.

'Who? Other than you and Emma, would have those photos?' he said, turning to face me.

'No one, there was only one of each photo, and I'm sure that I didn't bring them with me' I said.

'Did you put the photo there?'

'No, you know I didn't. Why would you say that?'

'Do you think she could be behind this?' he asks his eyes flashing with fury.

'Why would she?' I said, disliking his tone and suddenly feeling protective of Emma, but realising that I'd also thought the same thing. Even if the thought had crossed my mind. I never really believed that Emma could be behind this, despite our falling out.

'She hasn't been very nice since you moved here. Maybe we should mention it to the police, just in case' he said, his face grim.

'I'll try to contact her again first, maybe through some of her friends on Facebook', I said, hoping that he is wrong. I don't want all that has happened recently to be because of Emma and our falling out. Tom lets out a loud sigh as he runs his hand through his hair looking at me.

'Listen, I'm sorry if I snapped. It's just so frustrating all of these things that keep happening. I'm fucking sick of it, it's relentless' he said, his face softening.

'We should head back to the cottage, get a bite to eat and have an early night, ready for the solicitor in the morning' he said wrapping his strong arms around me.

Normally being close to Tom reassures me, but I'm irritated at what he said and his tone when he said it. Wanting to put some distance between us, I intentionally walk slightly behind him. The wind howls through the trees as we walk in silence back to the cottage.

***

Thankfully it was an uneventful night and through pure exhaustion I slept surprisingly well and woke early feeling refreshed. I didn't hear Tom get up; he was up extra early to milk the cows to give him time for the solicitor. I'm glad to see he's in a better mood when he arrives home an hour later.

***

'What do you think the solicitor wants?' I ask as I get into the car.

'Not a clue, but my gut says it will be that the farm is to be sold and I'll be out of a job' he said starting the car.

The atmosphere in the car is heavy as we arrive at the solicitors with plenty of time to spare.

'Good luck,' I said as he got out of the car.

'I just want to get this over with as quickly as possible' he said abruptly running his hands through his hair.

Waiting in the car while Tom is in with the solicitor. I decided to use my time trying to contact Emma again. I send several of her friends a message asking for her to get in contact. I don't believe that Emma is responsible for all that has happened. It doesn't take long before my phone pings; it's one of Emma's friends I'd messaged,

'Hey Eve, hope you're keeping well in N.I I'm a bit confused by your message. I thought Emma was with you. I haven't heard from her in ages and assumed she must have stayed after her holiday.

'When was she meant to be here on holiday?' I reply feeling very confused.

'Early March, didn't she come? I haven't heard from her. She's not on Facebook either.'

'No, I haven't seen her since I left over a year ago.'

Reeling from the message, my heart races, as I sit alone in the car.

'Emma is here' I thought, feeling very vulnerable.

I release a breath I didn't realise I'd been holding when I spot Tom coming out of the solicitors, crossing the road. He looks strange and I can't read his face as he gets into the car, sitting in silence, staring straight ahead.

'Fuck, it's worse than he thought' I thought anxiously waiting for him to speak wondering what has happened?

'What's wrong?' I blurt out, unable to wait any longer for him to speak.

'Nothing' he said, continuing to stare straight ahead his knuckles white as he tightly grips the steering wheel.

I'm unsure if he should drive, as I watch him trying to stop his shaking hands as he turns to look at me.

'Seriously Tom you're scaring me, what happened?'

'John left me everything, the farm, the house, the machinery and all the animals in his will' he said, turning to look at me.

'Turns out he and Morag were not married.'

He looks dumfounded and holds up a large set of keys.

'Seriously. The farm is yours? I said shocked.

He looks so devastated; I want to make him feel better.

'He must have thought a lot of you' I said.

'I know, it just feels weird and what about Morag? Where has she gone? What will I do when she comes back and finds out? I mean, they may not have been married, but she was there when I started working for John' he said, starting the car.

I don't want to tell him about Emma and upset him further as he's driving us home in silence refusing to talk about the farm. However as soon as we arrive at the cottage Tom announces that he's going to work and leaves me standing unsure what to do?

'Okay see you later' I call after him.

I watch as he walks slowly, his shoulders slumped and his head down, towards the farm. After Tom has left, I give the cottage a quick tidy up before remembering that I didn't feed the chickens before we left this morning. I make doubly sure to lock the cottage before I leave.

I can hear the hens clucking away as I make my way through the woods towards the coop. The hens rush forward and gather at my feet when I throw some food. After I've filled the feeder and the hens are happily eating, I enter the coop to gather the eggs. But my blood runs cold, something's wrong, all the eggs are smashed on the floor, there's not one egg that hasn't been smashed. I know eggs can get broken by the hens themselves, but this, this is something else altogether.

'This is not normal' I thought beginning to clear the gunky mess.

After clearing all the broken eggs, I leave the coop to get new straw. I scan the surrounding woods; my heart feels as if it could explode in my chest. I'm looking for any kind of movement and feel hyper-sensitive to all sounds, seriously considering whether we should get security cameras fitted?

'This can't go on; we can't carry on living in fear' I thought wondering what else we can do?

'EVE! EVE!' I hear Tom shouting frantically from the far side of the wood.

'I'm here' I call waving from the coop.

He is flushed and breathless as he rushes towards me.

'What's wrong?'

I'm trying not to sound too alarmed, but my adrenalin is quickly spiking and my heart thumping hard in my chest, I've had enough shocks for one day, wondering what's wrong with Tom?

'Someone has been living in one of the old sheds on the farm' he blurts out breathlessly, when he finally reaches me.

'How do you know?'

'Have a look at these' he said showing me photos he's taken on his phone.

181

It's plain to be seen from the photos that there has definitely been someone in the shed and it looks like they have been living there for a while. I flick through the photos on his phone confused about what this means.

'Come and have a look' he said turning abruptly and marching back in the direction of the farm.

As we walk to the shed, I tell him about the eggs, and my idea of security cameras as we walk.

'I'm phoning the police, this is something! it's trespassing! That's what this is, and I have photos' he said clenching his fists into a tight ball.

'I'm sick of all this bullshit, it's non-stop' he continues his nostrils flaring.

I'm breathless and sweating from walking so fast. Adrenalin courses through my body as we arrive at the shed. A shed, I didn't even know existed. I breathe deeply trying to calm the panic that's coursing through me as I glance around this new shed. I take my time as I walk slowly around spotting evidence everywhere that someone has been living here.

'Do you think they're gone?' I ask as I scan the shed noticing bits of torn clothing, rags, a saucepan and a camping stove.

'I don't think so' Tom said, showing me a half-used bottle of milk and smelling it.

'It's still fresh.'

'Phone the police now' I said, panic coursing through me as I listen hyper-sensitive to every noise.

I jump out of my skin when a chicken emerges from behind a bale of hay scratching the floor with its foot. The shed is filthy and there's a disgusting smell that makes my stomach lurch. As I walk around, I notice several buckets that are being used as a bathroom. Looking at the buckets I can see that they are on the verge of overflowing.

'I wonder if this is who trashed the cottage?' I said indicating the buckets full of human waste.

'Do you think who ever this is, has been living here all that time, watching us?' I said unable to keep the panic from rising.

'Probably' Tom said looking tense.

'There's no way this is Emma, she might be a bitch, but she wouldn't do this, for a start, there's no way she would live in a shed. She wouldn't even go camping with me' I said, certain Emma wouldn't willingly live in this shed.

'If you say so' he said sounding sceptical.

It doesn't take the police long to arrive, two officers come straight to the shed and begin gathering evidence. As the officers gather what they need, we walk back to the cottage with another officer who asks about everything that has been happening.

'I think someone's been in my caravan recently, there's photos, I'm certain I didn't bring to Northern Ireland that have been placed in it' I say realising how silly it sounds worrying about photos.

'Can you show me' the officer said?

'Of course,' I said.

Tom and I walk with the officer across the meadow, but as soon as the caravan door is opened, I notice straight away, the photos are gone.

'They're gone, the photos are gone, they were there yesterday and now they're gone' I said feeling my panic rising again.

Not wanting to go inside, I stay where I am in the doorway pointing to the place where the two photos were sitting.

'There were two photographs of me and my ex-housemate Emma sitting on the side, just there' I tell the police officer, pointing to the space where the missing photographs were.

'I didn't put them there; I don't even think I brought them with me when I moved here. The first one appeared after the first break-in, then another appeared yesterday' I said, feeling stupid stressing about photographs.

'It's okay, try to stay calm, can you check if there's anything else missing?' the officer asks as Tom checks the rest of the van.

'No, there's nothing missing only the photos' he said.

It takes the officers about half an hour to finish their search and they tell us to call if anything else happens. After the police have left, Tom, and I set about clearing the shed. We work together, dumping the filthy rags in a pile outside the shed ready for burning. Tom sets it alight and black smoke billows up into the air as I gather the last pile and notice something fall onto the ground.

'Tom, come and look at this' I call, as panic surges through me again.

I glance around looking for any sign of movement, as Tom steps away from the fire joining me in the shed.

'What's up?'

'Look' I said pointing at the ground, where at my feet is the photo of Emma and me, at the festival staring up at us.

'It fell when I lifted these rags' I said showing him the filthy bundle in my hands.

'Whoever this is, must've removed the photos, sometime between us being in the

caravan yesterday, and before the police
came today' I said.

My hands are shaking uncontrollably, and
my mind working overdrive, wondering who
on earth would do this? And why?

'And you're sure it can't be Emma?'
Tom said, his eyes fixed on me.

'I just don't think Emma would do this,
I'm sure she didn't.'

'Stay there, don't move' he orders,
before dashing out of the shed, returning
moments later with a Zip-lock bag.
Carefully he lifts the photo and places it into
the bag before calling one of the officers
who'd just interviewed us. I don't know
what to think as I examine everything in the
shed while Tom is talking to the police.
Glancing around taking in all the small
details, I notice rope near a pole, it almost
looks as if someone was being held here.

'The police want us to drop the photo
into the station today' Tom said, interrupting
my thoughts.

'What do you think about these ropes' I
ask, showing him the rope around the pole?

'I don't know, it looks like something was tied up' he said.

'Yeah, that's what I thought, it's almost as if someone was being held here, but now they're gone! Come on let's get out of here, this place is freaking me out' I said stepping out of the shed.

'Yes, we'll go home, get cleaned up and head to Ramtree' he said.

'When we're in Ramtree, dropping the photo off, I think we should look for some security cameras. What do you think?' I ask, and he nods in agreement.

'Yes, that's a good idea.'

Chapter 16. Intruder.

After dropping the photo into the police station, we head to a small hardware store in the town. Neither Tom nor I know anything about security systems, and we pick a simple system that the shop owner shows us how to set up before we leave.

'If you get stuck, setting it up, just give me a call' he tells us before we leave.

We've only been away from the cottage for about an hour, but as Tom is driving back down the road towards the cottage, I spot a cow in the middle of the road.

'Is that one of John's?' I ask, pointing.

'Looks like it. There's no one else with cows around here.'

'How do you think it got out?'

'No idea, but it definitely looks like one of ours.'

He shakes his head looking baffled and toots the horn driving slowly behind the cow until we reach the farm. However, when we arrive, it soon becomes obvious. That it's not just one cow, but the whole herd, that have escaped and are all over the farmyard.

'What's going on?' I said, feeling apprehensive with so many cows everywhere.

'It's that fucking squatter again! He's fucking with us again' Tom shouts, slamming his hands against the steering wheel.

'Call the police NOW' he yells.

Leaning away from him, I'm afraid at how angry Tom is. I have never seen him so angry.

'I'm not putting up with anymore of this bullshit' he shouts, parking the car abruptly, making the seat belt tighten against my chest.

He slams the door as he gets out and I watch him stride across the yard directing the cows back toward the field. Scanning the yard as I phone the police, I notice that there appears to be a large hole in the hedge it definitely wasn't there when we left. The hole has allowed the cows to escape from the field into the farmyard. I open the car door and lean out.

'Tom, look,' I yell.

'What?'

'Over there' I yell, pointing in the direction of the hole and watch as Tom walks to examine the damage.

Tom, come on, get back into the car. The police have asked us to stay in the car until they get here' I call.

As Tom sits next to me brooding, I'm thankful that it takes less than five minutes for three police cars to arrive. I notice one of the police cars has turned toward the cottage while the other two continue on toward the farm. As soon as the policeman reaches us in the car, Tom jumps out and starts yelling.

'You need to do something?' he yells pointing at the officer.

'I'm fucking sick of this' he shouts, stopping cows from bumping into the car.

'It's relentless. We are being harassed.'

'I need you to calm down, sir,' the officer said calmly.

'I can assure you that we are investigating, and we do have a lead that we are following.'

'Actually, I was about to call you. We need to talk to Miss Mullen.'

The officer turns to me, indicating that I should follow him. He pulls out the photo Tom had handed in earlier.

'You know this person?' he said, pointing at Emma.

'Yes, that is my ex-housemate, Emma Crosby.'

As I look at the photo, there's something niggling at the back of my mind. Something I can't remember about Emma.

'Do you have a contact number for Miss Crosby?' he asks writing in his notebook.

'I did, but she's changed her number. I tried calling her, but the line is dead.'

'Can you give us the old number anyway and your old address?'

'Yes, of course,' I said, giving him Emma's old number.

'Emma lives in England', I said, before giving him our old address.

'Have you been in touch with Miss Crosby recently?'

'No, she's changed her number and has blocked me on Facebook. We fell out before I moved here, and we haven't been in contact at all.'

'So, she hasn't visited since you moved here?' he asks.

'No, like I said, we fell out.'

'But I text one of her friends recently who thought that she was going to visit me here, but she never came' I said showing the officer the messages on my phone.

'Thank you, we will be in touch' he said, before joining his colleagues.

The police stay for about an hour, asking questions and searching all around the farm.

'We have all we need for now but remember to get in contact if anything else happens' the officer said, as he and his colleagues prepare to leave.

After the police have left for the second time, we have all the cows back in the field. Tom and I work together repairing and securing the hedge. However, as we work, I'm uneasy, certain that whoever is doing this has to be close by, probably watching us.

'The police checked all the sheds, didn't they?' I ask scanning the farmyard.

'That's what they said, but I can't help but think whoever is doing this is hanging around not too far away' he said.

He is very bad tempered as we work. I can tell that he's feeling as uneasy as I am. It takes the rest of the day; before the fence is secured, my emotions are raw and my body aches. I just want to go home when we've finished the fence, but the cows have been bellowing loudly for the past hour, letting us know they are ready for milking.

'I'm so tired I could drop,' I said, wishing we could go home.

'You go on. I'll finish up here and see you when I'm done,' Tom said.

'No, I don't want to be alone; also, we'll get it done quicker with the both of us working.'

The milking seems to take forever, and it's almost dark by the time we're finished. My body is aching, and my emotions are running high as we walk home. All I can think about is getting some food and going to bed. I burst into tears when Tom opened the cottage door and the smell hit me. I'd forgotten that I'd prepared vegetable soup the night before; it has been cooking in the slow cooker all day. The smell is delicious as we enter the cottage. I'm physically and emotionally exhausted.

'I'd forgotten about the soup' I sniff, wiping tears from my cheeks as my belly grumbles loudly.

'It smells good. Are you okay?' he asks, looking concerned, pulling me into a tight hug.

'Yeah, I'm just tired and emotional, I just wish everything would go back to normal.'

'I know, I feel the same, hopefully the police will find whoever is doing this soon.

If you're okay, I'm going to get showered before eating, you can start without me if you want' he said.

'No, I'll get showered after you and we can eat after.'

I'm exhausted and just want to sit down, but fear takes over and I begin checking everything, looking for evidence that someone has been here. I tread lightly as I walk around the cottage, anticipating the next problem. I don't expect anything to be as it should, anymore.

'This was supposed to be my quiet place' I thought, my eyes filling with tears again.

Standing in the middle of the cottage, I feel raw and sad that I don't feel safe here anymore.

'Why is this happening to us? Why are we being targeted? And who is doing this?'

I can't stop myself from checking every detail of the cottage. I know it's not helpful, but I'm looking for any small detail that might be different. It's a ritual, that I've taken to doing every day, and this time, thankfully everything looks normal. I've almost finished my ritual, when the bathroom door opens along with a bello of steam. Tom exits a towel wrapped around his waist and goes into the bedroom.

'Showers free' he calls.

The bathroom is still steamy as I enter. I turn the water temperature up high and scrub my hair and skin until it is red and painful. Spending longer than normal showering, I'm desperate to wash everything away. Tears run down my face, I want to get out, but I can't and instead I keep scrubbing, I need to scrub away all the horrible things that have been happening. My body still aches, and my skin is raw when I join Tom at the small kitchen table to eat our soup. Listening to the news, which is on in the background, my body aching. I look across the table at Tom and he looks as exhausted as I feel.

'I need this to stop, it's breaking me, I'm exhausted' I said, watching Tom as he sits in silence eating his soup.

I feel like he blames me for all that has happened.

'What if it is Emma, who's doing this?' I ask, watching Tom, who stops eating, lifting his head to look at me.

'I mean, where did the photo's come from? She's the only other person who had those photos.'

Even as I say it, I don't believe that Emma is behind everything that has happened, but I can't come up with any other explanation.

'It's all very strange, do you think she's here in Northern Ireland? I mean, this has been going on for months, since before the storm. She would need to be living here! do you really think she'd do this? Move to Northern Ireland to do all that has happened, also why would Emma cut a hole in the hedge to let the cows out?' he asks.

'Why would anyone? But you're right Emma is a real townie, she wouldn't want to touch anything dirty, let alone cut a hole in the hedge' I said glad that he doesn't think Emma is involved.

'I just don't know what's going on. It's all very strange. Where did those photos come from?' I said, feeling almost too tired to talk let alone think.

'You look tired, I don't think we should talk about it tonight, let's just watch some TV and get a good night's sleep. We can talk about it tomorrow' he said, gathering our bowls from the table before bringing them to the sink.

Chapter 17. Moving On.

It's been a month since we came back from Ramtree to find the cows had been let out. I'm grateful there haven't been any more shenanigans since then. Something changed that day; the strange things stopped happening almost overnight. The feeling I'm being watched has also almost stopped. I do still get a chill every now and again but it's nowhere near as often. It has taken a while, but I have finally begun to relax, to the point I'm considering finishing the last few things that need done to complete the cottage. I want to get the porch made; It will be my last low-cost project before I get someone in to do the roof. When I mention my plans to Tom, he agrees it would be good to focus on a new project.

'We can get started at the weekend, if you want?' he said.

'Sounds great,' I said looking forward to getting started.

Tom and I spend all weekend working on the porch. It's hard work, but I'm delighted at how lovely and rustic it looks when we're done. Standing next to Tom admiring our finished project, as the smell of our evening meal wafts around us, I'm feeling relaxed and happy.

'It looks great and will help protect against the bad weather,' I said.

'It does indeed' he agrees.

Later that evening, while we are enjoying our evening meal with a glass of Merlot. I begin thinking about the farmhouse.

'Now the cottage is almost finished. We could make a start renovating the farmhouse,' I said, watching to gauge his reaction.

Tom has avoided going anywhere near the farmhouse since he inherited it. We still treat the farm like John and Morag are living there and despite having the keys neither of us has gone into the house apart from to let the police in. I know that Tom, like me, still expects Morag to come home any day now.

'I know, we're waiting on Morag coming home, but when she does get back, she needs to know that John left the farm to you' I said.

'I don't know. It's not like we need it' he said, looking concerned.

'Even if we don't want to live in it, we could renovate it and rent it out; it could give us an extra income.'

'Yeah, I suppose. It's just, every day I expect her to come home. How am I going to tell Morag that John left me the farm?' he said, his head bowed.

'She has to be told that John left you the farm. She can live in the house, if that's what you want, but it belongs to you. John left it to you because he wanted you to have it' I said, watching his body language, I'm concerned he will hand it back to her.

'Yeah, I know. It's just, I'm still confused about why he left it to me and not Morag, even if they weren't married. Why didn't he leave it to her?'

'Something must have been up between them! John made a choice; he knew you would look after the farm and his beloved cows. You should honour his wishes. He knew what he was doing. It's what he wanted.'

'Yeah, I suppose. I'll just have to deal with Morag when she gets back,' he said, looking more relaxed as he raises his glass.

'Cheers'

'Cheers' I said, clinking my glass against his, enjoying feeling relaxed again.

'Does this mean, I can make a start on the farmhouse?' I ask smiling.

'Yeah, you might as well.'

'Brilliant, I'll come with you to the farm tomorrow.'

I'm glad that he's finally come around. It will be good to have a new project to get stuck into. Although I am nervous at the thought of going inside.

'Will you be okay going in alone? I'll come if you want me too, but I must admit that I've only recently stopped having nightmares about finding John electrocuted in his bed. I don't think I'll ever forget that smell,' he said.

'I do feel nervous about going inside, but it has to be done sometime and everything has settled down recently,' I said.

'Yeah, hopefully that's all behind us now.'

'It's hard to believe he's gone, isn't it?'

'It is, are you finished?' Tom says, changing the subject as he lifts my plate carrying it to the sink?

Tom has just finished washing the dishes and is about to join me on the sofa but before he gets a chance to sit down, we're startled by a clanging noise outside. My adrenalin instantly surges, terror washing over me as I stand up. I glance around the room, my heart beginning to pound in my ears. I'm grateful that after the storm, Tom put thick curtains up and no one can see inside.

'What do you think that was?' I ask, glancing at Tom.

'I don't know. I'll go and have a look, hopefully it's nothing' he said, looking for his torch.

'I'll come with you; I don't want you going out there by yourself.

'You're right. We should stay together,' Tom said.

I struggle to steady my breath, desperate to calm the increasing panic building inside me when I remember that we have cameras.

'What about the cameras? Do you think we should check them first? I don't know about you, but I really don't want to go outside.'

Relieve washed over Tom's face when he agrees,

'Yes, let's do that.'

I follow Tom into the bedroom, my heart racing as he turns the monitor on. There's four camera shots showing on the split screen, but each screen is dark and it's difficult to see anything at all.

'I thought they would be clearer' I said, focussing on movement I notice on one of the screens.

It's fuzzy, but it looks like there's a blurry figure moving away from the cottage through the woods.

'Look, do you think that could be someone?' I ask, pointing at the screen.

'It looks like it could be.'

We watch as the shape quickly disappears out of the range of the camera. Tom looks concerned and rewinds the recording to watch it again.

'It's so difficult to see' he said after the third time of rewinding and watching.

I'm phoning the police, I'm not waiting this time' he said, lifting his phone. It only takes the police ten minutes to arrive, but it feels like a lot longer as we continue to watch the screens searching for any kind of movement outside. The police search the farm and around the cottage but find nothing.

'This is so frustrating,' I said, watching as Tom paces the room looking furious.

He puts a new CD into the security recorder, giving the police tonight's recording.

'We will look at this, back at the station and get back to you' the officer said.

After the police have left, we're both too unsettled to do anything but watch the monitor. An hour has passed and I'm getting bored and tired of watching the blank screens.

'There's no one there' I said, yawning and stretching.

I want to turn the monitor off and go to bed.

'We don't know that' he said, yawning as well.

'Come on, turn it off we're both tired, let's get some sleep.'

I yawn again, before leaning over to turn the screen off leaving the room pitch-black. My tired eyes strain to stay awake in the dark.

Chapter 18. I Remember.

Waking with a start clutching my chest. I'm sweating, breathing hard and fast as I bolt upright instantly awake. I'm sweating trying desperately to catch my breath.

'What's wrong? Eve, what's wrong? Are you having a nightmare?' I hear Tom asking as he turns the bedside lamp on.

'The car' I gasp, still holding my chest that feels tight. I take deep breaths desperate to regulate my breathing.

I've woken with such a shock that my head is spinning. I try to steady myself by pulling my knees up and putting my head between them still gasping for air.

'The car we saw, the night of the storm, do you remember?' I said, still struggling to catch a breath.

'Yeah, I remember, the one in the hedge. What about it?'

He sounds confused as he rubs my back, trying to calm me down.

'Eve, what's the matter?'

'It's been at the back of my mind, annoying me since that night. I knew I recognised it, but so much has happened. I couldn't think straight.'

My breathing is beginning to regulate to a normal rate when I look up meeting Tom's gaze.

'The car we saw in the hedge. It's Emma's.'

'What? Are you sure? It was very difficult to see in the dark, he said, looking concerned and worried.

'I'm sure, it's been at the back of my mind and bugging me since the storm. I just didn't know why?'

'But now I remember, it was definitely Emma's car.'

He's giving me a strange look and I'm certain he doesn't believe me.

'Do you think she was coming to see you and got caught up in the storm?' he asks.

'What time is it?' I interrupt abruptly,

'Almost 5:30am'

'Where's my phone?'

I look around the bedroom, trying to see where I left my phone.

'I think you left it in the living room. I'll get it, stay there', he said, getting out of bed before returning moments later with the phone.

'Here,' he said, handing me the phone.

'What are you going to do?' he asks.

'I don't know. I was going to call her but then I remembered she's changed her number.

'Why did she .change her number and not tell me?'

'What does all this mean?' he asks, looking confused.

'I mean, if it's Emma's car and you're certain it is. That means she was definitely here, in Northern Ireland' he said looking intently at me.

'We need to contact the police.'

'Okay, but it can wait until the morning, don't you think?'

'Yes, it can wait. But I'm certain that the car we saw the night of the storm was definitely Emma's car.'

'And it was gone, by the time we returned after the storm. I know that it definitely wasn't there. I made a point of looking for it when we came home.'

I suddenly remember that Tom came back to the farm to milk the cows.

'Did you notice if the car was still there when you came back the day after the storm?' I ask.

'No, it definitely wasn't there, I remember looking for it. Because, I thought that someone must have crashed their car and would be back to get it.'

'The car has been niggling at me since the storm. I knew I recognised it when I saw it. There is a sticker in the back window from when we went to Glastonbury' I tell him, desperately wanting him to take me seriously.

'Do you think it's possible? Now we know Emma was definitely here that night. That she could be the one doing all the shit that's happened recently?' he asks, his face filled with worry.

'I don't know. I wouldn't normally think so, but why didn't she call? And why has she changed her number?' I said as a horrible sinking feeling in my stomach makes me feel very uneasy.

'I mean, her car was here the night when everything went a bit crazy, also the photos. She's the only person who would have those photos.'

Realisation suddenly dawns on me, that it has likely been my best friend who has been tormenting us these past few months.

'I just can't imagine Emma choosing to live, even short term in that shed. It's so unlike her, she would hate it.'

'Unless it is just a coincidence and someone else was living in the shed. But if she wasn't living in the shed, where is she? Why hasn't she called? I'm certain it was definitely her car in the hedge'

'Maybe she was hurt in the storm and no one knows who she is? She could be in a hospital somewhere? The car had ploughed right up that hedge,' Tom said.

'I'm calling the police. They can check all the hospitals in case she has been hurt' he said, looking concerned.

Rubbing the nape of his neck, anxiety etched on his face, Tom leans over to turn the security monitors back on. We watch as the four monitors appear on the screen and I'm instantly relieved they are clear. Leaning back, he lets out a small sigh as he lifts his phone to call the police again, I listen as he tells them what I remembered and asks if they could check the local hospitals.

'What did they say?' I ask when he hangs up.

'They're going to check the hospitals. The officer also said that they will call out later, they have more questions, about what you remembered' he said.

As I sit thinking about the night of the storm, I realise that is when everything changed. It's the night John died, and Morag

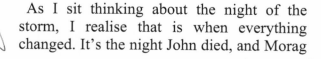

disappeared. We've since found out that somebody has been living in the shed watching and tormenting us. I just can't understand why Emma's car was here? and where has she gone? I'm feeling overwhelmed and confused by it all.

'It can't be Emma, surely she can't be the one who has been tormenting us? Can it?' I ask, looking at Tom, who shakes his head and shrugs his shoulders, looking as concerned and confused as me.

'I don't know what to think. I don't know Emma, she's not my friend, but after everything I've seen on Facebook. Well, most of that shit was messed up, honestly, I wouldn't be surprised to find out it was here' he said, his eyes flashing.

'She was definitely out to get you on social media. Do you think she would go as far as coming here, to Northern Ireland? To do all what has happened?' he asks.

'Normally no, but Emma changed after my mum died, she was drinking far too much, I was worried that she was spiralling out of control. The Emma I knew before would never do any of those things, but nothing is normal about this whole situation'

I said, feeling unsettled, watching as Tom gets out of bed.

'Are you okay to stay here alone? because it's nearly 6am and I need to make a move soon' he said.

The thought of staying in the cottage alone fills me with dread and I quickly decide to go with him to the farm.

'No, I think I'll come with you' I said, jumping out of bed to get ready.

I always find being at the farm therapeutic and feel instantly calmer and safer here.

'What do you think? should I start clearing the farmhouse?' I call to Tom who is walking the cows to the milking parlour.

'Yeah, if that's what you want. It's probably better too busy yourself while waiting for the police' he said ushering cows.

'You're right, I'll make a start, it'll help distract me.'

He kisses me on the cheek before I turn and walk in the direction of the farmhouse. This will be the first time either Tom or I have been inside the farmhouse since the storm. As I enter, the nauseating smell of electrocuted flesh hits me, and I begin to gag, feeling instantly sick. I'd thought that it would have died down a little. I take deep breaths in through my mouth trying to stop my stomach from lurching. I push the front door wide-open as I enter to let the fresh air in and the bad smell out. I feel weird being inside the farmhouse for the first time since the storm.

'Any wonder Tom doesn't want to come in' I thought, remembering that awful night.

'Poor John' I thought remembering sadly what happened and wondering where on earth Morag has gone?

'How has she just disappeared? it's so weird.'

The kitchen is freezing, but I open the windows to air the place and let some smell away. I shiver as I step further into the kitchen. There's an odour that's different from the burned flesh smell that's permeating the rest of the house. I open the fridge door and the smell of rotten food hits me. I pull my head away and, holding my breath peer inside. An uncooked beef joint looks decidedly green around the edges. There's a jug with slushy lumpy milk in it, I don't need to smell it to know it's off. Pulling out the vegetable drawer I see that the veg has turned into a pulp and there's liquid sloshing around in the drawer. As I look around, I can see that the farmhouse is quite run down. The kitchen is filled with a large wooden table, that has six wooden chairs around it. I step around the corner and find a large larder; the shelves are filled with tinned and packet foods. The kitchen definitely needs new windows, the wind is whistling through the rotten wooden frames.

'I'm surprised they survived the storm' I thought, picking at the rotten wood on the window in front of the sink.

I hear a creak and groan from somewhere in the empty house. It makes me jump and I stand still making sure that no one is actually here and once my heart has returned to a more normal pace, I let out a small sigh. It feels weird being alone in the house. I'm jumpy and have chills running down my spine as I slowly explore the downstairs rooms. I wasn't ever in the farmhouse much and before the storm I hadn't been any further than the kitchen. Cautiously walking down the dingy dark hall, I enter the first door next to the kitchen and find a small dining room. The dining room faces to the rear of the property and has a strong mouldy smell. It doesn't look like this room was ever used, there's just a large imposing table with six chairs no photos or any sign that anyone used this room ever. Across from the kitchen on the other side of the stairs I find a large living room. It's pleasant and bright with two large windows, one facing the front yard and the other facing the back across the field where the cows are. My heart begins to race as I step out of the living room back into the hall. Standing at the bottom of the stairs I'm wondering whether to go up or not? The potent burned flesh odour is permeating down the stairs and making me feel very nauseous. I know the smell is going to be stronger upstairs and need to either leave now and help Tom with the cows or go upstairs. Taking deep breaths through my mouth, I slowly climb the stairs that are covered with a deep, dark flowery carpet. Reaching the top, I scan the landing and see three closed doors what I assume are three bedrooms and a bathroom. The bedroom where we found John, is to the front of the house and the door is open. The room is dark, and I can see branches on the floor from where Tom cut the tree down and boarded the window up on the outside. Backing away from John's room, I cover my nose with my sleeve, as I cautiously walk across the landing. Opening the door next door to John's I poke my head in and can see what the police were talking about. Stepping in I can see the drawers have been emptied out onto the bed.

'It does look like Morag has left' I thought scanning the untidy bedroom and stepping back into the landing.

The bathroom is at the top of the stairs and next door to that opposite John's room there's another bedroom, that has a double bed, a large wardrobe and a fireplace in it. The house is freezing, and I decide to light all the fires upstairs. As I explore upstairs, I make sure to open the windows in an attempt to get rid of the potent stench. As I descend the stairs, I have a flashback to that dreadful night and panic, running the rest of the way and stand panting at the bottom of the stairs. When my racing heart begins to slow, I glance around and realise that while the house will need new windows eventually, other than that, it's not too bad. There's nothing a good clean and some paint won't fix. I've just stepped outside and I'm pulling the front door closed when a police car pulls up with two officers in it.

Chapter 19. Guilty or Not Guilty.

Standing on the doorstep as the police officers' head towards me, I spot Tom coming out of the parlour. He must have finished with the milking and is bringing the cows back to the field behind the house.

'Miss Mullan, we've some questions for you, do you mind if we go inside?' the police officer asks.

She's the same one, we spoke too, the night of the storm.

'Yes, come into the kitchen, sorry about the smell. Today's the first time I've been in here since the storm' I said noticing the officer's stern face.

I anxious as the female officer steps into the kitchen, noticing her colleague stays by the front door.

'It's like he is blocking the exit' I thought, unnerved at their demeanour.

'Miss Mullen, I understand, you've remembered seeing Emma Crosby's vehicle the night of the storm?' the female officer said, writing in her notebook.

'Yes, that's correct. The car had been bugging me, but I didn't remember whose car it was, until early this morning.'

'And you're certain, it was Miss Crosby's vehicle?' she asks in a direct tone, her face unsmiling and her eyes boring into me.

'It was the night of the big storm, and I saw the vehicle in the hedge, just down the road' I tell her trying to stop myself from wringing my hands.

But I can't. I don't know what it is. But I don't like her demeanour.

'I recognised the sticker in the back window, I just couldn't remember why I recognised it? In fact, I didn't remember about the sticker until this morning.'

Standing with the officers in the kitchen, I feel overly nervous and I'm glad when Tom arrives.

'With everything going on, it slipped my mind, but last night I remembered seeing the sticker and why it was significant? Emma bought the sticker when we went to Glastonbury, it was on the back window' I tell her, realising that I'm talking too fast as my heart thumps rapidly in my chest.

'Remembering seeing the sticker, reminded me why I recognised the car the night of the storm. I was asleep when I remembered that it was Emma's car' I said feeling like I'm rambling on.

'I also saw the car in the hedge, Eve asked me if I recognised it, but I didn't, I didn't know who the car belonged too? And we had more things to worry about that night than someone's car in the hedge' Tom said.

'It was dark, raining heavily and we could barely stand in the wind, so I didn't take that much notice. I just thought someone had crashed their car and would be back some time the next day to get it' he said, glancing at me.

The officer notes something down in her notepad then continues her focus on me.

'Had Miss Crosby told you that she was coming for a visit?' the officer asks.

She is making me feel uncomfortable, staring, watching my every move.

'No, we'd fallen out before I left England, and we've barely spoken since' I said.

'The thing is Miss Mullen, we've been trying to contact Miss Crosby, and no one has seen her. Her phone is disconnected, none of her friends or family have seen or heard from her. The last thing anyone seems to remember is that she was to visit you, here in Northern Ireland' she said, her eyes boring into me, I shift feeling uncomfortable under her stare.

'She didn't tell me she was visiting?' I said in a small voice.

'It was definitely her car, which means she was here, so where has she gone?' I ask looking at Tom for support, but he just shrugs his shoulders looking confused.

'Well that's the thing, no one seems to know. The officer said, writing something in her notebook.

'The only people to see the car, are the pair of you' she states looking at us both.

'Our investigation did find some evidence that a vehicle could have been in the hedge, but there wasn't anything there

223

the following morning when our team searched the farm and cottage' she states looking at me.

'It was there' I exclaim feeling panicked

'But it was gone when we returned home from the bed-and-breakfast. I looked for it on our way home' I said, uneasy at the way the officer is looking at me and her questions.

'Let me get this correct, you remembered about the car when you returned home after staying in the bed-and-breakfast. But you didn't think it was important to tell us then?' she said, looking at her colleague before turning her attention back to me.

'No, Yes,' I said exhaling loudly.

'I remembered, that I knew something about the car, but I couldn't remember what? I wanted to see it again. I'd hoped without the storm it would jog my memory about what it was that I knew? But the car was gone' I said, my palms sweating and my heart racing.

The officer closes her notebook and looks across at her colleague. I watch trying unsuccessfully to read their body language.

'Thank you for your time Miss Mullen, we'll be in touch and remember to keep us informed if you remember anything else' she said, her eyes boring into me.

'Okay, I will. But officer, if Emma is still here? do you think it could be her? Who has been doing all this stuff to us? You can look on my Facebook, she was being particularly unpleasant after I left England and moved to Northern Ireland' I said.

'We are monitoring the social media accounts. It looks like Miss Crosby hasn't been online for a while' she said staring at me.

'Oh, okay' I said, my heart thumping rapidly in my chest and pulsing loudly in my ears.

'We are investigating all avenues Miss Mullen. Has Emma contacted you at all?' she asks, writing in her notebook again.

'No. Like I already said, I haven't heard from her. She left me nasty voice and text messages on my phone, and nasty comments on Facebook, shortly after I moved here, but other than that, nothing' I said feeling exasperated.

'We haven't been in contact, but I'm certain it was her car in the hedge, the night of the storm' I tell her again, wishing this was all over.

'Okay, Miss Mullen keep in touch and contact us right away if you remember anything else. No matter how trivial you may think it is,' the officer said, tucking her notepad away in her coat and joining her colleague at the front door.

I watch through the window as Tom walk's the officers back to their car, returning with a grim look on his face.

'I think they're investigating me, that wasn't a friendly interview' I said, my voice quivering.

'They think I had something to do with Emma going missing' I continue unable to stop myself from pacing around the room, wringing my hands and watching his face intently.

'They're just doing their job, I suppose,' he said sounding concerned.

'We're the victims! it's us, who've had their home destroyed, been spied on and tormented. And it's looking more and more like my best friend Emma is the one who has been doing this to us.' I said my voice rising with hysteria, my heart racing and beads of sweat forming on my brow.

'Where could she be? She's obviously told people that she was coming here. But where did she go, if it was her staying in the shed, she's not there now?' I ask.

'She's probably staying in some hotel laughing at us' he said, scratching his head, watching me as I pace around the room.

'There's nothing we can do; we'll just have to wait it out' Tom said.

'What if I get arrested?' I said my panic reaching a fever pitch.

'Arrested for what? You haven't done anything; they can't just arrest you' he said wrapping his arms around me and pulling me into a hug.

I feel like I'm going insane, first all the eerie feelings of being watched. Then the cottage getting trashed, the photos appearing then disappearing and now this. I'm not sure how much more I can take. As I pace around the farmhouse kitchen, I'm wishing that I'd never came to Northern Ireland to live. It's been nothing but trouble.

***

I've been a nervous wreck since the last visit from the police a week ago. Every day I'm expecting them to land on the doorstep and arrest me, each day is worse than the last. Tom called the police this morning for an update and they just said that they'd be in contact if there was anything significant. It's torture waiting, if they're going to arrest me, I wish they would just do it already, at least then I may be able to sleep.

It's been ten days since the police last visited, and I've barely slept. I keep going over and over everything in my head. I'm annoyed that I didn't remember about Emma's car before. Since the last interview I had with the police, I've been thinking about what she said about Emma being missing. The more I think about it, the more worried I become. What if Emma was coming for a visit and didn't tell me because we'd fallen out and now, she is missing? I suddenly have a flash back to the shed where it looked like someone or something had been tied up.

'Something's not right and Emma is involved' I thought, deciding to phone her parents, hoping they will have some answers. My hands shake as I dial their number and wait for it to be answered.

'Hello'

'Hello, Mrs Crosby, it's Eve'

'Oh, Eve, thank goodness, have you seen Emma?'

'Err, no, that's why I was phoning. I remembered seeing her car not far from my home a few months ago, during a storm. The police told me last week, that she was supposed to be visiting me. But I never heard anything from her.'

I listen as Mrs Crosby, explains that Emma has been missing, that she had planned to visit me but that was the last they heard from her.

'Where has she gone Eve?' Mrs Crosby asks in a small voice.

'I don't know. I tried calling, but the line was dead' I said, a feeling of dread enveloping me as I worry for my friend's safety.

'I need to contact the police again, thanks for phoning Eve. It has been good to talk to you, keep in touch pet and let me know if you hear from her.'

'Yes, I will' I said.

When I hang up, I feel even more confused and wonder where on earth she could be? I phone Tom to tell him about the conversation I've just had.

'Tom, I'm really worried, I don't think it's Emma who has been terrorising us, I think she's in danger.'

'Remember, the night of the storm, someone was here. Whoever that was? followed us to the farm and slashed my car tyres. What if that person has harmed Emma? I don't know what to do?' I said noticing a thwap, thwap noise coming from outside and wonder what it is?

'I'll be home in five minutes, stay where you are' Tom said.

It takes Tom less than five minutes to get home. The thwap- thwap- thwap noise is getting louder and is coming from the direction of the farm. Tom is walking fast towards me, looking up at the sky.

'Is that a helicopter I can hear?' he asks looking at the sky.

'Yeah. Look' I said, pointing at the helicopter that has only just become visible as it appears over the hill.

'It looks like it's heading this way, I wonder what's going on?'

We stand looking up at the increasingly loudening noise coming from the helicopter. It is almost overhead now, looking as if it's landing in the field behind the farm.

'What's going on? Do you think I should head back to the farm?' Tom said, looking concerned.

Neither of us spots the police car until it has pulled up right in front of us. The police officer is out of his car and almost upon us before I have time to comprehend that he is even there. Distracted by the noise from the helicopter and the police officer in front of us. We completely miss the other two police cars that are heading quietly towards the farm. The deafening noise and the downwind of the helicopter drowning out all other noises.

'Miss Mullan can I have a word with you?' the officer asks.

I spot another officer as he appears around the corner walking quickly towards us. I'm immediately enveloped with panic. My heart instantly begins pulsating loudly in my head and my palms are sweaty. I feel Tom pulling me into the cottage.

'What's going on?' I ask, my voice breaking as I look at the officer's grim faces.

'Oh my god, this is it! I'm going to be arrested.'

Chapter 20. I'm Sorry.

'Continue straight for half a mile and you will reach your destination' states the Sat Nav.

Emma struggles to keep the car steady as she fights against the wind to steer the car around a hairpin corner. Just as she's exiting the corner, a large gust of wind blows the car sideways and she can hear a loud cracking noise. Looking up, following the noise, Emma spots a large branch falling towards her car and quickly swerves away ploughing up the bank towards a hedge. The car stops abruptly as she hits something hard and blackness envelops her. Blinking several times, her vision is blurred, and it is dark. Emma is groggy as she regains consciousness remembering what happened. Glancing around, she can't see much. It's pitch-black and the noise from the storm is deafening and disorientating. Emma twists to turn the light on inside the car, screaming in agony. Fear and shock course through her, when she sees the shape of her leg and foot. Glancing through the windscreen, it's too dark and Emma is struggling to see where she is? But she can smell smoke, noticing smoke coming out from under the car bonnet. Beginning to panic, she's terrified the car is going to blow up. Emma quickly undoes her seat belt and struggles to open the door, but it won't open; it's wedged closed with the grass. It takes all her might to repeatedly shove the door before it opens. Each jolting move causes excruciating pain in her leg and foot, unable to stop herself Emma screams in agony as she falls out onto the wet grass, landing in a lump on the floor. Her head slams into something hard before everything goes black again.

***

She's freezing and struggling to get a breath as the wind and rain pelt forcefully into her as she regains consciousness. Her body trembles uncontrollably as the cold takes a grip. It's pitch-black and she can't see anything. But all of a sudden, she can feel herself being pulled. As her body is roughly pulled, pain rips through her core and she lets out a stomach curdling scream. Emma is momentarily stunned when someone slaps her hard across her face, sending her sprawling face first into the dirt. Trying to focus her blurred vision, to see who is there? In the darkness, Emma can just about see there is a figure looking down at her.

'I'm Emma, I've crashed my car, and hurt my foot, I think it's broken' she tells the stranger.

'I DON'T FUCKING CARE, GET INTO THE CAR' the stranger roars.

'But I can't, I need to go to hospital' Emma said, before feeling another sharp blow to her head as she loses consciousness again.

***

Blinking against the darkness, pain sears through her body. Her foot and leg are agony and the cold is biting at her skin. Emma begins trembling uncontrollably as she tries to focus her vision. Panic takes over as she becomes more aware of her surroundings; she can barely breathe, paralysed with fear. Her head is foggy, and she's struggling to figure out what is happening? The last thing she remembers is crashing the car in the storm; it's still very noisy which tells her that the storm is still raging. The strong wind is gusting and the heavy rain battering loudly off the roof above her. Glancing around, she can barely see with the darkness but realises she's in some kind of warehouse. There's an annoying piercing high-pitched noise and Emma wishes it would stop. It takes a moment for Emma to realise that the noise she can hear is herself screaming. She sucks in air, taking long deep breaths trying to calm herself down.

'What is going on?' she wonders, looking around as her head thumps.

Attempting to stand up, Emma soon realises that she can't lift her arms; they're trapped behind her. She can feel something hard behind her back and uses it to push against, trying to lift herself up from the cold floor. But, as soon as she puts a small amount of pressure onto her foot. Intense pain causes her to crumple in a lump back to the floor. Lying slumped on the floor, screaming in pain and shivering uncontrollably in the cold. Emma is terrified and doesn't know what she can do, to get out of here?

'How on earth am I going to get out of this filthy place?' she thought, tears running freely down her cheeks as she shivers uncontrollably.

When somewhere in the warehouse, Emma hears a 'ping.'

'That's my phone' she thought, remembering putting the phone into her cardigan pocket and shoving them both into her bag. Hearing the ping has given her hope that she can get help. Emma doesn't know where her captor has gone. Or why whoever it is holding her here? But knows she's in danger and must get away.

'I must find my phone, at least then I can try to get help.'

Trying her best to see in the dark, where the ping came from. Emma spots something in the darkness. Staring at the shape, she soon realises that it's her car on the other side of the shelter. The driver's door is lying open. Desperation courses through her as she tries to stand, but her leg buckles unable to support her weight. Losing all hope of standing by herself, tears run down her face as she gives up hope of getting to her car.

'What's going on? Why am I being held?' she wonders, wiping tears and snot from her face.

The time passes slowly as Emma sits alone, in the freezing cold blackness. She is losing hope that someone will rescue her.

'No one knows where I am, so no one will know where to look for me. I must get to my car and phone?' she thought, knowing that this is her only way to get help.

As she sits trying to come up with a plan, she suddenly hears a noise outside.

'What's that?' she thought, her heart racing.

Emma sits unmoving straining to hear the noise coming from outside, wondering what it is that she can hear? It's only when the door is opened, a silhouette appears and enters the warehouse that Emma realises the noise was someone walking. Paralysed by fear, Emma struggles to breathe let alone speak.

'This is it, this crazy bitch's gonna kill me.'

Several minutes pass and the woman stands staring at her, not knowing what else she can do? Emma decides to try to reason with her. But as soon as she starts to speak, the woman screams at her, getting right up into her face, her sour breath an unwelcome warmth on Emma's cheek.

'If I stay quiet, maybe she will let me live long enough that someone can rescue me' Emma thought watching the woman.

Too afraid to say anything more and not wanting to antagonise the woman, Emma stays perfectly still sitting on the cold warehouse floor. Excruciating pain penetrates throughout her body, but despite trying to stay completely still Emma is unable to stop shivering in her cold wet clothes. The time is dragging and as the night draws on the storm continues to rage outside. Emma is glad that the woman has a torch and there's some light. She watches as the woman pulls her bag out of the car, dumping it on the ground, before using bales of hay to completely cover her car.

'Even if I was able to get to my bag. It's going to take me ages to get my car out from under all of that' she thought her hopes of escaping fading fast.

The noise from the storm is terrifying and every time there is a big gust of wind. Emma is terrified that the roof will rip right off. Her clothes are already soaking wet, and she doesn't want to be even more exposed if the roof gets ripped off.

***

As she blinks open her eyes Emma realises that she has been dipping in and out of consciousness. The pain coursing through her body is excruciating, and she knows she desperately needs medical help, and soon. Focussing her vision, as she sits on the cold floor Emma realises that while she's in agony, she can barely feel her foot anymore except when she tries to put any pressure on it.

'That's got to be a bad sign hasn't it?' she thought realising her foot is almost completely numb.

Emma doesn't remember falling asleep, but the bright sunlight wakes her. Looking around she can properly see her surroundings and immediately spots a large rat running across the dirty floor.

'That's disgusting! surely she can't keep me here much longer' she thought watching the rat.

Glancing around the warehouse, Emma spots the woman, asleep in the corner, wearing her clothes. Her bladder is overly full, and she tries to shift into a more comfortable position, but not being able to use a bathroom all night she is desperate and begins to panic.

'What am I going to do? I don't want to wet myself. But I don't want to wake her either.'

Without any other options, Emma realises that she has no other choice but to wake the woman.

'Hey' Emma calls, trying to wake the still sleeping woman.

'Hey, I need the bathroom,' Emma calls even louder, wondering if this could be her chance to escape.

Emma watches as the woman groans before stiffly sitting up. She stands and stretches before walking slowly towards Emma and slapping her hard across the face. It takes Emma a minute to realise what just happened, as the sting sits on her cheek.

'I need the toilet' she repeats watching as the woman turns and leaves the warehouse.

The woman returns moments later with an old rusty tin bucket.

'Use that and don't piss yourself' the woman snarls dropping the bucket next to her.

'I can't get up, I need help' Emma said, panicking as the woman pulls a wooden pallet box over.

'Use that to support yourself and no funny business' the woman said, loosening Emma's restraints before turning to look away.

Pain rips through Emma's body, not just her foot but everywhere. Her head is pounding, and she feels faint as she awkwardly positions herself over the bucket. After relieving herself she feels a lot better and is grateful that the woman has given her some hay to sit on. Watching the woman carrying the bucket away Emma notices that she doesn't empty it. But places it on the other side of the warehouse in front of where her car is buried.

'What is that crazy bitch doing?' Emma wonders, ashamed and disgusted at what she just had to do.

Curling herself into a tight ball around the pole she's tied too, Emma notices that she can't hear the wind anymore just the light pattering of rain. Listening carefully, she can hear the sound of vehicles in the distance.

'If I could just get myself out of here and onto a road, there's a chance someone will see me,' she thought.

The woman disappeared soon after Emma was finished going to the bathroom and has just returned. Staying completely still, Emma watches as the woman carries a small barrel of water in.

'Thank god' she thought, taking the cup of water offered, she'd been terrified that the woman was going to make her drink the urine she's storing.

'Why doesn't she just get rid of it? It's stinking' she thought watching the woman relieve herself and empty it into the bucket.

As the hours pass, Emma tries again to reason with her captor.

'I need medical attention, just dump me on the road. I will get help myself, I promise, I won't say anything' she pleads with the woman, who just ignores her.

It's been a long painful, humiliating day, and the light is beginning to dim.

'I'm going to spend another night in this god forsaken place' Emma thought, unable to imagine spending another night in the warehouse, her chest heaving uncontrollably as the tears roll silently down her cheeks.

The woman has left the warehouse taking the bucket full of urine and faeces with her.

'Thank god, it was stinking, but why did she leave it for so long?' Emma wonders, hoping that someone will find her soon.

'I have to get out of here, no one will know where to look for me. I have to get my wrists free' she thought, looking for something she could use to cut the ropes.

Determined to get free before the woman returns, Emma tries with all her might to stand. But she can't stop the piercing scream that escapes as the rope digs into her red raw wrists, the room blurring as dizziness and blackness envelop her.

***

The noise of the door opening rouses her, she can tell by the darkness that several hours must have passed. Realising what's happened, Emma is annoyed that she passed out and wasted her chance to escape. The woman reeks of urine and not wanting to draw attention to herself. Emma lies on the cold floor watching, trying not to be sick. She watches as the woman pulls more of her clothes out of her bag, stripping out of her filthy clothing before changing into Emma's warm clean clothes, discarding her own clothing in the corner along with other rubbish and waste.

***

The woman has been gone for many hours, but just as she returns, a 'ping' sound echoes around the shed.

'What was that?' the woman said in a quiet voice as she steps in through the warehouse door.

'WHAT WAS THAT NOISE?' she screams into Emma's face.

'I think it's my phone'

'Where is it?'

'In my bag, I think' Emma said, her heart racing.

The woman walks stiffly across the shed and lifts Emma's bag. Emptying the contents onto the floor. She lifts and shakes everything until Emma's phone falls out landing with a thud on the floor.

'What is this?' she screams into Emma's face.

'Open it. NOW!'

After Emma unlocked the phone, the woman forced her to close her Facebook account, before smashing the phone into tiny pieces.

'That was my only chance of escape' Emma thought, watching as the woman stamps all over her phone.

Watching her phone being smashed into pieces, Emma loses all hope that she will ever be found.

***

Emma believes that she has been trapped in this shed for about a week now, although it could be longer, she's lost all track of time. She's noticed that the woman has a routine, every evening, before it gets totally dark, she goes out to collect eggs and water. When she gets back from wherever it is, she goes? The woman always uses a camping stove to boil the eggs before offering her two eggs along with a cup of water. This evening however, instead of bringing eggs the woman is extremely agitated and won't stop pacing around. She smells disgusting and her wild grey hair has been getting wilder with each passing day. Emma just sits quietly hoping that the woman won't lash out and hit her again.

'I'm the victim, I don't deserve this' the woman mutters, pacing around the shed.

'What happened to you?' Emma asks.

'SHUT UP, IT'S NONE OF YOUR BUSINESS' the woman screams and begins pacing again.

'He thought he could beat me and get away with it' the woman said getting more and more agitated as she goes.

'No one suspected it was me, I was only thirteen after all' the woman mutters, before turning to look at Emma with a wildness in her eyes.

'I poisoned my father. I used the rat poison he kept in his shed. I was thirteen, and he was a mean drunk who beat the living daylights out of me and my mother' she muttered.

'Sounds like he deserved it' Emma said, her heart racing.

'He did deserve it, but my stupid cunt mother moved her bastard boyfriend in not long after we buried my father' she said, pacing back-and-forth spittle flying from her mouth.

'Her boyfriend was an evil FUCKER' the woman shouts.

'I hated my mother's boyfriend, he was worse than my father, he was creepy watching me all the time. He would whisper filth into my ear then grope my mother while staring at me as he touched himself. Many nights, I would wake up after feeling someone touching me and he would be in my bedroom completely naked masturbating. Aghaaa' the woman screams pulling at her hair.

Emma watches as the woman throws herself heavily onto the floor, sitting with her head in her hands.

'I hate that evil fucker; he still gives me the creeps' she said.

'What happened' Emma asks after several minutes have passed.

The woman looks so far away in her own thoughts that Emma isn't sure that she heard her.

'I didn't kill him, I wish I had' she said, lifting her puffy eyes to look at Emma.

'When I was nineteen, I married my boyfriend. I didn't want to, but I had to get away from that evil fucker. At the start of the relationship, my husband treated me well. I thought I'd escaped the abuse. My husband was a successful businessman, but his mood was always difficult to predict. Success brought out the worst in him, and the more successful he was the more abusive he became. He was always sorry after each beating, promising that it would never happen again.'

'Like a fool, I always believed him. But things changed one evening when he came home in a foul temper and took all his rage out on me. I thought he was going to kill me. I knew I deserved better, that my children deserved better' the woman said.

'No one should be treated like that' Emma said, hoping her captor will stop lashing out at her.

'I began adding a small amount of rat poison to his food, at first nothing happened but as the weeks went by, he began suffering stomach upsets. I thought my plan was going to work when he collapsed at work and was put in a medically induced coma. I prayed, every day, that he would die. I prayed, that me and my children would be free to live our lives without fear. Everything was going to plan, until the hospital called to tell me that the evil bastard had woken up' the woman said.

'What happened' Emma asks.

'NONE OF YOUR FUCKING BUSINESS' the woman screams before charging out of the shed.

'I hope she doesn't poison me' Emma thought, terrified at what she'd just heard.

***

Emma has been sitting for hours on the cold cement floor and her senses are heightened, she is hyper-sensitive to the sounds of the tiny nails from mice and rats scurrying around night and day. The daytime is bearable at least during the daylight hours she can see what it is that is scurrying around. During the night it is pitch-black, and Emma can barely breathe through fear. After what happened to her phone, Emma has given up all hope of ever being found, she doesn't know how long she has been here? Her hands and clothes are filthy and despite asking, the woman won't give her enough water to wash herself as well as drink. The days and nights are long, but Emma has noticed recently that the weather has been getting warmer. It's brighter, and the nights are not as long as they were.

'If it's staying brighter in the evenings, there's more chance that someone will be around. If I shout maybe someone will hear me. But I don't want to get hit again, if the woman hears me shouting, she will beat me' Emma thought, lifting her hand to her swollen lip and changing her mind.

***

This morning, Emma notices that there's a significant change in her captor's demeanour. The woman has just returned from wherever it is that she goes. Emma is curious when she realises that the woman is in a complete fluster.

'I wonder what's happened?' Emma thought, continuing to watch the woman as she paces back-and-forth.

'We have to move' her captor said before leaving Emma alone, her disgusting smell lingering long after she's left.

'Maybe this is my chance to escape?' Emma thought, desperately trying to come up with some sort of plan before her captor returns.

But as the hours pass, Emma begins to think that the woman has abandoned her and is not going to return. It's not until the daylight has almost completely gone, when the door is suddenly thrown wide-open, and her captor returns wheeling in a wheelbarrow.

'Get in, we're leaving' the woman said, loosening the restraints on Emma's wrists, pointing at the wheelbarrow.

As the restraints are loosened, all Emma feels is complete gratitude and relief, she is so happy she could cry. Just being able to move, without red-hot pain searing through her wrists. Wanting to do whatever the woman asks; Emma tries her best to stand. But she is unable to bear any weight and falls heavily in a lump on the floor. Excruciating pain sears through her foot, ankle and leg, as Emma crumples to the floor. She flies backwards hitting the back of her head off the concrete floor after the woman slaps her across the face, screaming at her.

'GET INTO THE WHEELBARROW NOW.'

Looking at the wheelbarrow from the floor, Emma knows there's no way she can do it, she's too weak. Her body aches and her face stings as she lies on the floor, when she notices a large swollen black lump, where her leg should be. Unable to control herself Emma lets out a high-pitched lung bursting scream. Filled with all-encompassing panic she continues to scream until there's an intense sharp pain across her face that stuns her into silence. She doesn't black out, but wishes that she had, the pain was so sharp she feared her jaw was broken.

'FUCK, I'm going to lose my foot' she screams at her captor.

Without warning there's another sharp sting on Emma's cheek, her ears ring and her head spins like she's been on a three-day drinking binge. Barely able to see in the dark and after a lot of balancing and heaving Emma eventually gets herself into the wheelbarrow. But as she sits carefully balancing as best, she can, Emma quickly realises that her captor's plan isn't going to work. The woman cannot push the wheelbarrow through the mud by herself and screams at Emma to get out and crawl.

'I can't crawl, look at my fucking foot. Can't we just stay here?' Emma asks pleading with the woman to let them stay.

But before she realises what's happening, Emma's hurtling towards the floor. The woman has overturned the wheelbarrow and pain shoots through Emma's body as she lands in a lump in the mud.

'Now start crawling' the woman orders in a low clipped voice.

Letting out a low painful groan she lifts herself as much as she can out of the mud and begins moving herself slowly forward. Emma can't comprehend what's going on and focuses all her energy on keeping moving and not the excruciating pain that stabs her with every movement. Emma's hands and knees sink in the dirt under her weight, making every jolting move excruciating. It's pitch-black and Emma can't stop shaking terrified at not being able to see where she is going. She pleads with the woman to stop but the woman doesn't listen and keeps her moving forward. She keeps thinking that this is her only chance to get away, but she has no clue where she is, it's pitch-black and she's already going as fast as she can despite the agony.

'There's no point, I'll not be fast enough' she thought gritting her teeth to stop the scream from escaping.

Desperate to stop and rest, Emma doesn't think that she can go on much further, but she is terrified that she'll black out and the woman will kill her. Despite the agonising pain Emma continues to move slowly forward. When all of a sudden, the ground changes under her hands, it has become firmer and she can feel leaves and twigs. Lifting her eyes Emma realises that they have reached a wooded area. The woman has stopped walking and is now pulling at branches and plants in front of her. Realising that they have reached their destination, Emma sits down gasping for a breath, she watches as the woman pulls and pulls at the bushes. The woman pulls back enough bushes and shines her torch that Emma can see a gap in the dense woods that she can crawl through. Using the last of her strength Emma follows behind the woman until they reach a dilapidated type of barn.

'Get in' the woman said breathlessly, shoving Emma forward.

Not wanting to upset her captor, Emma tries but fails to squeeze through the tiny entranceway. That's the last thing Emma remembers, before there's a sharp sting on her cheek, everything spins, before going black.

***

Blinking her eyes open, red-hot pain pulsates at her wrists. Emma pulls at her arms but realises she's been tied up again. Blinking several times to unblur her vision, she notices the woman, pacing back-and-forth. Emma stays quiet, watching her captor realising she is struggling to walk, and looks to be experiencing great pain with each step. Emma tries to position herself in a comfier position, but red-hot pain sears through her red raw wrists. Unable to stop herself, Emma lets out a piercing scream and begs the woman to untie her.

'Please, loosen the ropes, I promise I won't try to escape' she said.

Silent tears trip down her face. She's in so much pain, both her wrists, her foot, ankle and leg are unbearable.

'I just want to die, I wish she would just let me die' Emma thought sadly, giving up all hope of escaping.

***

She has been drifting in and out of consciousness and doesn't know how long they have been here? It has been days since the woman last left the barn and she hasn't given her any food since she stopped going out, only small sips of water. Emma is exhausted and her mouth and throat dry as she watches her captor peering through a small hole in the side of the barn.

'What is she doing?' Emma thought, trying to shift into a more comfortable position, without drawing the woman's attention.

It doesn't work, and before Emma can react, the woman is limping in her direction. The nauseating smell hits Emma, long before her captor is even close, she is filthy and smells vile, a mixture of urine and body odour. It makes Emma's stomach lurch, but she hasn't eaten in days and just wretches. Emma sees the hand coming but is too exhausted to speak or move. Pain ricochets as the hand strikes her face, sending her plummeting forward. Her head spins and her ears ring, before blackness envelops her.

As she regains consciousness, Emma is aware of an orange glow shining on her face.

'That feels nice' she thought, lying on the cold hard floor enjoying the warmth on her face.

As she blinks her eyes open, she can see a lovely stream of light shining through a gap. Emma stares at the light, her body heavy, a feeling of tranquillity and peace surrounding her, her pain has gone, and she knows this is the end. Hearing movement from the other side of the barn, Emma turns slightly to look at her captor, who is still watching through a hole in the wall. Smiling slightly as her breathing slows, Emma knows her time is up. She won't be here much longer and welcomes the release, as she closes her eyes for the final time.

Chapter 21. Morag.

Morag hadn't meant to target John; she hadn't meant to target anyone. Her goal had been to stay under the radar and find somewhere safe for her and her children to live. But John was so easy to manipulate, right from that very first unexpected meeting.

Three days before she met John, Morag had fled her life in Scotland and had been hiding in an abandoned old barn terrified that someone would find her. She'd run out of supplies and was rushing, trying to get everything she needed and get out without being recognised. On her way out of the supermarket, she wasn't looking where she was going and tripped in the car park. John happened to be on his way in and caught her before she hit the ground. Morag immediately sensed a vulnerability in John and began to watch him from afar. It didn't take long before she discovered that he lived by himself, deep in the countryside on a farm and she set about befriending him. John made it obvious right from the start that he wanted more than friendship, but Morag had no intention of making a life with him. He was just a means to an end; She had no doubt his kind demeanour would go as soon as she let her guard down. There was no way she was letting that happen again. No way. Being invited to stay at the farm had been a welcome comfort after living in the cold barn for the past six weeks. To pay for her board, Morag insisted on working on the farm, determined that she will never be a victim again. She'd only planned on staying with John for a few weeks, but as the months went by, she began to think that the farm could be the forever home she was looking for. The only problem was John; he was not part of her plan.

'I must get rid of him, then I can go and get my children and we can live here on the farm' she thought, after discovering John was an only child.

Knowing that both of his parents had passed away, Morag soon realised that there would be no one to contest the farm and immediately began planning how she was going to get rid of him. She tried to poison him, but unlike her father, John wasn't a drunk, and when he got sick, he went straight to hospital. His illness was put down to severe food poisoning, but Morag quickly realised that she would need to be more careful with how she dealt with John, otherwise she was going to risk getting caught.

***

It has been fifteen years since Morag moved into the farm with John and to her surprise, he has been nothing but a gentleman. Nevertheless, she still can't bring herself to trust him; she knows the only reason he hasn't become violent is because she hasn't let her guard down. And after what she saw last week, Morag knows that she was right to be cautious. Last week, John brought an estate agent over to value the farm. She knew he would turn on her and now he has, he's planning on selling the farm, her forever home.

'How dare he do that to me?' she thought her anger seething as she stands hidden beside the bedroom door barely able to control her rage?

Her rage has been building since she saw the estate agent last week and she is ready to explode as she turns, silently walking back down the stairs to the kitchen.

'Slow and steady wins the race' she thought, trying to stick to the plan.

Desperate for things to progress faster, Morag is unable to stop herself from adding an extra drop of anti-freeze to his porridge. Seeing John with the estate agent has unsettled her, but she knows that she must stick to her plan. Morag has prepared and made all the meals for the past fifteen years. But for the past couple of days, she makes sure to add just a small drop of anti-freeze to each of John's meals. John was a strong, well-built man when she first met him. This past week, however, with each anti-freeze treatment he's become weak and confused, his health fading with each passing day. Watching him struggling with his failing body, Morag takes pleasure in knowing that it won't be long now before John's out of the way and she can begin to have a normal life. Only a handful of people in Northern Ireland know she exists, but she will play the grieving widow for a while before putting the rest of her long-term plan into action. Her original plan had been working perfectly; the farm was a perfect forever home where she could bring her children. At one point she had considered telling John about bringing her children to Northern Ireland. But when she saw him with the estate agent, Morag was furious, she couldn't believe that he'd betrayed her. Thinking about that moment, rage courses through her body, Morag is so angry she could push him down the stairs.

'I knew he would betray me, everybody does' she thought seething.

Morag's knees are aching, and she's annoyed she can't just sit down and rest. John has been trying to have 'a chat' ever since that estate agent was here last week, but Morag doesn't want to hear what he has to say.

'That silly old fool thinks he can sell my home without even telling me' she rages.

There's no way, Morag is going to let that happen, no matter what he thinks. The rest of her life relies on this plan working, and it has been a long time coming. But, with John trying to sell the farm behind her back, Morag knows she will have to work faster. She will have to make sure John is dead before that estate agent comes back.

***

Morag sleeps in the bedroom next door to John and could hear through the wall that he'd been vomiting for most of the night. Getting up earlier than usual, she has just brought him some porridge laced with an extra drop of anti-freeze. Not wanting him to wake up and see her, she carefully places the porridge on the chest of drawers next to the bed before tiptoeing back out.

'This is her home, how dare he?' she rages from outside the bedroom, watching through the slightly ajar door as he wakes and struggles to sit himself up.

The wind is howling loudly outside, blowing the curtains through the rotten window frames in the bedroom. Morag is terrified that everything she has been working so hard for, may slip out of her grasp as she tiptoes silently back down the stairs. It's not just John trying to sell the farm behind her back that is grating on her nerves her. It's also that pesky girl, who moved in next door. John thinks she can do no wrong. But Morag wants her to stay away. She's worried that the new neighbour could identify her. Morag had hoped the girl next door would return to wherever she came from, but it's been over a year now and it looks like the neighbour is planning on staying.

'If she doesn't leave soon. I'll have to deal with her, I'll make her leave one way or another. I just have to deal with John first, I can't allow him to put the farm on the market.'

Morag is furious that her plans are being messed with and she will not let that happen. It's been two days since she last actually spoke to John. As she reaches the top of the stairs with his porridge, she can hear he's in the bathroom.

'Good, I don't have to talk to him. There's no way this farm is being sold and we are not talking about it' Morag silently rages as she hurries back down the stairs.

Her mood is black, and she can barely look at John without wishing him dead.

'If he would just die, then the farm would be mine. I could start to rebuild my life and reconnect with my family' she thought.

***

The weather has been stormy all day. As darkness draws in, the noisy wind continues to rush in through the rotten frames in the kitchen window. At one point, Morag thought the windows were going to smash with the force of the wind. Sitting at the kitchen table, rubbing at her painful knees. Morag wishes the weather would ease up; her arthritis always plays up when the weather is bad. The constant aching in her knees makes it difficult for her to walk, even when the weather isn't bad. Nevertheless, she is determined to make her new neighbour leave and if she isn't going to leave willingly Morag will do whatever it takes to make her leave. Over the past few weeks, Morag has taken pleasure watching and noting her neighbours every move.

'No one knows her here; she won't be missed' Morag thought knowing she'll need to pick a time when it'll be awhile before anyone will find the neighbours body.

'I know I can easily keep Tom working at the farm, but I'll probably need to get rid of him as well, perhaps a car accident, that would get rid of both of them at once' she thought.

This weather is very stormy, and it's making everything difficult, especially with the pain in her joints. This evening however Morag has taken great pleasure in letting her neighbours know that someone is watching them. She has been in and out in the torrential weather all day and has spent the day soaking wet, freezing cold and exhausted with trying to stay hidden. Morag gave up trying to stay dry after the first time she went out, she couldn't believe it when she'd almost got caught. John and that fucking farmhand had returned before she'd gotten back. After John went upstairs to lie down, Morag was unable to stop herself and took a risk venturing out into the storm one more time. She made sure to leave the torch on in the caravan before returning home for the last time this evening.

'That should get them thinking, but I'm not going out in that weather again' she thought, grateful to be back indoors.

Her wet hair clings to her face as she sits huddled at the kitchen table in front of the fire with a hot cup of tea, listening as the wind whistles through the windows. Rubbing her throbbing and swollen knees, she makes a mental note to store some clothing downstairs in the future. Shivering with the cold as she sits in her wet clothing, Morag takes a sip from her tea, there's a loud cracking noise coming from outside. But she's startled by a thunderous crash that makes the house shake and all the lights go out. A deafening gust of wind gushes down the stairs, through the kitchen door that swings open slamming against the wall.

Morag gasps, 'What's happening? She said aloud wondering what the thunderous crash upstairs was. But, by a stroke of luck, the storm was on her side.

Chapter 22. A Stroke of Luck.

Morag didn't know what to expect as she climbed the stairs, her heart racing as the wind blows forcefully in her face, pain stabbing at her knees with each step. On reaching the landing, the wind increases dramatically, catching her breath, whipping her wild grey hair across her face. Holding on to the bannister to get her bearings, Morag lifts her head, noticing a large tree that has crashed through John's bedroom window. She can hear a crackling noise and can see sparks, quickly realising that the tree has brought an electric cable with it. Morag immediately sees her opportunity even with the chaos caused by the gale force wind and glass shattered everywhere. The electric cable is just hanging and sparking right above John. Morag can hardly believe her luck and acts quickly, carefully edging into the bedroom. She can see him watching her, the whites of his eyes flashing wide with terror.

'Morag, please' he said in a small voice.

Morag ignores him, all she has to do is reach over, using the wooden broom. Slowly and carefully, she pushes the cable down until it touches his side. She keeps the broom steady, holding the cable in place, watching as he contorts in pain and sparks fly. The bedcover momentarily catches on fire, just as a large gust of wind knocks her sideways releasing John from the electrical cable. He continues to twitch on the bed as the smell of cooked flesh fills the room. Her stomach lurches as she staggers into the landing feeling momentarily shocked. Morag can't believe what has just happened and is delighted it was so quick, she barely had to do anything, he was too weak to resist.

'It was as if he had already accepted his fate' she thought, watching as John twitches and smoulders on his bed.

She knows he is not yet dead but has no intention of helping him. Euphoria fills her every pore as she stands in the doorway watching and waiting for him to die. It doesn't take long before his laboured breathing stops, but she waits a little longer to make sure he is definitely dead. Filled with adrenalin, she knows she must act. She must leave the farmhouse until the police have taken John's body away.

'I can't risk being identified; I'll be arrested for the attempted murder of that evil bastarding husband fifteen years ago' Morag thought knowing she must go into hiding until everything settles down.

'There's no way I'm going to risk being found at the farm; I've worked too hard to stay hidden for the past fifteen years.'

Standing at the top of the stairs Morag can barely believe that John is finally dead, and she can begin to rebuild her life. Her heart aches when she thinks about the children she left behind. Over the years, she has often wondered what happened to them? Would they want to see her? Would they forgive her? But now with John out of the way, she finally has the forever home she always wanted. It has taken a long time, but now she can begin to repair her broken life. Thinking about all she can offer her children Morag can feel the euphoria building. She's on a complete high, barely able to comprehend how everything has worked out so well. Tilting her head back she begins laughing, and can't stop, her sides hurt. This is the first time she has laughed properly since before she fled Scotland.

'How dare that lousy lying piece of shit, get away with almost killing me and I'm the one who has been on the run for fifteen years' she thought?

A smile spreads across her face, Morag can't stop grinning from ear to ear when she realises that for the first time since she'd tried to kill her abusive husband. She has an actual chance to have a normal life. Relief floods her, as she turns away from John still smouldering on the bed, walking out of the bedroom. She suddenly feels tired and emotional as she steps carefully into her own room, pulling clothes from the wardrobe and the large wooden chest of drawers. As she roughly stuffs the clothes into a small bag, she notices something glinting through the window. Spotting lights coming down the road, she quickly realises there's a car coming, and leaves most of her stuff, speedily zipping up her bag.

'Who could this be?' she thought ducking down, peeping out the window.

'It's that fucking farm hand and the bitch whore from next door' she thought, furious that they dare to mess with her plan.

'What are they doing here?'

Morag lifts her bag and hurry's as quick as her knees will allow down the stairs and out the front door. Ducking into the woodshed at the side of the house just as the car pulls into the yard. Her knees are aching as she crouches silently watching with rain dripping in through a hole in the roof. Barely breathing, she stays completely still until they are both in the house and certain that they won't see her.

'Nosey bastards' Morag thought, as she steps out into the pelting rain.

The fierce wind and icy rain sting as it pelts relentlessly into her face as she strides determinedly towards the car parked in her yard. Making sure to keep an eye on the house, Morag pulls out a pocketknife that she always keeps in her coat pocket and takes great pleasure in slashing all the tyres.

'Maybe there will be three people that die in the storm tonight' Morag thought.

Determined to finish what she started this evening; Morag moves into the darkness. It isn't long before she hears her neighbours coming back down the stairs. She can't have these two idiots messing with her plan and has decided that they both must die tonight. Icy rain is being blasted with the wind into her face; Morag knows she must stay in the shadows until she sees the right moment to pounce. However, she didn't anticipate how fast the idiots would be. Watching as they run right past her and jump into the car before she has a chance to move. But she keeps her cool, knowing that they won't be able to go far, Morag watches as they begin to drive off, certain that they will return to the house soon.

'Sit tight, they will be back, and you will be ready' she thought.

Soaked to the skin she continues to watch her prey without moving, the wind causing her to lose her breath momentarily. Huddled down in a crouched position, her penknife unlocked in her hand as the car stops at the farm gate. Shifting her position so she can see better, Morag watches as the farmhand gets out to check the tyres.

'Come on, I've a nice surprise for you both.'

Holding her knife close, she's anticipating taking him out first.

'It will make it easier to get her' she thought.

Rain drips down her face and the icy wind bites at her skin. Morag is determined to finish what she has started, but she's freezing, and her knees have locked. She tries to stand but pain courses through her, as she continues to silently watch the farmhand and her neighbour.

'Something's not right, what are they doing?' she thought.

Clenching her fists, Morag is furious they're not doing what she thought they would, instead they're leaving, running away from the farmhouse.

'They must be going back to old Mrs Thompson Cottage.'

Morag watches the pair of them running away in the rain and returns to the shelter of the farmhouse. The smell hits her as soon as she steps through the front door.

'For fucks sake, it's stinking in here, it'll take me ages to get rid of that smell' she thought.

Morag angrily wipes the rain from her coat, water pooling on the kitchen floor. Pure rage courses through her, as her plan to drive her neighbours out looks like it is failing. She has spent the last couple of months, making her neighbours lives a misery, making things so uncomfortable that they would not want to stay in old Mrs Thompsons place anymore. It took ages to get rid of old Mrs Thompson, that woman was going to live forever, and she took ages to die. But Morag is smart, learning with each kill. She has learnt to be patient and knows she can get better.

'I'm no longer a victim' she thought furious at the stupid girl for moving in and messing with her plans.

Morag had tried to talk John into buying the land, but he wouldn't. He told her that he wanted to downsize not buy more land. She has spent months watching their every move and learning their routines, they are both so stupid.

'Seriously, who leaves keys hidden under a rock?' she thought, shaking her head at how easy everything has been.

'They deserve everything they get' she reflects, hoping they will die in the storm before they get home.

'Maybe I should make that happen. Perhaps a branch falls and kills them both' she considers.

Believing that the storm came to help her with her plan, Morag is determined to finish what the storm started tonight. Pulling on a dry waterproof coat Morag steps out ready to battle the wind and rain following the direction her neighbours took. She's moving slower than she would like, but the rain is stinging her face as it blasts into her with the force from the wind. The weather along with the pain in her knees make it difficult for her to move fast. She isn't out for long when out of the corner of her eye, she spots something glinting up ahead with her torch light.

'What is this? is it a light?' she thought, quickening her pace.

Morag pushes against the wind and rain, continuing past the turn off for old Mrs Thompsons cottage. Continuing further up the road until she reaches the shiny thing.

'It's a car that's crashed into the hedge' she realises circling around it, spotting a person.

The person has half fallen out of the driver's side and is slumped half in and half out, their leg sitting in a funny angle on the floor. She lifts the persons head to check if they are alive, noticing that it is a young woman, and she is breathing.

'I could use this car, but I have to get rid of the driver' she thought.

'Get out of the car' she tells the woman, who can barely lift her head.

'GET OUT' Morag screams dragging the woman by her hair out of the car into the road.

'WHO ARE YOU?' Morag continues to scream at the woman.

'I crashed my car, my leg and foot are hurt' the woman said sobbing, trying to lift her leg.

'I CAN FUCKING SEE THAT' she screams at the sobbing woman, furious at this inconvenience.

'What a fucking idiot' Morag thought, rage searing through her body when she realises that this woman may be able to identify her. Also, someone may recognise the woman's car if she leaves it here.

'FUCKING LET ME IN' she screams at the sobbing woman, grabbing her by the arm, pulling her back into the car as she struggles to manoeuvre herself into the driver's side.

Despite the smoke coming from under the bonnet, the car starts after a few tries and Morag manoeuvres it slowly towards the farm keeping the lights off. Morag doesn't want anyone to see the lights even though she is struggling to see where she is going. It's pitch-black and the heavy rain is pelting off the windscreen. Morag has an idea to hide the woman in the old barn where she stayed when she was watching John all those years ago. She drives slowly and carefully before stopping the car, knocking the woman unconscious and turning and driving down a small narrow dirt path.

S.J.C. RATCLIFFE

Chapter 23. The Prisoner.

'*What is this place*?' the woman asks, her words slurring as she regains consciousness tugging at her restraints.

'I don't want anyone looking for you' Morag tells the barely conscious woman as she unpacks the bag that she'd found in her prisoner's car.

'Ah, this is perfect, a friend of Eve's I see. My lovely new neighbour EVE' Morag said, holding up a photograph that she'd just found in her prisoner's bag.

'*Yes, yes, Eve's my friend, you know, Eve?* The woman asks her words slurring as she struggles to keep her head upright.

'Oh, yes, I know Eve' she said, pulling out another photograph from the woman's bag.

'*I've hurt my foot. I think it's broken*' her prisoner said, her voice barely above a whisper.

'I DON'T CARE ABOUT YOUR FUCKING FOOT' Morag screams, furious at this inconvenience.

'I don't want to hear about your foot,' she said, placing the photographs in her pocket before zipping up her coat. Morag steps back out into the rain, leaving the woman in the old barn. Just as she is about to set off, the woman begins screaming and shouting hysterically.

'LET ME GO, WHO ARE YOU? YOU CRAZY FUCKING BITCH. Where's EVE?' the woman screams from inside the shelter.

Worried that her prisoner might be heard, Morag furiously steps back into the shelter and slaps the woman hard across the face to shut her up.

'Who does this crazy bitch think she is? Morag thought, watching the woman slump, whimpering to the ground.

'It's noisy outside, and it's unlikely that anyone will hear her, but there's no point in drawing any unnecessary attention' she thought, contemplating how long she should let this idiot live?

'Don't you ever talk to me like that again' she snarls at the woman, who is sobbing hysterically on the concrete floor.

Morag makes sure that the woman is properly restrained before stepping out into the storm again. The force of the wind is strong, and it's difficult to breathe as she tries to stay upright. But the storm is on her side, and she has a plan. Despite the weather and the pain in her knees, Morag pushes herself to walk as fast as she can, to a small unused barn behind the milking parlour. Where for the last couple of months she has been storing buckets of urine. Morag has been planning this for a while, knowing that she has to get rid of that irritating English bitch.

'I must make Eve leave, so I can be completely sure that no one can identify me, and I can begin to rebuild my life' she thought.

Morag hadn't planned on doing everything in one night, but the storm is proving to be invaluable. Lifting the buckets of urine and faeces before tramping through the woods until she reaches the cottage gasping for breath. The buckets are heavier than she thought they would be, glad to be putting them down. Morag had got the spare key for both the cottage and the caravan, when Eve had invited her and John over for a 'moving in' party.

'That was such a shit night, having to be nice to those idiots, and John telling everyone that he wanted to sell the farm' she remembers, her anger bubbling ready to explode.

'Maybe I will have a moving out party when they're gone' she thought.

Checking her pocket, she makes sure that she has her knife with her.

'The friend could come in useful; I could make it look like they killed each other,' she thought, remembering the argument they were having online, contemplating her next move.

Being careful to stay hidden as she looks through the cottage window. Certain that no one is home, Morag uses the spare key to open the door and let herself in, making sure she is definitely alone before taking fifteen years' worth of rage out on the cottage. She takes pleasure throwing the buckets of urine all over their precious stuff. Pulling open all the drawers and emptying them all over the floor. When the buckets and drawers are empty, Morag smashes all the crockery she can find and uses their clothes to spread faeces on the walls.

'Hopefully this will make them leave' she thought, hatred coursing through her every pore, as she steps out through the front door, gagging with the smell.

She makes sure to close the front door but doesn't lock it when she leaves. Exhausted after all her hard work, she desperately wants to go home to the farmhouse, but knows that she can't, not yet. She must bide her time and stay hidden until the fuss dies down.

'Good things come to those that wait,' she thought, heading across the meadow towards the caravan.

Morag is pleased with her days work. She hadn't planned on moving so fast, but the storm has turned out to be a vital part of her plan. Without the storm, the tree wouldn't have crashed through the window, and she would never have found the woman in the car.

'I don't know what I'll do with her yet, but for now, I will keep her alive, she has already shown herself to be invaluable, by providing the photographs.'

'As long as she is useful, I will keep her alive.' Struggling against the wind, Morag walks across the meadow towards the caravan. Using the stolen key, she enters the caravan and places the photograph, slightly hidden, on the side.

'Eve will never know where the photo came from?' she thought.

'It's disappointing I won't see her face when she finds it', she thought, contemplating hiding and watching from her usual place.

Planning her next move, Morag knows that she will have to be extra careful, for the next couple of weeks.

'I need to do as much as I can tonight. I won't get the chance after the storm has passed.'

Morag had spotted the new chicken coop on her way over.

'I'm going to fill it for them,' she thought, furious that John gave the coop away without asking her.

Soaked to the skin and freezing cold, Morag tramps back to the farm, gathering several hens by their necks.

'I will let them know that they are not welcome here' she thought.

Rage courses through Morag as she wrings all the chicken's necks, throwing their limp bloody bodies into the coop.

'How dare John give her chicken coop away' she thought.

Staring at the dead bodies in the coop, Morag wipes rain from her face while fighting to get a breath as the storm rages on.

'It's not showing any sign of stopping' she thought.

Tiredness overwhelms her and while Morag realises that the storm has been working in her favour. Now her adrenaline has dropped, she is exhausted, cold, and her knees are aching.

'I need to get things moving' she thought.

Walking slowly and purposefully through the woods back to the farmhouse. She notices that the front door has been left wide-open, and it's banging in the wind. Stepping into the farmhouse she's grateful for a reprieve from the weather as she wipes rain from her coat and face before lifting the phone to call the local newspaper. The call is answered on the second ring and she leaves an anonymous message about a fallen tree crashing through a local farmhouse.

'That should cause some distraction and get things moving' she thought.

Stepping back outside into the storm, the wind knocks her sideways and the rain pelts into her face as she looks for somewhere to hide. Branches dig into her side and scratch her face as she pushes herself through the thick woodland looking for somewhere to shelter while she waits. Her breathing is laboured, and there is a strong smell of urine that splashed against her during her rampage of the cottage. The smell is making her gag, and she's annoyed that she has to wait to change.

'At least I've got some spare clothes back at the shelter' she thought, trying to ignore the smell.

Morag knows that after her phone call, the police and the press will be here soon and squats low in the hedge, to rest, and get some shelter against the weather. Over the years she has become an expert at watching and waiting. Morag knows that sometimes she has to stay deathly still for a long time before there is any action. But not this time, this time she gets lucky, and it's not long before she spies lights coming down the road. The press arrive at the farm first with their cameras and reporters. They are followed shortly by the ambulance and the police. She was surprised that the first police car to arrive went straight to Eve's cottage rather than the farm.

'I wonder what they're up to?' Morag thought, watching as an ambulance followed by two more police cars go straight to the farm.

She decides to stay where she is to keep an eye on the farm rather than the cottage, knowing what they will find in there.

'Perfect, I can't believe how perfect tonight has been. Hopefully it won't take too long for them to process his body and I can return to my farmhouse' she thought. Soaked through to her skin, Morag is unable to control her chattering teeth as she watches the paramedics emerge from the house with a covered body.

'I knew the press would be a good distraction' she thought, watching the press that are all over the police and paramedics.

The cameras are flashing brightly in the dark trying to get a picture. She takes great pleasure watching the police struggling to do their job while swerving questions from the journalists and fighting against the weather.

'Yes, I definitely did the right thing' she thought, enjoying the show.

As the paramedics' struggle against the weather to load John's body onto the ambulance, she realises that this is what she has been working towards for the last fifteen years.

'It will take some time, but it won't be long now before I can move back into the farmhouse, and I can give my children a forever home' she thought.

Sheltering under a bush her whole-body trembling in the cold, she realises that there won't be too many at John's funeral.

'He was the last one in his family and I will have him cremated as soon as possible' she thought.

Despite the cold Morag is delighted at how well her plan is working.

'It's taken a long time, but there will be no one to contest the farm' she thought.

The wind, rain and the cold continue to make her feel uncomfortable, but she doesn't want to miss the show and hunkers down further trying to protect herself against the weather.

'I hope I can stand up, when all the fuss dies down here' she thought rubbing her throbbing knees.

Sitting with the rain pelting into her face, Morag hopes her neighbours will not return from wherever they have gone? She hopes that she has got rid of them for good. A fierce gust of wind knocks her sideways, and a tree falls in the wood behind her. The deafening cracking noise makes her jump and Morag knows, for her own safety that she should go, she has been hunkered down for several hours in this bad weather. As she watches the police begin to clear out, every part of her body is aching, she is soaked through to her skin but feels satisfied that she has seen all she wants. She reluctantly decides to go back to the shelter, to the woman who is securely tied up. It takes her longer than expected to get back, sitting in the cold has worsened her pain and she can hardly walk. Also, the weather has worsened significantly as the night has progressed, and because of the police presence she had to take a longer route, through the thick hedgerow. But when she eventually arrives back at the shelter, the woman is lying unmoving on the floor.

'Don't you be dead, you stupid bitch,' she thought, feeling too sore to deal with another body today and in pure frustration, she kicks the woman in the side.

The woman lets out a low painful groan, rolls over and opens her eyes.

'Let me go' the prisoner groans barely able to speak,

'I won't tell anyone about you, I just need to get my foot seen by a doctor, I will tell the truth, that I was in a car accident. No one will think anything else with this weather' she continues in a quiet voice.

'SHUT UP' Morag screams slapping her prisoner across the face.

'It shut her up last time, hopefully she will stay quiet now' she thought, watching as the woman's head slaps heavily onto the floor again.

Morag's hand pulsates with pain after slapping the woman in the face again.

'Please let me go, I promise I won't tell anyone'

'STOP TALKING' Morag yells trying to listen to the vehicles she can hear in the distance.

The noise from the vehicles is reducing and she can tell that they are moving away from the farm.

'They must be finishing up' she thought, still trying to listen over the noise of the still worsening storm.

It takes some time, but she is grateful when her prisoner finally quietens down. Suddenly feeling exhausted, Morag tries to find somewhere comfy to sit, but she's soaked to the skin. Now that she has stopped moving, she is freezing and doesn't want to show weakness in front of her prisoner, but her teeth won't stop chattering. She can't feel her fingers and considers making a small fire but worries that the smoke will be seen.

'I don't want anyone looking in this direction' she thought noticing her prisoner is not moving, giving her a shove with her foot, but the woman doesn't move.

'You better not be dead' she said using her hand to feel the woman's neck trying to find her pulse.

It's slow but she can definitely feel it.

'She's alive, must have passed out.'

The warmth Morag got from touching her unconscious prisoner emphasises how cold she feels. Glancing around she finds the bag she'd packed earlier realising that she only has a few items and knows that it's too risky to go to the house to get more of her own clothes.

'The police are likely to still be around' she thought, looking around the barn.

Morag spots her prisoner's suitcase and pulls it apart taking all the clothes she needs, changing out of her sopping clothes, into the woman's clean dry clothing. The warmth helps her feel better, despite the wind whistling under the side of the shelter. Her body is weary as tiredness takes over; Morag spots a wall of hay along the back of the shelter behind the car that she'd parked in the corner. Pulling a bale down she spreads it around the woman, then does the same for herself, preparing to settle down for the night. But as she sits down, she notices her prisoner's car and realises that she should try to hide it.

'Just in case someone comes,' she thought using all the strength she has left, to bury the car with bales of hay.

***

Morag has just returned from gathering more eggs and water, but as she steps through the shelter door, she hears a noise that startles her. It's a strange unfamiliar 'ping' noise.

'What was that?' she said, her senses on high alert, as she listens, her eyes darting around the shelter following where the unfamiliar sound came from.

'WHAT WAS THAT' she screams at her prisoner.

'My phone, it's in my bag.'

Morag begins to frantically search the woman's bag as she hears another high-pitched 'ping'. Pulling all the clothes out on to the floor, she shakes everything and eventually a mobile phone drops out.

'How did I miss this?' she thought, staring at the phone.

Morag quickly realises that her prisoner can be traced with the phone.

'Open it, NOW!' she barks at the woman.

Morag can see that her prisoner is barely conscious, her head hanging limply in front of her.

'OPEN IT NOW' she screams into the woman's face.

Morag pulls the woman's head up using her hair to hold her steady, as she struggles to key in a number.

'FUCKING FACEBOOK' Morag screams into the woman's face.

Scanning all the missed notifications on her prisoner's phone Morag begins shaking with fury.

'WHY DIDN'T YOU TELL ME?'

'Shut down your account now' she said, into her prisoner's face, her voice barely louder than a whisper.

The woman fumbles with the phone before handing it back to her. Morag takes the phone and smashes it with her foot until there are tiny broken bits of phone all over the floor. Agitated at what just happened she begins pacing back-and-forth, memories from her childhood and past, begin flashing through her thoughts.

'Get out of my head' she yells slapping her head desperate to stop remembering.

'Are you okay?' she hears her prisoner ask.

'SHUT UP' she yells, wondering if it would matter if she told her?

'She won't be alive for much longer anyway' she thought, beginning to tell her what she'd done.

The voices and memories in her head are driving Morag crazy and she has to get away. She checks the woman's restraints before lifting the bucket of urine and faeces, heading out into the woods bringing the spare keys with her. She stalks carefully through the woods, heading around the back of the cottage, peering through the window at the back of the property to make sure there is no one there. Morag is careful as she stalks, treading softly, watching for any movement as she moves against the side of the cottage around to the front door, listening carefully for any unusual sounds. As Morag opens the door, her stomach lurches, the stench is disgusting. Taking a deep breath, she steps through the door and walks to the living room, pouring the bucket containing the urine and faeces all over the rug in front of the fire. She makes sure to leave the cottage unlocked before leaving. As Morag steps out of the cottage, she can hear a noise and quickly realises that there's a car coming.

'I wonder who that is?'

Moving slowly and stiffly she walks towards the woods, spotting Eve and the farmhand as they drive towards the cottage. Smiling to herself she walks purposefully towards a large tree, peeping out slightly to watch, just as the blue Golf pulls into the drive outside the cottage.

'It's them, they're back' she thought desperate to see their faces when they enter the cottage.

As much as she wants to stay, she doesn't want to risk getting caught. Reluctantly she turns and heads purposefully back to the shelter careful not to leave any trace behind. Morag is only back to the shelter for a short while when she smells smoke. Stepping outside she spots black smoke billowing up from the direction of the cottage.

'They must be burning everything' she thought, pulling the woman into a sitting position, and opening the door so she can see the smoke

'That is your friend burning all her belongings because you pissed and shit all over her stuff' she said, roughly shoving the woman back onto the floor.

The woman is barely conscious and unable to hold her weight and falls, smacking her face as she lands.

'Are you still alive?' Morag asks, shaking the woman, who gives a small low groan.

'Good, don't go dying on me' she said.

Morag is euphoric as she sits outside the shed door watching the smoke. However, it doesn't take long before her euphoria turns to panic. It dawns on her that now that her neighbours are back, there's a good chance that she could be found if she stays in the shelter. She knows that the stupid one could come looking for hay or something else in the shelter.

'We must move' she tells her prisoner, who is still slumped unmoving on the floor.

'She'll be hard to move' Morag thought, shoving the woman trying to gauge how heavy she is?

'Why couldn't you have been skinny like your friend?' she snarls at the woman kicking her with her toe.

'Just leave me here, it will be easier for you to go alone' the woman groans gasping for a breath.

'No chance, you are part of my plan, you're not getting away that easy' she tells her prisoner, trying to figure out how she is going to move her?

The time is moving slowly as Morag waits until the noise from the milking parlour stops and it is dark enough to leave the shelter. Her knees and knuckles are throbbing as she ventures out to the farm. Morag searches the barn behind the parlour until she finds an old wheelbarrow.

'This is just what I need.'

Staying vigilant as she pushes the wheelbarrow around the back of the farmhouse. Morag has remembered a time when John had told her that he used to play in an old barn, in the woods behind the farmhouse, when he was a kid. She has never seen it and doesn't even know if it is still there. Barely able to see in the darkness, she drops the wheelbarrow and pushes herself up the steep hill through the dense woodland until she meets something solid. Morag immediately begins pulling at the ivy, until she has cleared enough that she can feel a wooden structure. It is pitch black, but Morag uses all her strength to pull at the ivy until she has cleared a small patch. She kicks and kicks until the wood breaks and there's a gap in the side. The gap is small, but she pushes until she's able to squeeze her bulky body into the barn scratching the side of her face as she goes.

'This place is perfect, I wish I'd remembered about it before' Morag thought, wiping the blood running down her cheek.

Stepping cautiously into the barn trying to let her eyes adjust to the darkness, she notices that the sides of the barn are solid and secure. However, looking up she realises that most of the roof is missing, with only a small area that will offer shelter from the weather.

'This is where we will stay for now, until I can get rid of those two idiots next door.'

Chapter 24. The Old Barn.

After pushing her way back out of the barn and through the woodland in the pitch-black. Morag gets down on her hands and knees feeling around until she finds the wheelbarrow. Pain stabs at her knees as she straightens up and pushes it around the back of the house. Not wanting to be seen, she makes sure to take the long road across the edge of the cow field to the shelter. Gasping for breath, her mouth is dry as she struggles to pull the doors open wide enough to get the wheelbarrow in. Entering the shelter, she's annoyed to see that her prisoner has turned her torch on.

'WE HAVE TO LEAVE NOW,' she screams, not in the mood to put up with any bullshit.

Morag immediately cuts the restraints from her prisoner's wrists momentarily shocked at how raw they look.

'GET IN THE WHEELBARROW, NOW,' she screams, when the woman doesn't move, just sits rubbing her wrists.

'GET INTO THE WHEELBARROW, OR I WILL HURT YOU,' Morag yells, furious that her prisoner isn't doing as she is told.

'I can't. I'm not strong enough,' the woman said.

'I said, GET IN!'

Startling at being shouted at, the woman begins to move, struggling to lift herself into a sitting position. But immediately tumbles over falling flat on her face. Morag is furious that she has to practically lift the woman into the wheelbarrow herself. When she eventually has her prisoner where she wants her. Morag pushes with all of her might and they begin moving slowly out of the shelter. But as the wheel lands in the muddy field outside the door, it abruptly stops. Morag quickly realises that her plan is not going to work. She can't move the wheelbarrow forward in the mud; it's stuck, and they've barely moved at all. Leaning forward Morag gasps for breath, unsure what to do?

'You have to get out and walk' she tells the woman, before abruptly tipping her on to the ground.

'I can't walk' the woman whispers from the ground where she's curled into a ball crying.

'Are you still whining about your FOOT?'

Morag shines the torch at the woman's swollen, misshapen purple and black foot. The woman raises her eyes following the light, glancing in the direction of her foot and begins screaming.

'Aghaaaa Aghaaaaa Aghaaaa, MY FOOT,' the woman screams.

The woman's deafening screams knock Morag sideways

'SHUT UP, SHUT UP,' Morag begins screaming, terrified her prisoner will be heard.

Desperate to get moving and wanting the woman to stop wailing hysterically, Morag pulls her onto her hands and knees.

'I SAID GET MOVING,' she screams, as the woman steadies herself on her hands and knees screaming out in pain.

'Now get moving.'

Morag shoves her prisoner forward, guiding her slowly in the direction of the old barn. It's a slow journey, the only noise her prisoner's quiet sobs. Morag is frustrated with how long it is taking, but grateful, forty-five minutes later when they arrive at the woods surrounding the old barn. The whole time the pair of them are out in the open, Morag is aware that they could be seen or heard before she can get them both hidden again.

'It's going to be difficult to get the woman through the small hole,' Morag thought, wishing she could just sit down and rest.

The agonising pain in her knees has become unbearable and the constant stopping and starting on the uneven ground is making everything worse. Morag's glad when she finds the woods surrounding the familiar barn. She uses her body and the protection from her coat to hold the brambles backward as her hostage struggles to clamber through the small crack. It is difficult for the pair of them to manoeuvre through the dense brambles, but before long Morag spots the cleared area. She is glad that they have made it to the old barn unseen. Morag is drained and wants to sit down and rest. Her knees are so swollen that she can barely put any weight on them. Rubbing her painful knees, she's not sure that they will ever go back down to their normal size. Holding back a large lump of ivy, Morag tells her prisoner to wriggle through the small hole.

'You must squeeze through the crack.'

'But there's no way I will fit. I can't get through there,' the woman said.

Sick of listening to the woman making a fuss, and worried about being heard. Morag loses her temper and smashes the woman's head off the side of the barn, knocking her senseless. Completely fatigued, Morag uses all of her strength to drag the limp body through the gap.

'Someone was going to hear her whining, I had to shut her up' she thought.

Barely able to stand with exhaustion, Morag drops the woman onto the muddy floor and drags her across the barn, before securing her unconscious prisoner to a large pole that holds the barn up. It is the only part that has some roof. Morag's knees are trembling, excruciating pain ricochets through her with every step she makes. Her knuckles are also throbbing, and she is exhausted, slumping down heavily onto the wet muddy floor. Morag is not sure how much more of this she can take as tears slowly drip down her face.

'I must be strong. I deserve to have a normal life' she thought, sniffing as she wipes the tears from her face.

Sitting on the cold wet floor, she hopes to return to the farmhouse soon.

'We can't stay here long, I must find somewhere else to stay' she thought, her eyelids heavy.

Morag wakes on the dirty floor, heaving herself up into a sitting position. She blinks against the sunlight pouring through the open roof. Glancing around, she spots her prisoner lying in a lump on the floor. Leaning forward onto her painful fluid filled knees, Morag stiffly crawls to a spot where she can see daylight shining through a gap in the side. Peering through the small hole she realises that the barn is position high above the farm, the woods have grown below acting as the perfect cover. From this position, she can see out, but no one can see her without climbing through the undergrowth.

'This place would be perfect if it had a roof and wasn't so uncomfortable,' she thought.

Morag prepares to escape the barn, checking that the woman is still safely secured. First thing is always her worst time for pain and as she squeezes her bulky body through the small gap, excruciating pain rips through her swollen knees. She heads slowly down the steep hill through the thick woods towards the cottage determined to find out what is happening?

'I wish they would just leave' she reflected, wanting to get into her hiding place before everyone gets up.

Careful to stay low Morag spots the caravan, wondering whether to leave the woman in the outbuilding and live in the caravan herself. Realising that it will be awhile before anyone gets up, she decides to have a look. Bracing herself for the agony she pushes herself up onto her knees and slowly edges towards the caravan, using the undergrowth to hide behind. As she reaches the caravan, she makes sure no one is around before pulling out her key and enters unnoticed. Shuffling around inside, her mouth is dry, and she tries the tap, but nothing comes out.

'Damn, there's no water.'

Her belly grumbles as she opens the cupboard doors, finding a bar of chocolate and some crisps but nothing else.

'Well, this will keep me going for a little while, ' she thought, looking for something to carry water in.

The only thing she can find is a mug, making sure to bring it with her when she leaves. She takes a risk filling the mug from the tap behind the farmhouse before returning to the barn.

***

Morag has been keeping a close eye on her neighbours, toing and froing from the old barn to the caravan for the past week. She's certain no one has seen her but can tell they are getting edgy.

'I need to find somewhere better to stay' she thought, glad the weather hasn't been too bad.

THE COTTAGE

Sitting at her viewing spot Morag watches the comings and goings on the farm intently. Her senses on high alert as she listens for every noise. She hears shuffling and a low groan coming from the back of the barn. Turning toward the noise Morag notices the woman huddled in a ball on the floor her badly swollen black foot sticking out from underneath her.

'Her foot is disgusting, I wish she would put it away' Morag thought, her stomach grumbling loudly.

'I need to get out of here and get some water and something to eat' she thought turning back to her viewing spot.

She spots the stupid one and Eve looking as if they're moving into the farmhouse.

'HOW DARE THEY? IT'S MY FARM MY FOREVER HOME' she yells, furious her plan to drive them away hasn't worked.

Behind her, the woman lets out a low groan as she tries to move. Morag doesn't know what to do with her prisoner. She's become less and less responsive and has barely moved at all these past few days. Watching her prisoner Morag realises she must find somewhere better to stay and leave her here. It's unlikely anyone will find her and without food and water she won't be strong enough to escape. Contemplating her next move Morag is suddenly startled when she hears the sound of a branch breaking and quickly turns to look through the hole in the wall. She spots the stupid one directly below her walking along the edge of the wood towards the direction of the old shelter.

'I'm so glad the undergrowth is so thick' she thought, holding her breath as she watches until he disappears.

'That was close, I knew, I was right to move' she thought, sliding down onto the muddy floor her hands trembling.

'They would have caught me, had I stayed in the old shelter.'

Terrified that she is going to be found, Morag vigilantly watches her neighbours as they go back-and-forth to the barn. Determined to keep an eye on the goings on Morag doesn't move from her viewing spot and is exhausted as night falls. She doesn't remember when she fell asleep, but she has woken early this morning and noticed the stupid one checking all the barns he doesn't normally go in. How dare he, he has no right to go in there.

'I need them to leave, I need them to leave for good.'

Her mouth is dry as she swills the last of the water around in the dirty mug she'd taken from the caravan. Morag feels unnerved after almost getting found and doesn't want the stupid one, snooping around her farm.

'I need to distract him with something else, but what?'

Hearing a car start, she waits until she can see the car drive off down the lane.

'This is my chance'

Afraid of getting caught but knowing that she has to act while she can. Morag leaves the safety of the barn and pushes through the brambles stumbling down the steep slope until she breaks free from the woods. Wanting to stay hidden, Morag ducks down, keeping close to the back wall of the farmhouse until she reaches a small barn.

'Thank fuck it's here' she said, pulling out a chainsaw.

Weak from hunger and thirst her head is light as she uses all of her energy to carry the weighty chainsaw to the other side of the field. It takes several tries to get the chainsaw to go, but suddenly there is a loud roar as it ignites to life. Her arms vibrate as she begins cutting a hole in the hedge. Standing back to examine the gap, sweat dripping down her face and back, she is satisfied that the hole is large enough. Being naturally curious creatures, many of the cows are already surrounding her and she directs them through the hole. She'd hoped that the cows would get further, but before she has them all out of the field. Morag hears the sound of a car coming down the lane. Eve and the stupid one have returned quicker than she'd expected. She'd almost got caught again as she struggled to move quick enough to get away.

'Those fucking idiots have called the fucking police over a bunch of cows. What sort of idiots are they?' she rages.

Unable to settle herself with so much police presence, Morag hobbles back-and-forth, keeping an eye on her prisoner.

'Make sure you don't make any noise' Morag snarls into the face of the woman lying unmoving on the floor.

***

The police don't stay long, but their presence is enough to send Morag into a raging panic.

'I've got to get out of here. What am I going to do? If I don't find somewhere safer to stay, they're gonna find me' she mutters quietly as she paces.

Pacing back-and-forth helps the pain in her knees, but she needs to know what's going on? Sitting in front of the hole again Morag can see Eve and the farmhand walking back towards the cottage.

'I wish that they would just leave' she rages.

All the commotion of the last couple of days has unsettled her, and she decides to lay low for a while. She takes one last trip to get as much water as she can carry.

'There's no point risking going near the chicken coop, there's never any eggs in there anymore' she rages.

It is pitch-black and Morag can barely see in front of her face as she slowly fills the water bottle as quietly as she can and hauls it back to the safety of the barn.

'This should keep us going for a couple of days until everything settles down.'

Chapter 25. Times Running Out.

Morag looks through the rations she has left. Including the three water bottles she has just filled, there's half a rusty bucket of rainwater and three eggs. She didn't bring the camping stove when they moved so they've been eating the eggs raw. She knows that there's another barn belonging to the neighbouring farm about two miles away, but Morag is unsure what to do? She doesn't want to leave her prisoner in case she escapes.

'I'll have to kill her, no one will find her body here', she thought, looking at the woman lying unmoving on the filthy wet floor.

***

Morag has lost all track of time, during the day she watches the farm through the hole and at night she paces back-and-forth planning when to leave. She doesn't know how long she has been here but thinks it has been several weeks. Her food and water rations completely ran out three days ago. Through sheer desperation, Morag has resorted to collecting rainwater and gathering condensation off the leaves in the barn. She is weak and disorientated with hunger. Morag knows she'll have to leave her hiding place soon, but she's afraid that she won't be strong enough to get water and get back again.

'It's just too risky' she thought abandoning her plan to leave for the third night in a row.

Morag knows that she must be patient; she must be strong and wait just a little longer. Spending all day stooped at the hole watching the farm intently, certain that it won't be much longer, and this hell will be over.

'Soon I will be able to move back into the farmhouse and begin to make a real life again.'

Tears run down her cheeks when she realises that she can't let her kids see her like this.

'I will have to get well before I bring them here' she thought.

Morag knows that her health has deteriorated since living in the old barn. As she sits staring through the hole, she feels a warmth spreading down her legs.

'Not again!'

Morag looks down as the dampness spreads down her legs, producing another tide line on her trousers, creating a puddle at her feet. Her incontinence has become a real problem lately. Morag doesn't even know it's happening until she feels the wetness and warmth. It was bad enough when it had happened occasionally before. But here, in the old barn, she doesn't have any spare clothes to change into. Not wanting to risk getting caught, she just sits quietly watching, waiting for the moment when she can make a move. Unable to change her clothes, the skin on her thighs has reacted to the repeated urine exposure. She has developed blisters and her skin is red raw. The blisters have started festering, and every time she moves the putrid smell rises, making her empty stomach lurch. She knows she must get the infected area treated, but with so much police activity on the farm, there is nothing she can do, but wait. There's no way she can risk getting caught by leaving her hiding space. It's not just the raw skin on her thighs that's causing agonising pain, but her knees and knuckles are also red and badly swollen, so swollen that she can barely use them. Everything happened so fast the night of the storm that she didn't pack enough clothes and forgot to pack her arthritis medication.

'I never expected to be here for so long' she thought.

The increasing police presence has left her without any other options. Morag doesn't know why the police are still there. But she is careful to be vigilant, barely moving or sleeping, just watching the farm. The gap is positioned uncomfortably low and makes her stoop, but it's the only spot where she can watch the farm.

'I'm so thirsty' she thought, swiping at a blue bottle.

Realising that her body can't take much more, Morag is almost ready to give up; she is exhausted and every part of her body aches.

'I can't give up just yet. I must be strong and stay hidden,' she thought, shifting uncomfortably.

Gagging on the putrid smell that has been released with her movement. Morag swats away a bluebottle that keeps landing on her, glancing around she realises that the barn has filled with flies. There's a distinct buzzing from their wings; the flies are everywhere.

'It must be because the weather is warming up' she thought swiping another bluebottle away.

It is warm in the barn with the sun shining through the missing roof. Morag has noticed that the weather has been getting warmer for the past few days.

'I must leave soon. I must get water, without the rain there's nothing to collect.'

***

Growing more and more disorientated with thirst, hunger, and pain as each day passes. Morag knows that she must leave soon, but there's still so much police activity on the farm.

'I must be strong and bide my time' she thought, hoping to get out later tonight.

Blinking her eyes open, everything is blurry as she wakes up. Morag is standing with her head pressed to the side of the barn the warm sun on her face. Disappointment fills her, as she realises that she has slept all night, missing her chance to get water yet again. As she wakes properly, Morag senses that something has changed.

'What is that? What can I hear?' she thought, stooping to look through the hole watching as police car after police car arrive at the farm.

'Why won't they just leave?' she thought, pain tearing through her as she crouches down.

Morag tries to move into a more comfortable position, releasing an aroma that makes her wretch. Sitting on the floor listening, she can hear a new noise in the distance; it distracts her. Sitting completely still in her urine-soaked clothes listening carefully. No matter how hard she listens, she doesn't know what the noise is? Rage fills her every pore, furious with this new noise and the extra police presence that are preventing her from leaving again. Her lips are chapped and dry, she is weak and getting desperate.

'I must get some water soon' she thought, but I can't go yet, I can't risk being found.

Frustration penetrates her every pore as she resumes her position in front of her watching spot.

'I will make a break tonight.'

Unable to settle herself, Morag stumbles around the old barn. Her knees buckle and excruciating pain sears through her raw skin with every step. Morag tries to come up with a plan that will not leave her exposed. As she stumbles around the barn, Morag swats at the flies buzzing around her face. Noticing a pile of dirty rags on the floor where her prisoner is lying. Morag turns to look at the woman curled up in a ball, her bony back sticking out, wondering what she should do with her?

'I wonder if she's dead' Morag thought realising her prisoner has been quiet recently.

'I suppose, it would make things easier if she was already dead' Morag thought giving her prisoner a light kick.

Whatever happens, when she leaves tonight Morag knows that she cannot risk leaving her prisoner alive in the barn.

'I've no other option, but to make sure the woman is dead before I leave tonight.'

'What is that noise?'

Standing deadly still, she listens carefully, trying to identify the strange noise that has been getting progressively louder. Listening carefully, she suddenly realises it's a helicopter flying above.

'What is that fucking helicopter doing? it feels like it has been out there for hours' she rages, wondering whether to take the risk and just leave the barn.

'I should probably wait until that helicopter has gone. There's no point taking unnecessary risks.'

Morag sits down preparing to wait it out. But it doesn't take long before she begins to get agitated.

'What are they doing? Why won't they go away?'

The helicopter noise continues to get increasingly louder.

'Where is it? And why is it out there?'

Morag continues to sit listening to the noise of the helicopter as it gets closer and louder. She is frightened and doesn't know what to do? Using all of her strength, Morag pushes herself into a standing position. Pain ricocheting with every movement, she moves slowly and painfully around the barn trying to see through the gaps in the wooden sides. Fury courses through her when she is unable to see anything, Morag turns to look at her prisoner. Staring at the woman, Morag is certain that her prisoner must be responsible for whatever this is?

'She must have done something' Morag thought. Shuffling across to the woman, she crouches down and screams in her ear.

'WHAT HAVE YOU DONE?' she screams at her unmoving prisoner unsettling a flurry of bluebottles.

The helicopter noise is deafening, and it consumes all sound. Terrified at what is happening and not knowing what else to do? Morag presses her hands hard to her ears. Moving stiffly away from the woman on the ground she hobbles to the other side of the barn. Morag tries desperately to see through any of the small gaps in the side. Disorientated, afraid and unable to hear

325

anything but the helicopter. Sitting stiffly down on the cold hard floor with her head between her knees. Red hot pain pulsates throughout her whole-body.

'What's going on?' she thought, wishing the helicopter would leave so she could get away.

But the deafening noise continues, and she pulls herself into a ball on the cold floor, pain searing throughout her body. Her heart racing in terror, and her hands pressed firmly on her ears desperately trying to muffle the deafening noise.

Chapter 26. Capture.

The noise from the helicopter consumes all sound when suddenly, there's another loud banging and cracking noise that startles her. It's coming from the direction of the small makeshift opening. Afraid of what is happening, Morag attempts to find somewhere to hide, but she is in too much pain to move. She curls up into a ball on the floor, lifting her head slightly to peep through her fingers. Her heart races as she looks in the direction of where the noise is coming from. Lying perfectly still on the floor, watching as panels of wood come flying in and a large hole appears in the side. The barn suddenly fills with police officers. It takes her a second to understand what has happened.

'They've found me, the helicopter and the police cars, that was all about me' she realises.

Morag continues to lie curled in a ball on the floor, filthy, cold and soaked with urine.

'How did you find me?' she said quietly to the officer standing in front of her, too tired to fight any longer.

'STAY WHERE YOU ARE, STAY DOWN ON THE FLOOR' someone shouts.

Following the direction of the voice, Morag can see someone standing beside the hole that has been smashed into the side of the barn. The light is streaming in from behind him, making it difficult for her to see anything but a silhouette. She watches as more officers continue to rush in.

'STAY DOWN AND PUT YOUR HANDS BEHIND YOUR HEAD' shouts the officer again.

She can feel her arms being pulled roughly behind her back, and hard cold metal as an officer handcuffs her wrists. Morag listens as he states her legal rights, but she doesn't care. Lying face down on the floor with her hands cuffed, she is strangely relieved that they have found her.

'I can finally stop running' she thought.

For the first time in fifteen years, Morag relaxes her body, her breathing slows as she listens to the noisy footsteps around her. Placing her face down onto the cold filthy floor, Morag closes her eyes and feels euphoric as she watches her children playing as she runs to hug them. Her euphoria is short-lived when she is abruptly brought back to reality when she hears an officer shouting.

'I've found someone; it's a woman. She doesn't have a pulse. No, wait a minute, I've found a slight pulse, it's weak, but she's alive, CALL AN AMBULANCE NOW' he orders.

Lying on the floor Morag watches as he unravels her prisoner from the ball, she was tightly curled in.

'I think it could be the missing woman from England' he continues, holding the barely alive woman.

Chapter 27. Discovery.

Tom and I are distracted by the noise from the helicopter and don't see the police officer until he is standing right in front of us.

'Miss Mullan, Mr Davis can I have a word with you both please?'

'Um yes,' I reply, glancing at Tom, who looks as shocked as I feel to see him.

As we walk the officer to the cottage, my heart thuds rapidly wondering what's going on?

'Miss Mullan and Mr Davis, I'm here to tell you that we have arrested a suspect for the break-ins and vandalism. I can't disclose any details, but I need to ask that you both stay here at the cottage; someone will come and talk to you in due course,' the police officer said.

Stunned at what we'd just been told, Tom and I watch as the officer joins his colleagues and they stride off in the direction of the farm. As we are watching, police car, after police car speed past, towards the farm.

'This all seems a bit much, don't you think?' I said as the last police car speeds past.

'You'd think so, maybe someone has been trespassing again, why else would they be going up there?' he said looking as confused as I feel.

'There's not much we can do, but wait and see what happens,' I said, pulling out a chair for him to join me at the patio table.

I'm just about to head in to get us both a cup of tea when I hear sirens coming from the direction of the farm. After a few seconds, an ambulance speeds past its sirens blaring and its blue lights flashing.

'I wonder what that's all about?'

'No idea, but are you getting some tea or what? I'm dying of thirst over here,' Tom said, smiling.

Not long after the ambulance sped past, we hear the helicopter starting up again and watch as it flies off.

'I guess they have whoever it is.'

'I wonder if there was someone hiding in one of the farm outbuildings again. I hope the cows are all right' Tom said, his brows furrowed.

'Yeah, I hope so, all this noise won't do them any good.'

I'm confused and worried as we sit outside quietly drinking our tea. A few minutes after the helicopter flew off, two police officers walk around the corner and stride towards us. I nudge Tom.

'Look, here they come. Maybe we'll find out what happened?'

'Miss Mullen and Mr Davis, can we have a word?' the first officer asks when they reach us.

'Of course,' I said, inviting them into the cottage, curious why they're here.

'What's happened?'

'Do either of you know a person named Morag Edwards?'

'Morag Edwards, no, I don't think so' I said, shaking my head confused.

I look at Tom to see if he knows this person, but he is shaking his head as well.

'No, I don't know anyone of that name.'

'We believe that we've found the person who damaged your property.'

'Who is it? And what's going on at the farm?' Tom asks, looking from one officer to the other.

'We have arrested a woman named Morag Edwards. We believe that she lived with John Bamford at the farm until recently.'

'Morag?' I gasp, turning to look at Tom.

'I didn't know her surname; she's been missing. Morag went missing the night John died in the storm,' I said, reaching across to grasp Tom's hand.

'Are you sure it is Morag?' Tom asks.

'Miss Mullen, you mentioned your friend Emma Crosby when we interviewed you last. Have you heard from her?'

"No. I haven't heard anything at all' I said, wondering why they are asking about Emma?

'Miss Crosby was reported as a missing person, a couple of months ago' the officer tells us.

'I only found out a few days ago that Emma is missing?' I tell them, my mind racing trying to remember the last time I had contact with Emma.

'The thing is, we've found a woman being kept in terrible conditions in an old dilapidated barn behind the farmhouse. Can you tell me the last time you had any contact with Miss Crosby? Any contact at all, we are trying to establish a timeline of when she was last seen or spoken too' the officer asks directing his question to me.

'It's been a long time since I had any actual contact. I tried to phone her again after Mrs Crosby told me Emma was missing, but the line was dead,' I said, lifting my eyes to meet his.

I don't move a muscle as I stare at the officer and ask, the woman you found, is it Emma?'

'Unfortunately, we've not been able to identify the woman yet. But Morag Edwards has been arrested in connection with the damage caused to your property and the kidnap and holding of an unidentified female.'

'We believe that Miss Crosby had been on her way to visit you. But she got caught up in the storm and crashed her car. The car you saw in the hedge, but that's where the trail dies. Miss Crosby and her car haven't been seen since' the officer said, making notes in his notepad.

I'm stunned and look from one officer to the other, certain that this must be some kind of mistake. The storm was months ago. Surely, I would have known if Emma had been missing all that time? Wouldn't I? Why didn't anyone contact me?

'So, it could be Emma that you have found?' Tom asks, squeezing my hand.

I open my mouth, but words won't come out. I glance at Tom, his brows drawn together as he rubs his chin. I just can't comprehend what we are being told.

'I'm afraid the woman we found is in a bad way. She has been held in terrible conditions and was badly dehydrated. But she is alive and has been taken to hospital' the officer said.

'It's important we identify the woman as quickly as possible. And if you're up to it, it would be helpful if you could come to the hospital and identify if the woman is Miss Crosby. Do you think you could do that?'

'Yes, yes of course' I stammer, my heart racing.

'Are you free to come to the hospital this afternoon?

'Yes, I'm free'

'In that case, I will meet you outside the room' the officer said giving me all the details before leaving.

I don't know how I feel about what I'm about to do. What if it is Emma? part of me hopes it's her, because that means she's been found, but then another part of me hopes it's not, I don't want her to have suffered.

'Will you come with me?' I ask.

'Of course, I'm not letting you do something like this by yourself' he said wrapping his arms around me.

Chapter 28. Who is it?

On the drive to the hospital, I struggle to calm my racing heart, anxious about what I'm about to see.

'What if it is Emma?' I said, realising she was only in Northern Ireland because of me.

I'm feeling extremely guilty about how things have been between Emma and me.

'We'll just have to wait and see,' Tom said, as he pulled into a parking space in the hospital carpark.

As we enter through the revolving doors, I'm reminded about when I had to identify my mother. My heart thuds loudly in my head as our footsteps echo down the corridor to the room where the officer said he would meet us.

'If it is Emma, please let her be okay.' I pray silently as we get closer to the room.

As we turn the corner, I see the officer sitting outside a door, standing as we get closer.

'Thanks for coming Miss Mullan.'

I nod, keeping my eyes on the floor. My heart is racing, and I want to run away.

'Are you ready?' he asks.

'Yes. No, not really,' I said, welling up.

'What if it is Emma?' I said tears running down my face.

'Miss Mullen, if it is Emma, then her parents can rest knowing that their daughter has been found. Alive,' the officer said.

'You can help end their suffering.'

I take deep breaths to compose myself.

'Okay, I'm ready. I just needed a minute.'

As the door is opened, I step through and immediately see that it is Emma lying on the bed.

'Yes, it's her.'

'Can you confirm that the person you are identifying is the missing woman Emma Crosby?'

'Yes, it's Emma Crosby'

As I stand staring at Emma in the bed, I can't believe how dreadful she looks. It's definitely her, but she doesn't look like Emma. Emma is loud, in your face and full of fun. This person is just a shell attached to numerous tubes and machines. I feel a tap on my shoulder and turn,

'Excuse me, Miss Mullen, thank you for your help. But I have to ask you to leave now. The medical staff insist that Emma is allowed to rest.'

***

I barely remember leaving the hospital, but as we arrive home, Tom tells me that the police are coming over to talk to us.

We are only through the door when the police car pulls up outside.

'I wanted to thank you for what you have done. I know it wasn't easy for you. But with a positive identification we have been able to inform her parents that their daughter is alive.'

'Are you sure, it was Morag, John's Morag, who kidnapped Emma and broke in and destroyed the cottage?' I ask, unable to believe what has happened.

'Morag was found in the barn where Emma was being held captive and was immediately arrested. She will be questioned about a number of crimes spanning the last fifteen years, along with John's death and the vandalism to your property,' the officer tells me.

'But I don't understand? it was us, Tom and I, we found John. He'd been electrocuted after a tree crashed through the window,' I said, gasping for a breath between sobs.

'The thing is Miss Mullan and Mr Davis, I know this is difficult for you both. But John's autopsy report has shown high, lethal traces of ethylene glycol in Mr Bamford's system.'

'What is ethylene glycol?' Tom asks.

'Ethylene Glycol is more commonly known as anti-freeze and there was a high level in Mr Bamford's system. We are investigating the possibility that he was being poisoned,' the officer said.

I'm stunned. I look across to Tom, who looks as confused as I feel.

'John had been poorly for a while,' I said.

'We are investigating everything,' the officer said as he put his notebook away.

'Thank you again. We will be in touch if we need any more information.'

'Just one more thing. You should expect to see a high police presence in the area for a while. Turning to look at Tom, he said,

'We will need access to all areas of the farm.'

'That's not a problem, search wherever you like' Tom said, as he walked the officers to the door.

'Before you go, do you know when we can visit Emma?' I ask.

'The hospital staff have said that Emma can have visitors but only for a short time. You have to phone before you go, to let them know when you are coming,' the officer said, handing me a note with all the details before leaving.

Tom and I stand staring at each other, not sure what to do with all the information we've just received.

'I need wine,' Tom said, grabbing a bottle of Merlot and two glasses.

'It was Morag, she did everything. She kidnapped Emma, and it was her who was watching us. She trashed the cottage and probably killed John' I said tears running down my face.

I'm bewildered at all that has happened today.

'Why would she do all of those things? How did we not see it? Do you think it was for the farm?' I said blowing my nose.

When Tom doesn't answer, I turn to look at him, but he's staring straight ahead.

'Tom, are you okay?'

'I think John was on to her. Why else would he have left the farm to me?'

'Maybe he was, he must have been feeling unwell with anti-freeze in his system.'

I'm stunned and not sure whether to feel happy Emma has been found or devastated at what she's suffered at the hands of Morag. I watch as Tom takes a large gulp of wine and notice his hand shaking.

'This experience has been rough on us both,' I realise as I take a sip of wine enjoying the feeling.

We drink in silence, hoping the answer lies at the bottom of the glass and then the bottle and then the next bottle. And so, the night drags on. Few words are exchanged between us. And the words spoken are slurred and useless.

***

The following morning, my eyes sting as I try to prize my heavy eyelids open, my stomach heaves and I only make it to the bathroom before lurching forward onto my knees as chunks of partially digested chicken spew out of my contracting stomach. My head feels like it is exploding with every footstep, my whole-body shaking and my throat like sandpaper as I make myself a cup of coffee.

'Why the fuck did we do that last night?' I thought feeling sorry for myself.

I glance around looking for Tom, realising he's not home.

'Where is he?' I wonder spotting a note on the coffee table telling me that he's gone to milk the cows.

I can't stop shaking, my hangover feels like a balloon under my cranium, slowly being inflated. I splash water on my face and instantly wish I could wash my brain free from the toxins. I'm overly apprehensive about seeing Emma today and really wish I didn't feel so rough. I'm still finding it hard to believe that she was kidnapped and held so close to the cottage. She has been here for months, in a dirty old shed being held captive by a crazy woman. She must have been terrified. My hands won't stop shaking and my heart is racing when I remember that Morag was here in this cottage, socialising with us.

'I invited a psychopath into my home, she was a bit grumpy, but I never would have thought that she would do that. What on earth happened to her to make her do such a thing?' I wonder, my stomach lurching and gurgling again.

The aching in my skull ebbs and flows like a cold tide, yet the pain is always there as I shakily get myself dressed and ready for visiting Emma.

'Why would Morag kidnap Emma? She didn't even know her' I thought, still trying to make some sort of sense of what has happened?

'None of this makes any sense.'

I can't stop myself from impatiently pacing around the cottage as if determined to wear a hole in the rug, too agitated to eat or stay still. I finally understand why they call it a hangover, for it feels as if the blackest of clouds are over my head with no intention of clearing. I'm still pacing when Tom arrives home. He looks as rough as I feel, there're beads of sweat glistening on his furrowed brow.

'I don't know about you, but I feel like shit, like there's been an axe planted in my head. Also, there's fucking police all over the farm' he said.

'Yeah, I'm not feeling well either. I still can't believe that she was being held so close and we didn't know.'

'I know, it's mental.'

'Do you think Emma will be awake?' I ask my mind still surging perplexity.

'I don't know, I suppose, we'll find out when we get there.'

I can't settle, I'm hungover and apprehensive at our impending trip to the hospital.

'I can't believe this is how you are going to meet my best friend' I said, picking at my breakfast before pushing it away my stomach churning.

'I know, it's all a bit weird, isn't it? he said a muscle twitching involuntarily at the corner of his right eye, his mouth formed into a rigid grimace.

'I'm going to go and get cleaned up, then we can make a move' he said.

My head thumps relentlessly and I can't sit still. I begin pacing again unable to focus on anything until Tom returns dressed smartly in jeans and a bright blue shirt.

'You look nice.'

'Well I do have to make a good impression on your best friend, even if she's in a coma?' he said smiling.

'Come on we better get going, I know you're nervous but putting it off isn't going to make it any easier' he said giving me a hug.

Chapter 29. The Hospital.

All the reasons not to do this come flooding in; my nails are already bitten down to the quick. Yet I continue to nibble at their frayed, edges like a famished mouse.

'This happened to her, because she was coming to visit me' I said, rubbing my puffy eyes that fill up again when I think about what my friend has had to go through.

'This isn't your fault. Morag is responsible; she didn't have to do any of what she has done.'

I clench my fists into tight balls, squeezing so tightly my nails dig into my palm. My heart is throbbing against the cage of my chest as we arrive at the hospital, unable to stop myself, tears begin rolling down my cheeks as Tom parks the car.

'Come here, she is alive, and she is in the best place she can be,' Tom said, pulling me into a tight hug.

The hospital is overly hot, and the air has an undertone of bleach, my head is pounding and there's a vomit taste at the back of my throat. I'm flustered and nervous as we walk down the corridor toward Emma's room. I don't know what to expect. Emma was bad yesterday, but she'd only just been found. I'm hoping that there will be an improvement today, that she may even be awake. The nurse has told us we can see Emma, but we're not to stay for long. She explains Emma was severely dehydrated and malnourished when she was brought in, also that there's an unidentified infection spreading throughout Emma's body. Because of the severity of her condition, Emma has been medically sedated until her condition improves. Our footsteps echo in the corridor as we follow the nurse to Emma's new room. As we approach, I notice there is a police officer guarding the door; he takes our details before allowing us in. The room has a strong bleach like smell and unlike yesterday when the first thing I saw was Emma's sunken face. Today the first thing, I notice are the sounds from all the machines she's attached too. There's an IV, a heart monitor, and an oxygen tank. Glancing around, I notice an old TV set hanging from the ceiling.

'There are so many machines,' I said quietly, scanning the room.

Gripping Toms hand as we walk closer to the bed, I see her properly for the first time.

I can't control the floods of tears. My chest heaves uncontrollably as I stare at my friend. I barely recognise her. She's lost so much weight, looking tiny in the hospital bed.

'I can't believe how frail she looks,' I said between sobs.

Yesterday her face and hands were still dirty, but the nurses have cleaned her up and the bruises on her face are more obvious. I can't believe what has happened to her, as I stroke her long blond hair that is still matted and tangled. Watching my barely recognisable friend as she sleeps, on her face there are great purple welts that stand out against her ghostly skin. Her arms are covered in red marks along with purple welts scattered like a disease. There are dark circles under her sunken eyes and her cheeks hollow. I notice a dark purple bruise at the top of the cast propped up on pillows.

'This is my fault, Morag did this too her because of me. She wouldn't have been here if it wasn't for me,' I said, tearfully looking at Tom.

'This is not your fault; you didn't do this' he said, placing the flowers and chocolates on the bedside locker.

'Morag is sick, mentally unwell, nobody sane would do this' he said sounding tired as he sits down on the chair next to me.

'I don't know what I expected? but I didn't think she would be this bad.'

'I know, she's in a bad way' he agrees, rubbing my back looking at Emma.

As I sit in the overly hot room, listening to the rhythmic noises of the machines, I find the noises strangely therapeutic. I'm reassured these mechanical noises, tubes and liquids are helping her recover and get well again. Neither Tom nor I say anything more as we watch Emma lying in the hospital bed. I'm startled when the door opens, and a nurse enters

'I'm sorry but visiting times over. Emma needs to rest' the nurse said, standing at the door waiting for us to leave.

Looking at my friend so frail and small, the reality that we could so nearly have lost her hits me. Wiping the tears running freely down my cheeks, I'm reluctant to let go of her hand and say a silent prayer before we go.

Yesterday when I returned home after identifying Emma, I phoned her parents to let them know. The police had already called them with the good news, but I promised to phone them after I visited the hospital today.

'Hello, Mrs Crosby, it's me, Eve. I've just been to see Emma; she's sedated but doing well.'

'Thank you for calling dear. I'm so glad she's okay and has someone with her. We've been out of our minds not knowing where she was, I'll not settle until I see her though. We've a ferry booked for tomorrow morning,' she said.

'You must stay in the cottage, Tom and I can stay in the caravan,' I said, giving her directions.

I've an overwhelming need to have them close after what's happened to Emma.

'I'm just relieved that she has been found, but I will feel happier when we get to Northern Ireland' Mrs Crosby tells me.

We chat for half an hour and she explains that Emma had planned to surprise me, and they'd asked her to let them know when she'd arrived safely. But when they didn't hear from her, they initially thought in the excitement she'd forgotten.

'You know what she's like, but, when she hadn't contacted us after a day, I tried to phone her, but she didn't answer. It wasn't like her not to answer her phone or return a text message. Also, I'd heard about the storm on the news which worried me' Mrs Crosby said.

She explains that Emma had planned on staying in Northern Ireland for a week, and when she didn't return after the week. They were frantic with worry; it was only then that the police took their concerns seriously and Emma was classed as a missing person. The police in England, were unable to locate her, despite there being a record of her booking a ferry to Belfast. There was no record of her actually arriving there.

'She hadn't used any of her credit cards or booked any hotels, we didn't know if she had actually got on the ferry?'

Mrs Crosby explains that it wasn't until I remembered seeing Emma's car the night of the storm they were contacted by the police in Northern Ireland.

THE COTTAGE

Chapter 30. Sentencing.

It has been more than a month since Emma was rescued, and she is still being kept in a medically induced coma in hospital. The nurses tell us she is improving but is still too weak to be woken up. Every day we are told to be patient, but I'm losing hope that she will ever wake up.

It's a beautiful day, the sun is shining, and I'm uncomfortable dressed in a smart navy-blue trouser suit, Tom is next to me in a smart pinstripe suit. We are standing side by side, looking up at the steps in front of us that lead to the imposing High Court building that is towering above us. I'm still in shock at all that has happened this year. We're at the court today, because the jury are to give their verdict on whether Morag is to be found guilty or not guilty of her charges. Today is the day we find out if the person who made our lives a living hell for months, kidnapped Emma and kept her in horrendous conditions, and was arrested for the murder of our friend John. Today we will find out if that person will be sentenced to prison. Today is a big day.

My palms are sweaty, and I feel overly hot as we sit in the middle pew seats towards the back of the court room. I can see Morag sitting at the front, next to her solicitor. It is the first time I have seen her since before the storm. As I watch her, I can see that she has lost a lot of weight. She looks very skinny, sitting with her head down, looking at the floor. Her long grey hair is hanging limply, covering most of her face.

'She looks old and unwell' I thought, unable to take my eyes off her.

As I watch her, I realise that she is very unwell and looks as if she will die soon. I'm disappointed that she will not live long enough to suffer the consequences of her actions for very long. I feel eyes on me and scan the room, noticing a man staring. He is sitting directly behind Morag; I think he is with the woman sat next to him. The woman is crying, the man stares at us, until I catch his eye, when he quickly turns his face away.

'I wonder who they are? I've never seen them before. But who would feel sorry for Morag? She's hardly the victim, is she?'

There is a flurry of commotion as the jury enter the court. All, but one of the jury have sat down, the one who is standing at the edge of the jurors seating area, holds an envelope and waits for everyone to settle. The judge has asked the jury if they have reached a verdict?

'We have, your honour,' the juror said.

He clears his throat and opens the envelope before addressing the room. He begins reading in a loud clear voice.

'Morag Edwards, for the crime of the kidnapping, holding and torture of Emma Crosby, the jury find you: Guilty.

For the crime of causing malicious damage to the property of Eve Mullen, the jury find you: Guilty.

And, for the crime of murder in the first degree of John Bamford. The jury find you: Guilty.'

The judge thanks the juror and waits for the commotion to die down before turning to Morag and stating in a stern voice.

'What I have heard here in court these past couple of weeks, I have found this to be one of the most callous and selfish of crimes. All the crimes against you Morag Edwards were committed because of greed. You

wanted John's farm and were going to do anything to get it, including slowly murdering him, kidnapping and torturing a person you didn't even know and making your closest neighbours' life a living hell. You committed all of these crimes in the hope that you could keep the farm for yourself. I find your actions deplorable. On the evidence presented to the court and on the juror's verdict; You, Morag Edwards, are sentenced to serve twenty years in Her Majesties Prison for the kidnapping and torture of Emma Crosby. You are also sentenced to serve 12 months for the malicious damage to the property of Eve Mullen. Finally, I sentence you to serve twenty years for the most deplorable murder of John Bamford. All sentences are to be served concurrently, effective immediately.'

As the judge addresses Morag, I notice she doesn't react at all; she just continues to stare at the floor. That is, until the police officer moves in behind her and places the handcuffs on her wrists. At that point she slowly lifts her head and turns to look me directly in the eye, staring for a while before giving me a small smile as she is walked out.

Her eyes are wild, and her smile sends a shiver down my spine, making me remember that awful feeling of being watched. She really is evil. Relief floods me and I feel reassured that she can't hurt anyone anymore. At least now we can forget about Morag and focus on getting Emma well again. She still has a long road to recovery, but at least the person who harmed her will be in prison for the rest of her life. Tom and I step out of the court and begin walking down the steps, but as we almost reach the bottom step, the man and woman who were sitting behind Morag stop us.

'Excuse me,' the man said.

I turn to look at the person speaking and instinctively step away not trusting him.

'What do you want?' I said, anger and fear surging through me.

'Sorry if I frightened you' he said, gauging my reaction.

'What do you want?' Tom asks again.

'It's just, Morag Edwards is our mother. We just wanted to apologise for everything that has happened,' the man said.

His sister stands beside him, her head down tears streaming down her face. As she looks up, the anguish is written across her face.

'I'm so sorry for what she has done' the woman said between sobs.

'But Morag is our mother, and she disappeared years ago; our father told us that she was dead' the woman continues.

'We just wanted to say sorry.'

The man takes his sister's arm and guides her down the rest of the stairs.

'Morag had kids, a family, a whole other life, what on earth could have happened? that she would leave them and do all this?' I said, looking at Tom.

The sadness of the situation overwhelms me as my eyes fill with tears, my chest jerks up and down as I fight to control the sobbing. Tom pulls me close and holds me tightly in his arms, as my body heaves and shudders with sadness. I'm crying for John and what he must have suffered, for Emma and all that she has and still is going through. Also, for all that Tom and I have been through. As the sobbing subsides, I feel relieved that it is over, but I'm also sad at how many people are victims of a very sick woman's awful actions

'I know it's irrational, but there's a part of me that feels sorry for Morag's children,' I said, as Tom guides me down the stairs away from the courthouse.

'Come on, we need to go to the hospital and let Emma's parents know what's happened' he said squeezing my shoulder.

Chapter 31. Waking Up.

There's a bright light, and it's hurting her eyes. There are voices calling her name, but she can't see anyone it is too bright. She can feel someone gently shaking her arm and calling her name. Emma wishes that they would stop and just let her sleep.

'Emma, can you open your eyes?' a strange voice asks.

'Emma, come on, Emma open your eyes' the voice continues.

Emma can hear other noises but doesn't know what they are? The bright light is really annoying her now. She wants to tell them to turn it off and just let her sleep.

'She's starting to wake' the voice said gently shaking her arm.

'Come on, Emma. You can do it, open your eyes.'

The light is too bright. Emma wishes that the voice would go away. As she tries to open her eyes, the bright light blinds her.

'That's it, Emma. You're doing great, just open your eyes.'

The light is so bright she can't see anything; she can just hear the voices and see shapes.

'Where am I?' she asks, straining against the light, trying to see the person speaking to her.

'You're in hospital, Emma. You're safe now' the voice said as a nurse comes into view.

As her vision becomes clearer, Emma scans the room and can see that there are several nurses and a doctor standing looking at her.

'Why am I here?' she asks feeling confused, as her ordeal slowly seeps back into her memory.

'The woman' she gasps.

Emma grips the bed looking all around. Panic rising through her body, she is ready to scream. The nurse closest to her, grips her hand and calmly tells her,

'You're safe, no one can hurt you here' she said calmly.

'She is locked up; you are safe now' the nurse repeats continuing to hold Emma's hand.

Emma can feel something heavy and looks down the bed at her leg, realising it's in a cast. All of a sudden, everything comes flooding back to her in a rush. The storm, the car crash, the woman, the barn, the filth. She can hear a loud annoying high-pitched sound, and it takes her a minute to realise that the annoying noise she can hear is herself screaming. Unable to stop screaming, she watches as another nurse pushes some liquid into the canula on her arm. Everything is becoming blurry as she softly drifts back off to sleep.

The light is bright, but not as bad as the last time. Emma blinks her eyes open against the bright light as she fully wakes up. As her vision focuses, she spots a nurse at the bottom of the bed checking her chart.

'How long have I been asleep?' Emma asks, realising how weak her voice sounds.

'Just over a month' the nurse replies looking up from the chart

'A month, really?'

'Yeah, you were very unwell when you were brought in. We woke you briefly yesterday, but your body is too weak to take too much strain at one go. So, we mildly sedated you again to wake you at a slower rate and reduce the strain on your body' she said.

'Am I in Northern Ireland?'

'Yes, you're in Northern Ireland. The doctor's will be here to see you soon. They will explain everything to you.'

'Would you like me to get you something to eat or drink?' the nurse asks.

Emma hadn't realised it, but the more alert she becomes, the more she realises that she is starving. Her stomach grumbling at the thought of food.

'Yeah, I'm kind of hungry,' Emma said.

'That's a good sign. I'll get you some tea and toast. Would that be okay?

'Sounds great.'

It doesn't take long before the nurse returns, and the room fills with the smell of toast. That smells so good, Emma told the nurse her stomach grumbling loudly.

'Here you go, get stuck in.'

'You know you've had visitors while you were in the medically induced coma' the nurse said.

'Really, who?' Emma asks, wondering who would have been to visit her in Northern Ireland.

'Well, there's been Eve and her boyfriend, Tom. Your parents have also been here every day' the nurse said, smiling.

'My parents are here?'

'Yes, a lot of people have been worried about you.'

'Eve knows I'm here?' Emma said, feeling confused.

'Yes, and she has been here every day since you came in. She has been very worried about you. I'm sure she will be in later.'

'And my parents, they're still here in Northern Ireland?'

'Yes, they're here, they've come to the hospital every day as well'

'They must have been so worried, what month is it? Emma asks, realising that she has no idea what day it is? let alone what month it is.

'It's July.'

'July.'

And I've been in the hospital for a month, is that right?

'Yes, that's right.'

'So that means, I must have been missing for about three months, is that right?' Emma said struggling to remember.

'I remember booking the ferry to come to Northern Ireland in March. I wanted to visit Eve, I wanted to surprise her, to say sorry and make up with her. I was awful to her and I feel terrible. My parents must have been out of their minds. They'd asked me to text when I arrived to let them know I was okay.'

'Yes, everyone has been very worried about you, I'm sure your friends and parents will tell you everything, also the police will need to speak to you when you are a little stronger.'

'Why do the police need to speak to me?'

'Do you remember what happened? About being kidnapped.'

'Yes, I remember all of it.'

Emma felt the panic begin like a cluster of spark plugs in her abdomen and her breaths come in gasps before the heartrate starts to alarm.

'You need to calm down, there is no point getting worked up, your body can't take it' the nurse said silencing the alarm.

'The police want to speak to you about what happened, you don't need to worry. The woman who was holding you captive is in prison, she was to be sentenced today. I haven't heard how it went yet, I'll let you know as soon as I hear anything.'

'Okay, thank you. Do you know what her name is? the woman who took me?'

'Her name is Morag Edwards, she was arrested for many crimes including, kidnapping you, damaging Eve's property and murder.'

'Poor Eve, is she okay? I overheard the woman who was holding me, talking to herself. She was plotting to kill Eve, and her boyfriend if they didn't leave. The woman didn't want anyone to know that she was there and damaged Eves property to make her move away.'

'Well I'm very pleased to tell you that Eve is fine, and she is still living here in Northern Ireland, Morag's plan didn't work.'

'When do I have to speak to the police?'

'You will have to speak to them soon, they can wait until after visiting hours, or if you feel up to it, you can speak to them now, get it over and done with before your visitors come. I'm sure your friends and family will be delighted to see you awake.'

'I know it's silly, but I feel kind of nervous at seeing them, I don't want Eve to be cross with me.'

'Trust me, when I tell you this, Eve is not cross with you, not even close. She will be delighted to see you awake, they all will, you have many people who love you and have been very worried about you.'

'It's almost visiting time, do you want to go to the bathroom? we'll get you comfortable for when your visitors come.'

Chapter 32. Emma's Awake.

For the past month, Emma's parents have been staying in the cottage while Tom and I are in the caravan. It's been a squeeze, but I wouldn't have it any other way; it's nice having them so close. I can't imagine how hard this situation has been on them. We've all been going to the hospital every day for the past month since Emma was found in the barn and Morag was arrested. Emma's parents asked if Tom and I would go to the court today to hear the verdict. It was just too much for them and we arranged to meet at the hospital before visiting hours. When we arrive at the hospital, we meet up with Emma's parents in the coffee shop to discuss the case. Tears spring to my eyes and my voice catches when I tell them the verdict.

'She's been sentenced to life; she will die in prison.'

'Oh, thank God. At least now we can move on, knowing that awful woman will die in prison,' Mr Crosby said, hugging his wife.

'Cheers to that' Tom said, raising his coffee cup.

'Cheers' the rest of us reply clinking our cups off his.

The news of the verdict is like a weight has been lifted. Even with Emma still unconscious, we're all lighter. It's almost visiting time by the time we've finished our coffees. As we walk towards the nurses' station, I sense that something is different. I initially thought it was because of the sentencing, but we've barely made it to the nurse's station when Emma's nurse immediately reports that Emma is off sedation and is awake and talking.

'That's wonderful' I exclaim, bursting into tears, looking across at Emma's parents who are standing in shock tears tripping down their faces.

We take a minute to compose ourselves before the nurse walks us to her room. The police are outside Emma's room, waiting to talk to her. I can't believe what I see when we enter. Emma is sitting up, she looks frail, but her blue eyes are alert. Both, myself and Mrs Crosby burst into tears, as her dad pulls her into a teary hug followed closely by her mum.

'I'm so happy you're awake' I said relief flooding me.

Her parents stand back to look at her as I pull her into a hug. I lean back to look at her properly now that she is awake. She smiles holding on to my hand weakly. I notice that her hands still look very red from the cold they were exposed too, while she was held in the barn.

'I missed you' she said, in a voice so quiet I can barely hear her.

She smiles at us all, turning to Tom, holding out her hand.

'I'm Emma,' she said quietly.

'Pleased to meet you, Emma, I'm Tom' he said, leaning over and pulling her into a hug.

'And we are very happy to see you awake. You had everyone worried there' he said, smiling kindly.

The nurse enters and explains that now Emma is awake only two visitors are allowed in the room at a time.

'Just until she regains some strength,' the nurse said.

'Can we stay after visiting hours?' Emma's dad asks.

'Yes, you're next of kin.'

Emma's parents immediately stand up, pulling Emma into a hug, then hugging both Tom and me before leaving. After Emma's parents leave, Tom and I sit beside her bed just chatting about the hospital and how she is feeling. It feels so weird that I burst into tears, overwhelmed that she is sitting up awake. I'm so grateful that Emma has survived her ordeal and looks as well as she does. It is a miracle considering all that she has been through. But so far, we have avoided talking about what happened. But I have to know what she remembers.

'Do you know what happened?' I ask gently, hoping that I don't upset her.

'I had to give a report to the police shortly before you came, and the more I talk about it the more I'm remembering, it's coming back in flashes' she said in a quiet voice.

'I missed you and hated how horrible
I'd been, so I decided to surprise you with a
visit. I wanted to apologise in person. I
waited until March, before booking the ferry
hoping that the weather would be better. But
I picked the worst time to arrive right before
a storm.'

She is looking at her hands and takes a
deep breath before continuing.

'The storm was getting worse and
worse the longer I drove. I was aching and
tired, but the Sat Nav told me that I was
close. But as I turned down a narrow road.
There was this big gust of wind that brought
down a large branch into the road right next
to me. I remember swerving away from the
branch and losing control. I crashed my car
into the hedge' she said, her voice quiet and
weak.

'I must have blacked out, because the
next thing I remember is that awful woman
dragging me out of the car and dumping me
in a dirty old barn.'

Worried about her health as the tears roll
down her face, I place my hand on her arm
and tell her,

'You don't have to say any more, if you don't want too.'

'No, it's okay. I remember trying to tell her I'd hurt my foot, that I thought it was broken. But she just went crazy, screaming and shouting at me' she said, a rawness in her gasping sobs.

'She tied me up and left me there, it was freezing, and my foot was too painful and swollen for me to put any weight on it. I tried to get up and get away, but I couldn't get free. She had tied my wrists to something, and I was so cold' she continues her tears subsiding.

'You know she took all my clothes and left me with barely anything. I was freezing and could see her wearing my warm jumper.'

'I can't believe you were so close, and we didn't know,' I said.

'If it wasn't for me, she would never have been here' I thought, an overwhelming feeling of responsibility crushing me as I continue to hold her shaking hand.

'How far away was I?' she asks.

'About a two-minute walk away' I said glancing at Tom, guilt sitting heavily on my chest.

'She moved me; you know from the first place to somewhere new' she said blinking, lashes heavy with tears.

'She thought someone was going to find us, I was terrified she would kill me' she said weakly, her eyes closing and her breathing labouring.

'She told me that she'd killed her father after he abused her. She'd tried to kill her husband, but he survived, that's why she was hiding, I told the police this earlier and they didn't know anything about any of the earlier crimes.'

'She killed someone else as well! I heard her talking to herself when she thought I was asleep or unconscious. She was talking about how perfect it was, about how no one would know because the storm gave her the perfect alibi' she said, closing her eyes and drifting off into a light sleep.

'We should go and let her rest' I said quietly looking at Tom.

'Yeah.'

Tom rubs Emma's shoulder to wake her and let her know we are going.

'We're gonna go, let you get some rest' I said gently.

'I'm sorry about everything. For being such a bitch' she said as we hug goodbye.

'Me too, I'm sorry too. But, let's not worry about all that. You just focus on getting better' I said wrapping my arms around her bony shoulders.

Emma's parents are waiting outside with the police officer.

'How is she?' Mrs Crosby asks her eyes filled with worry.

'She's good, just tired' I reply squeezing her arms.

My mind is working overtime on the drive home. I can't stop thinking about the impact all of this will have on Emma and her parents.

'I hope Morag lives a long miserable life in prison, that evil, sick woman has caused so much damage. I hope she's locked away in solitude for life' I said, my heart heavy.

'How did life get so complicated?' I ask exasperated.

Chapter 33. The Aftermath.

It's September, and it's been three months since Emma was found. She woke up two months ago and yesterday the doctors said she is well enough to go home. When she gets out of the hospital, Emma is to return home with her parents, but not before coming to see the cottage and the farm. I've been trying to distract myself by cleaning and making the cottage look as nice as possible for Emma's arrival.

'I really want her to like it, after all if it wasn't for me, she wouldn't have suffered all that she has gone through' I thought, the guilt returning again to haunt me.

The least I can do is show Emma. She would have had a nice time if everything had gone to plan.

Emma's parents left for the hospital about an hour ago and are due back anytime now. Tom is at the farm, and I made sure that we have some nice treats for everyone when they get back. I'm buzzing with nervous energy and keep fluffing cushions and tidying unnecessarily to keep myself occupied. I'm sick with nerves and keep fluffing the cushions. I'm wishing they would hurry up when I hear a car pull up outside. Dropping everything, I rush out to meet the car, delighted to see they've made it back safely. Emma has lost so much weight during her ordeal that she's literally half the person she was. Steading herself as she gets out of the car, she begins to walk unsteadily on crutches barely able to put any weight on her damaged leg. I notice she's relying heavily on the crutch to hold her weight. The doctors explained that she may never fully regain full usage of her leg. It was so badly damaged in the accident and had started to heal in a funny angle whilst she was being held captive. The surgeons needed to re-break the bone and pin it is using titanium rods to hold it in place. She will need many months of rehabilitation, but we're hopeful that she will recover.

I rush to her side, she looks so frail, I wonder whether she should be out yet?

'Are you okay?' I ask glancing at her parents who have a bag full of medicines.

'Yes, just weak. This is the first time I've been outside of the hospital grounds. It feels weird like I've escaped' she said, smiling.

'So, this is your new home.'

She is standing at the front of the cottage looking across the meadow.

'I like it. I can see why Mum and Dad have been raving about this place' she said, smiling.

'Look at you' we hear Tom calling from the road as he strides towards us.

As he reaches Emma, he wraps his arms around her, pulling her into a hug.

'It's great to see you out, come on in' he said, linking his arm through hers and guiding her towards the cottage door.

Before they get a chance to enter Emma stops abruptly, looking behind her and around at the meadow.

'Where was I kept?'

'It wasn't here. It was at the farm, just down the road,' I said, pointing back towards the road.

'Let's get a cup of tea, then we can take you up to the farm. If you want, we can show you the barn where you were kept for at least some time. The other barn is just a heap now. It collapsed after the police kicked the side in when they were investigating,' Tom said.

'I didn't even know it existed until after you were found. It was hidden deep in the woods; I probably would never have found it' he said.

Emma loves the cottage. She uses her crutch to walk around, touching everything only stopping to look out of the kitchen window.

'You can see the chickens from here', she said excitedly, pointing at the coop through the kitchen window.

'Can we feed them?' she asks childlike.

'Of course, they'll never turn down food' I said watching her looking excitedly through the window. It makes me glad to see her looking so happy.

'Give me a sec to clean up, then we can go and feed them,' I said.

Keeping pace with Emma, we walk slowly and carefully through the woods to the chicken coop. Emma gives a squeal of delight when we reach the coop.

'I can't believe you have chickens' she said grinning from ear to ear, taking great pleasure in throwing food for the hens.

I decide that while we're here, I might as well see if there are any eggs. As I leave the coop with a basket full of eggs, I'm distracted trying to avoid standing on a hen and don't notice Emma. But I'm shocked when I hear her gasp loudly and look up to see her looking aghast, staggering away from me.

'What's wrong? What's happened?' I ask, confused about what has upset her as I walk towards her.

She's struggling with her crutch backing away from me.

'No. No. The eggs' she stammers pointing at my basket.

'Is this where she got the eggs?' she said her eyes darting all around before pointing at my basket.

'The woman, she fed me two boiled eggs every day, until we moved then we ate

385

them raw because she forgot the cooker'
Emma said, her eyes full of fear as she scans
all around her.

'I don't know where she got the eggs?
but most likely the farm, there's plenty of
hens up at the farm. It's unlikely she got
them from here, I would have noticed if any
eggs were missing' I said passing the basket
to Mrs Crosby, who turns and hurries with
them back to the cottage.

'She is gone, Emma. She will never get
out of prison. She can't hurt you anymore'
Tom tells her.

'Are you sure you want to go to the
farm?' he asks, glancing his eyes filled with
worry at me.

'Yes, I think I need to, or else I'll never
be able to come back' she said.

'Okay, if you're sure you're up to it,
let's make a move.'

Emma holds Toms arm as he walks her
slowly towards the farm. We take the now
easily defined beaten pathway through the
wood. As we reach the farmhouse, Tom
slowly guides Emma and her parents around
the side of the house and down a small

pathway into the first barn where she was kept. There are marks left from where the police removed Emma's car after she was found. The car was returned a couple of weeks ago and is now parked in the carport next to the farmhouse. The car is staying here for now, Tom is going to repair it for when Emma is ready to drive again.

'I recognise this place' she said her eyes scanning the inside of the barn.

She shows us the spot where she was kept tie to a pole.

'That woman, talked to herself all the time, I'm sure she forgot that I was there half the time. There was one time when she was rambling about her perfect anti-freeze plan. Saying no one would know what she'd done' Emma tells us.

'I was terrified she would poison me as well, but I was too hungry and thirsty not to eat and drink whatever she gave me.'

'I still don't know why she took me?' Emma said tears running slowly down her cheeks.

'Morag had been poisoning John, the police said his autopsy found lethal levels of

387

anti-freeze in John's system. Thankfully, she was charged with his murder along with your kidnapping. The police are also investigating a cold case that they believe she was also involved with' I said.

Seeing how upset Emma looks, I'm not sure how much I should say about her kidnaper, not wanting to upset her further.

'I believe she would have killed me, if I hadn't been found, but her health was failing. I could tell she couldn't take much more' Emma said her muffled sobs echoing in the now empty barn.

'I know the barn where we were found was demolished, but how far away from here was it? I was held here for a few weeks but that crazy bitch panicked and insisted we move. It was so difficult; my foot was broken, and she wasn't strong enough to push me in the wheelbarrow, so made me crawl through the mud in the pitch-black, dead of night, I don't know how I did it.'

'It's a fair distance from here. I don't think we should walk it today' Tom said.

His face is aghast at what Emma has had to endure.

'We didn't even know it was there, it had been long forgotten, and the trees grew and completely covered it' he tells her as we walk back to the farm.

'So, this place is yours now Tom?' Emma asks, looking up at the farmhouse.

'Do you think you will move in?' she said.

'It needs a lot of work; I plan on making it my next project' I said smiling, glad the conversation has changed direction.

'I can see why you like it here' she said, looking around the farmyard holding her face up to the sun.

'When I get better, I wouldn't mind spending some time here in Northern Ireland. Maybe visit some touristy places' she said.

'Really? I said delighted,

'It would be great if you did come and spend some time here' I said, unable to believe what I'm hearing.

Emma hates the countryside; she's always been a real townie.

'When I get the farmhouse tidied up, you could stay here, for however long you like. Have an extended holiday' I said grinning from ear to ear, glancing at Tom who is nodding in agreement.

'Yeah, I like the sound of that, it's gonna take me a while to recover, but I'd like to spend a bit of time here' she said looking around.

'I really am sorry for how I treated you, but, after your mum died, I just couldn't handle it and started drinking too much. I just wanted to block your obvious pain out' she said looking at me her eyes full of tears.

'I just didn't know what I wanted to do? and I'm nowhere near as brave as you. There is no way I would have moved to Northern Ireland all by myself. You, Eve Mullen are the bravest person I know' she said sniffing and pulling me into a tight embrace.

'I don't want to spoil the mood, but we'll have to make a move soon' Mr Crosby said looking at his watch.

'Yes, of course, I wish you could stay longer' I tell them all and genuinely mean it.

My heart is heavy at the thought of them leaving today and when Emma and her parents are packed up and everything is loaded into the car, I feel an overwhelming sense of loss.

'I really will miss you' I said, leaning through the car door hugging Emma tightly hoping that she will return soon.

'Take care, and get well, and remember to keep in touch. Let me know if you do fancy a change, you're very welcome here anytime' I said as we hug goodbye.

Tears are tripping down my face and my heart feels heavy as we watch them leave,

'Do you think she will come back?' Tom asks

'I don't know. I'm not sure I would, if I'd been through what she has' I said, genuinely hoping that she will, even for a little while.

'Honestly, I think it would do her good spending some time with this country air' I said.

I take a long sniff of the air, smelling the fresh grass and pine tree smell that I still adore.

'You know, it was the smell of the air that sealed it for me'

'Sealed what?'

'Buying this place, I loved the smell, the smell of the grass and the pine trees. It was the smell that hit me when I first got out of my car, and I fell in love' I said smiling, feeling hopeful for the future.

Chapter 34. A New Start.

There's a nip in the air as autumn begins and Tom and I have been busy since Emma and her parents left. Tom has started reintroducing some rare breeds into the farm. He's also spent every spare minute fixing Emma's car and today he's finally finished.

'What do you think?' he said getting out of the car looking very proud of his finished work.

'It looks great. She'll be delighted,' I said, walking around the car, admiring his work.

The car is running perfectly, and the scratched paintwork has been repaired. He really has done a good job. I have spoken to Emma almost every day since she left, and while she has been frustrated at her slow progress, she seems to be recovering well.

'It's the least I could do after all she has been through' he said, lifting our shared suitcase placing it into the boot.

Our plan is to take the ferry at the weekend and drive the car across to Emma's parent's house for a surprise visit. Tom has asked our neighbour to look after the animals while we are away.

'It's going to be weird not having to get up early,' he said.

'There's no chance, you won't be up early' I tease, laughing.

'Are you sure that she hasn't guessed we're coming?' he asks smiling.

'Definitely not, she hasn't a clue' I said looking forward to seeing Emma again.

Since Emma and her parents left, Tom, and I have been working hard, renovating the farmhouse. This morning, the glaziers have arrived to install new windows throughout the farmhouse. It's been a lot of hard work, but the windows are the final piece to complete the renovation. The new heating system was installed last week; the farmhouse was freezing, no matter how many fires I lit.

There have been some big changes at the farm, and when we get back from our trip to England, Tom and I are going to move into the farmhouse. Shortly after Emma and her parents left, I got a pleasant surprise, when I found out that the exhaustion and nausea, I'd been experiencing wasn't down to all the stress I'd been through. But I was in fact pregnant. It was quite a shock; we hadn't planned to have a baby so soon, but we're delighted. The cottage will be too small for us to raise a baby in which is why we've decided to move into the farmhouse. I was going to tell Emma as soon as I found out, but Tom and I decided that it would be nice to tell her the exciting news in person.

**

The trip to England was lovely. Emma was delighted to see us and surprised to get her car back, thanking Tom over and over. She was also surprised but delighted at my news, telling me that I would be a great mum. I'm delighted at how well she looks; she's put on some weight and can now walk, if a little stiffly without a crutch. Emma gave us a surprise of her own when she announced that she was coming over for a few months early in the spring. It was lovely seeing how well she is doing and I'm looking forward to seeing her when she visits in June.

When we got back from our surprise trip, we moved straight into the farmhouse and have been living here for a week now. Despite moving all our own stuff in, everything still feels weird. I thought it was because it was so new, but something doesn't feel right. I'm uneasy and on edge here, I don't feel like it is our home yet. There's an eeriness about the place I don't like, I don't want to admit it and I'm certain it must be my imagination, but I've been getting a feeling that I'm being watched again.

'She's in prison. She can't be watching us anymore.' I tell myself certain it's my imagination.

Since moving into the farmhouse, I've started working full time with Tom on the farm; the days are long and tiring, but I enjoy everything about working here. Along with working on the farm, I've also been working on my novel and hope to have the first draft finished soon. I want to get it finalised before the baby is born. I haven't been back to the cottage since we moved out. But I'm heading over this afternoon to light the fire, I want to make sure that it stays aired over the winter ready for Emma when she visits in the spring. It's weird, maybe it's my pregnant brain, but I'm on edge as I reach the cottage. It looks the same just a little overgrown outside. I'm on edge as I glance around, my spine tingles, I feel like I'm being watched.

'Not again' I tell myself, certain it's all in my head.

When I enter the cottage, there's a fusty smell I don't like and instantly set about lighting the fire.

'I suppose it's been a while since anyone was in here' I thought, but as I straighten up, I spot something which puts me instantly on edge.

'What is that?'

Walking to the coffee table, I lift the battered-looking envelope and pull a crumpled note out.

'No, it can't be' I thought, paralysed with fear as I read the letter.

I can't breathe; it feels as if someone is choking me. My heart is racing as I pull out my phone and call Tom.

'Hey babe, what's up?'

'You have to come to the cottage. Now'

'Are you okay? Stay where you are. I'll come now.'

I just stand staring thinking that I have lost my mind.

'How?'

'What's wrong?' Tom calls as he rushes through the front door, looking everywhere.

'Look,' I said giving him the letter.

To my darling babies, I am so sorry, but I have to go away for a while. I promise that I will return soon when I have found us somewhere safe to live. I love you both so much, it breaks my heart that I have to leave you.

Love you forever, Mum. Xxx

He runs his fingers through his hair and his jaw is clenched tight when he asks,

'where did this come from?' after reading the letter.

'It was on the coffee table when I came in, look at the other side'

This was the letter my mother left me when I was six years old. My father gave me the note when the police told us she was alive. The next time I got to see her was in court when she was sentenced to life in prison. BECAUSE OF YOU!!!

'I'm phoning the police, it's Morag's children' he said, striding around checking all the rooms in the cottage.

'I had that horrible feeling that I was being watched again on my walk over here' I said.

'Let's go back to the farm and call the police' he said locking the door as we leave.

As we enter the yard at the front of the farmhouse, I realise something's wrong and notice the front door is wide open and turn to look at Tom.

'Was the door open when I called you?' I ask

'No, it was closed, I called in quickly to grab my trainers. Look my wellies are on the doorstep. I closed it; I know I did.'

'Call the police. Now!' I said.

Not wanting to do anything until the police get here. Tom and I stand in the yard my eyes are darting all around looking for any kind of movement.

'I can't believe this is happening' I said, as we wait for the police.

Thankfully, it doesn't take long before a police car pulls into the farmyard and two police officers get out.

'Good afternoon, shall we go inside to discuss what you found' the police officer said indicating the house.

'I think you should check inside first; the door was open when we arrived back' Tom said, and I nod in agreement.

The two officers enter the house while we wait outside in the yard. As we're waiting another police car pulls up and two more officers get out and stand with us until their colleagues return.

'The place is clear' the officer said as he and his colleague join us in the yard.

'Come on, there's no one in there' he said, indicating that we should follow him back inside.

Standing in the kitchen my heart races as I watch Tom handing the letter to one of the officers.

'Will you show me where this was found?' the officer asks.

'Yes, it was Eve who found it, in the cottage' Tom said, leading him out to the cottage to show him where it was found.

I stay at the farm waiting with the other officers until they return. The officers take down some more details reassuring us that they will be investigating the incident.

'The letter would indicate that Morag's family are involved. But I don't want you to worry, we are taking this very seriously' the officer said, before putting his notebook into his pocket.

Tom and I walk the officers out to the yard, and we watch as both cars drive away.

'I thought it was in my head, the eerie feeling that I've been feeling recently. I've been feeling like I'm being watched again' I said yawning.

'It is weird though, isn't it? How did they get into the cottage and here? I checked the cottage door and there's no damage. It's as if the door was left unlocked' Tom said, looking confused.

'Do you think they have a key?' I said.

'I don't know, I just hope the police are able to find them, it took them long enough to find Morag didn't it?'

'We never did find the missing keys, did we?' I ask wondering if we should get the locks changed.

'No, but that was long before Morag was caught, she wouldn't have the keys in prison' he said.

'I suppose, Morag's kids are devastated about what's happened.'

'Yeah, I get it, it must be hard on them. But they can't start messing with us. None of this was our fault' he said a tightness in his eyes.

'Listen, are you okay? Because I need to bring the cows in soon, you can come and help if you don't want to stay here by yourself?'

'I'm not okay, but I'm tired, this pregnancy has me exhausted. I know the police have checked everywhere, but I'm going to lock the door when you go.'

'No probs, I'll get you a cup of tea before I go. You go, lie down, and I will lock the door behind me when I leave.'

'Okay thanks.'

Despite my worry, my brain is on a five percent battery as exhaustion takes over and I have to lie down. I try to stay alert but struggle to keep my heavy eyelids open. The energy is being drained out of me, like every muscle is giving into gravity.

Chapter 35. It's all Over.

I wake suddenly, confused about where I am. As I sit up and look around the room, I remember lying down earlier and realise why I'm so confused. It's dark, I must have slept for hours. What time is it? Where's Tom? checking the clock on the mantle, I realise that it's almost 7pm.

'He's normally back by now.'

Dragging myself into a sitting position, I stretch and turn all the lamps on. Even though I have just woken, my head is foggy, and I'm exhausted as I look out of the window. This pregnancy is wiping me out, I glance through the window across at the parlour where I can see all the lights are on.

'He must be working.'

Pulling my coat on, I unlock the door and poke my head out. Something doesn't feel right; I'm probably uneasy after what happened earlier but…

'It's too quiet' I thought.

My footsteps echo as I walk across the yard, the closer I get, I realise I can hear running water.

'He must be washing everything down. That's why it's so quiet and late.'

The lights are harsh, and I spot a hose on the floor spraying water down the middle of the parlour. Turning off the tap, glancing around, I'm confused as to where Tom is?

'Tom, where are you?' I call, looking all around.

'This is weird, where is he?' I thought, searching my pockets, realising, I've left my phone back at the house.

Wishing I'd put wellies on, I take a step down the middle of the parlour, a discomfort in my chest, my heart pounding, deep down I know something's not right.

'Where could Tom be?'

A chilling tingle runs down my spine and I turn to look behind me, I can't see anyone and I'm about to return to the farmhouse when I spot something out of the corner of my eye.

'What is that?'

Feeling uneasy, I cautiously walk toward the swirling on the floor. As I get closer, I realise that whatever it is, was being washed away with the hose, but since I've turned it off, something that looks like blood has started to pool. A feeling of dread courses through me, standing stock still, I'm unable to stop watching the darkening liquid pooling on the floor.

'I need to find Tom' I thought watching as the colour on the floor continues to darken becoming a deep red.

I follow the direction where the liquid is coming from and curiosity gets the better off me. What is it?' I follow the trail with my eyes to one of the stalls, unsure what to do. I want to look in the stall, but where is Tom?

'Tom, where are you?' I yell wondering what on earth is going on as I take a small step towards the stall, stopping before I reach it to look behind me when I hear a noise.

'Who's there?' I call, certain that someone is watching me again.

My heart is racing. I don't know what to do. Unable to come up with a better plan, I decide to check the stall and return to the farmhouse to wait for Tom.

'He's probably looking for me,' I thought, walking slowly and cautiously, my heart pulsating loudly in my ears as I take the last few steps to the stall.

'Oh my god,' I gasp, dropping to my knees.

There's a noise behind me and I turn, watching the shape of a person running away into the field.

'Oh my god. TOOOOM,' I scream, fear coursing through me, my chest tightens, and tears run down my face.

I can't think straight, this can't be right, brain synapses are firing like a bomb exploding in my head as the reality of what I'm seeing hits.

'TOOOOM,' I scream again until all the air has left my lungs.

I can't stop looking at him lain splayed on the straw. The stall is filled with dark red blood. There's a deep cut running across his neck. Turning to look in the direction of where the person ran, fear fills my every pore as I stand up and run as fast as I can back to the farmhouse. Unable to stop shaking, I grab my phone, dropping it twice before I'm able to call the police.

'I need the police; my boyfriend has been murdered.'

Dropping to my knees, I let out a stomach curdling scream. Screaming until I have no more air left in my lungs and crumple into a heap on the floor. I know Morag has done this; I don't know how? But she has done this. She's never going to stop until I leave.

'I HATE YOU MORAG EDWARDS, I HOPE YOU ROT IN HELL.'

About the Author

S.J.C. Ratcliffe lives in Northern Ireland enjoys the outdoors, including walks in the forest, camping and cycling. S.J.C. Ratcliffe often uses the countryside and life experiences as inspiration for her writing.

My new book Blackcliffe Island a nuclear apocalyptic thriller is available now from Amazon.

Follow me on

Twitter: @Samanth25513868
@SJCRATCLIFFEAU1

My Blog: sjcratcliffe.home.blog.
Webpage
https://sjcrat79.wixsite.com/website

.

Disclaimer.

59926233R00243

Made in the USA
Middletown, DE
13 August 2019